The Ice Cream War

a mystery of murder

and hot fudge

by

Paul Janson

Published by JM Publishing

All characters, events and organizations contained in this book are fictional. Any resemblance to persons or organizations is entirely coincidental

 Published by JM Publishing May 2014

Cover Design: Kevin Gierman

Author Photography: Sarah McGrath

All rights reserved

For more information contact

Paul Janson
JM Publishing
36 Elm Street
Georgetown, MA 01833
Paul_janson@AOL.com

PaulJanson.com

ISBN 13: 978-0990742401

Copyright 2014 Paul Janson

Acknowledgements

This book was written not by me alone, but with the help and guidance of my family and friends. I would also like to acknowledge my family: my wife Mary, and my daughters: Maria and Emma. Mary's sisters, Ruth and Sally provided guidance as well. I would like to mention Linda and Ralph Boragine and Debbie and Dave Hennessey for their assistance in making the ice cream shop in this book real. My gratitude to you all.

Other books by Paul Janson

Mal Practice: a mystery of medicine and murder: Awarded finalist in the IPNE 2014 Book Contest in Genre Faction

Scratch a young adult novel of magic and feline fantasy. This novel was given a four star review by IndieReader making it "IndieReader Approved".

and

The Child In Our Hearts, a series of picture books about adoption, to be read to or by young children. They include versions for families with a mother and father, two mothers, two fathers and for single parents, either a mother or a father. There is now a version for assisted reproductive technology births also for families with a mother and a father and for two mothers. These books have been translated into Spanish and Italian.

Dedication

This book is dedicated to the Jeffrey Boragine, and to Maria and Emma Janson who are now operating Jeff and Maria's Old Fashioned Ice Cream and Food Shop with Mary and me in Groveland, Massachusetts.

# Chapter 1

"Hot weather is always so much fun," Mary said. "One scoop or two?"

Three people began to answer at once.

"Two," said the youngest, a girl of six.

"I think one will be enough," said the mother.

"I was thinking three," said the father. His wife looked at him, and then at his stomach, and frowned.

Mary looked from one to the other, finally resting her gaze on the youngest. "Two all-around then?"

There were reluctant nods from the two adults, and enthusiasm from the youngest customer.

"Same flavors as usual?" asked Mary, and she began to scoop when this question elicited nods from all three.

"Jerry's opened up his stand across town, hasn't he, Mary?" asked the gentleman. His wife frowned at him again.

"Re-opened, yes," replied Mary. "He had it open for two weeks last year."

"Not a worry to you though, a renewal of the ice cream war?" he asked. The wife's scowl went unnoticed, at least by her husband.

"He won't last. It will cut into his surfing." Mary shrugged.

"Heard his prices are way lower than—" he began to say, as Mary started to hand out the ice cream cones.

His wife shoved some money onto the counter, interrupting him. "We're going to eat outside. Thanks, Mary."

"I was going—" began her husband, looking at the empty tables in the shop.

"Eat your ice cream outside, or wear it inside," replied his wife.

Their child giggled, and they started for the door.

"But it's cooler in here," he was saying as they walked out into the heat of the evening.

"No it isn't," said his wife. "It just seems cooler right now. If you keep talking, it will get hot soon enough."

"What do ya mean?" was the last thing Mary heard any of them say. She was alone in the shop now.

Seven thirty at night, hot mid-summer evening, and an empty ice cream shop.

"Damn," she said softly to herself. Jerry, Jeremiah Wilson, had done this same thing last year. It was the middle of the summer, and he'd arrived in town to visit his aunt May. Next thing anyone knew he had opened an ice cream shop across town in his aunt's old store, which had been closed for years. His aunt was going slightly senile; which was Jerry's fault, Mary was sure. Aunt May had kept the licenses up-to-date just in case she wanted to open the business again...after only four years closed. But she was losing track of time as well as losing track of her nephew.

So just about this time last year Jerry had shown up, opened the shop a couple weeks later, and then started halfheartedly selling ice cream. The halfhearted part was that he "sold" it for less than Mary sold it for—a lot less. Mary was sure it was far less than it cost him to buy it. He sometimes even gave it away! Well, not really gave it, but he let people run up a tab and never collected the tab thus run up. Mary had tried to cut her prices, but couldn't come close, and couldn't sell it and...well, ended up having to throw out some of her stock.

Then Jerry had just closed up with no explanation. He didn't seem to realize he had almost put her out of business. He came by to say goodbye when he closed, and wish her well and to say he was sorry he hadn't gotten by sooner and to say how nice she looked and...*oh yeah, ya want my leftover ice cream?* Mary was so surprised she hadn't known what to say, but Jerry must have thought she said yes because the next day, he dropped by in a borrowed van and unloaded several tubs of his leftovers and just drove away.

Where he went, no one seemed to know, any more than they knew where he came from or why or...well, anything about him except that he had grown up here in this small town, gone to high school and then gone somewhere else. California, someone had said. He talked a lot about surfing.

She smiled as she thought of that day. Half the ice cream was melting and had to be thrown out right there, and she was sure he had never come close to making any money at his shop. He had the strangest collection of flavors, many never opened. "Mint chip root beer" was the one she remembered most, and as she did, she laughed. Where had he even found a supplier with that to sell? If he had left because the business wasn't making money, he showed no disappointment at this, and that just begged the question—where had the money to start the business come from in the first place?

No one seemed to know, but his aunt had little money that wasn't in a strictly controlled trust fund, and the rumor was that Jerry had paid cash for his stock.

Maybe he ran out of money, or maybe someone was afraid he was getting into his aunt's money. There were a few other relatives who hoped she had some money left when she died. The Wilsons were a sentimental lot, especially about money, but the rumor also said that someone might have paid him to leave.

If Jerry's aunt was a little less "addled", as Mary's father called her senility, Mary would have suspected she had paid him to leave. The ice cream wasn't very well served at Jerry's shop, often melting or mixed flavors, and the shop was always dirty. There was a musty smell about it probably from so many years unused, but Jerry never seemed to manage to get rid of it. It was said that the Board of Health had been by with some "suggestions" that ended with the phrase: "… or you will have to close." By the time Jerry left, he was becoming a running joke in this town, to his other relatives' embarrassment, socially if not financially. Maybe Jerry's aunt wasn't as senile as she appeared to be and had paid him to leave.

Whatever the cause, the ice cream war had lasted only two weeks. Two costly weeks for Mary, though.

Her father walked in just then to end her musing.

"Pretty busy here tonight. Think I can push to the head of the line, Mary?" he said, smiling.

"No you may not," Mary replied, motioning toward the empty shop. "This crowd has been waiting hours to get a chance to buy my ice cream instead of the sh—…instead of what Jerry is selling."

"*Giving* is a more accurate term. *Grand opening* I think he called it. A *thank you* to his loyal customers."

"His loyal customers?" replied Mary. "They haven't been in his shop for a year!"

"His shop hasn't been open for a year. Am I goin' ta have to pay tonight?"

"Damn right you are. And it's only been eleven months and three weeks since he closed last year." Mary stared at her father defiantly. "Three weeks and two days."

"How many hours, or are you just keepin' a rough estimate? Can't I at least get a family discount?"

"No, you can not, and you better leave a tip, too. I'll figure the hours since Jerry left, while I wait for you to go to the ATM for that tip if you want."

"I don't know if the ATMs are open on holidays, Mary."

"They're always open, even on holidays and furthermore, today is not a holiday."

"Even if Jerry is giving away free ice cream? That ought to count as a holiday."

"If I give you a free ice cream, will you go away?"

"That's a deal I can't refuse."

"Damn right you can't refuse it. Murder is the only other option."

"Really? Who's going to get killed?"

Mary just glared at him. "Maybe Jerry, if I can't find anyone else to kill. Please order an ice cream so I can close the shop and go over there tonight. You were planning to order tonight, weren't you?"

"Oh," replied her father. "Yeah, about that ice cream. Ya got any mint chip root beer? In a dish, not a cone."

"No. I'll give you mint chip and you can get your own root beer."

"Ah, okay. You weren't planning to kill Jerry tonight were you? I gotta work in the morning ya know."

Mary began to scoop the requested mint chip into a dish, and answered without looking up or stopping, "By work you mean sitting in your office pretending to be a lawyer?"

"I am a lawyer. Got papers all framed an' everything on my wall ta prove it."

Mary stood and stared at him. "Forged, I'm sure. Here's your mint chip, John Burke, Esquire. Now pay up."

John Burke, Esquire or not, knew when to leave...before, not after you pay. "Put this on my tab, will ya? I just came by to see if you were married yet so I can retire."

He was out the door as his daughter yelled after him, "I am *not* married yet, and you do *not* support me, so retire whenever you damn well please. And I want some DNA testing before Father's Day, do you hear me?"

"Wonder if Jerry's givin' out free root beer?" John Burke, Esquire replied, and got into his car.

Chapter 2

It took less than another half-hour in her empty shop for Mary to decide that the ice cream could spend the rest of the evening alone. She turned the "OPEN" sign on her door to display the "CLOSED" side. She turned off the lights inside so that they would waste no more of their luminosity tonight, following which she turned her key in its lock and headed...well, anywhere but where she was.

Where she ended up was with her father at *Jerry'd Ice Cream*. That's what the sign on the door said, and Mary was outside the crowded shop waiting to ask Jerry if he knew that his sign was misspelled. It had obviously been written on a computer, and the "d" is next to the "s" on the QWERTY keyboard; but how unprofessional could he get? This was her competition, and he was likely to put her out of business with his misspelled sign and free ice cream; life was not fair.

"Hey, Mary," said her father. "Got a free root beer here from Jerry."

"That will leave you enough money to pay your tab."

"Might." He took a spoonful of his mint chip ice cream and washed it down with a swallow of root beer.

When his mouth was empty again he looked at his daughter and asked, "You didn't come by to kill anyone, did you, Mary? 'Cause if you did, I'd like to leave before you do."

"So you can dig a grave to help me hide the body I'm sure."

"Well...I got an early morning tomorrow ya know."

"You mean you'll be going to work before noon tomorrow?"

"Maybe I should say 'an early day.' You're not really going to...?"

"Kill Jerry? No, suicide is so much easier."

"That's a relief. So what are you doing here?"

"I thought I would do the suicide thing here and ruin Jerry's business the same as he's ruining mine. All's fair in an ice cream war, ya know."

"You sure?" asked her father.

"Oh, Dad, you sentimental fool. I wouldn't really commit suicide."

"I meant about your suicide ruining Jerry's business. It might just get more people to come by to see the place, ya know."

Mary looked around her. "I'm not sure there could *be* any more people. Isn't everyone in town already here?"

Her father looked around too. "I see one or two that I don't see."

"That makes no sense, Dad, even for a lawyer."

"Might be someone should check on 'em. Might be sick or somethin' if they're not here."

"I'm going to talk to Jerry and point out to him that there's a misspelling on his sign," replied Mary.

John Burke took another spoon full of mint chip ice cream and a swallow of root beer. "Fix the sign?" he said, looking at it as it hung crookedly on the door. "That'll get those last two of 'em in here all right."

Mary ignored her father and walked inside to stand at the counter. There was a lull right then, and when the people at the counter saw Mary come up, they seemed to find the outside more inviting. It might have been some discomfort on their part for coming here instead of going to her shop for ice cream, or possibly it was the scowl on her face, or possibly it was that Jerry had no air conditioning so it was hotter inside than out.

Mary was about to speak, but Jerry beat her to it. "Oh, hi! How are ya…?" Only his blank expression was left to say he didn't know who she was.

"Mary?" she offered.

"Yeah, yeah. How are ya, Mary? Can I get ya some ice cream?"

"Why don't you give me all of it?"

"What? Oh, ya mean ya want three scoops? Different flavors, right? I'll start with the mint chip root beer. That's real popular tonight."

"Jerry."

"Yeah?"

Mary just shook her head. "Your sign's got a misspelling on it, and you don't recognize me, do you?"

Jerry looked first at Mary, and then at the sign. "Yeah, I got to fix that sign, and I do recognize you, I just don't know who you are."

"Mary," she said again.

"Oh yeah. Of course. Mary." Jerry smiled. It was a nice smile but there wasn't even a hint of recognition anywhere on his face. "Ya want some ice cream?"

"You still don't have the foggiest idea who I am, do you, Jerry?"

"Sure I do. You're Mary." He paused, and it looked as if there was some effort going into thinking beneath his bushy blond hair.

Mary just shook her head again. "I'm Mary Burke, and I probably have more ice cream than you do. I own the ice cream shop over the other side of town."

"Oh, sure. I remember. You're the one I came back here to see! I've been thinking about you since last year. Real nice of ya ta come all the way over here just to welcome me back. I mean like, that's real nice."

"Yeah, well, thanks. And I thought you just came back to renew the ice cream war and destroy my business."

"What?"

"Never mind," replied Mary.

Jerry just smiled. "Let me get ya some ice cream, okay? What about a triple mint chip root beer?"

"No, that's okay, Jerry. Are you going to keep giving the ice cream away?"

"Well, no. Maybe just tonight."

Jerry wasn't tall, maybe only an inch or two taller than she, and might outweigh her by only a few pounds. Tanned and blond-haired, he could be a major threat on the surfing scene. Certainly on the covers of the surfing magazine, if there were any of those anywhere to be on the covers of. Did surfers read? Did they know *how* to read? She looked at the misspelled sign on the door again. Did Jerry know how to read? And more importantly, why was he back here in this little town in Nebraska trying to put her little ice cream shop out of business?

Mary thought for a minute and nodded. Yeah, he wasn't that big. She could probably take him down easily in a fair fight. Maybe they'd use ice cream scoops as weapons.

When she looked up, Jerry was still standing there, smiling. She had expected the smile to have faded a little. The tan should have faded a little too, as long as she had been standing there.

"So, would ya like that in a bowl or a cone?"

"It's all right, Jerry. I can go to my own shop if I want ice cream."

"But mine's free." He looked truly disappointed.

Mary shrugged. *Okay, she would take him down tomorrow. Too many witnesses tonight anyway.* "Just one scoop, in a cup, not a cone."

"Mint chip root beer, right?"

"No. Just strawberry."

Jerry smiled broadly. "That's my favorite, too. What a coincidence!" He seemed really pleased. Mary wasn't.

Damn, she thought. *It would be his favorite.*

Chapter 3

So there she stood, eating Jerry's favorite ice cream and cursing every bite. She might never eat strawberry again.

She was alone for only a minute, however, before a new arrival came in to stand next to her.

"Hey, Prentiss," said Mary, as she looked at the very big, very muscular, bearded man in jeans, a tee shirt and work boots. He only offered a grunt in reply.

"So..." said Mary, smiling. "How are you on this hot summer night, Prentiss? Come to get some ice cream?"

A smiling Jerry was standing in front of them, with the counter between. Mary glanced at Prentiss Forrest, specifically at his face, and thought it was a good thing there was at least a counter between them. The venom on that face said the counter might not be enough, but Jerry didn't seem to appreciate that threat.

"Hi," Jerry said. "Can I get ya some ice cream?"

"No," replied Prentiss. Those who hadn't moved outside did so now and quickly, and those already outside moved a little further away.

"A soda, maybe," offered Jerry, still smiling broadly.

"No," Prentiss repeated.

Jerry frowned a second. "I know. I'll get you a taste of the mint chip root beer. The tastes are free."

"Isn't all the ice cream free tonight, Jerry?" asked Mary, but Jerry was already heading toward the cases to scoop a taste.

"Damned fool," said Prentiss, looking after Jerry.

"Now with that I would have to agree," said Mary. "My reason has to do with an ice cream war and a shop across town that will be bankrupt soon. What's your reason, Prentiss?"

Prentiss didn't shift his stare from the man scooping ice cream as he spoke. In fact, there was no hint that he was actually speaking to Mary or anyone else. Maybe he wasn't. "I could have had this place bought 'n' paid for, weren't for that bastard."

"Well," said Mary, taking a taste of the ice cream in her cup. "I wouldn't have minded if you had bought it, but I'm not sure May, the aunt of the bastard in question, would have sold, even to someone as charming as you are Prentiss."

"She would've, or Rufus would've," replied Prentiss Forrest, appearing not at all charming right now. He turned to look at Mary for the first time since he arrived. "May ain't no fool," he added, speaking directly to her. It was almost a challenge.

Mary frowned a bit. She wondered if she could take down Prentiss in a fair fight. Maybe not a *fair* fight, but this wasn't anywhere close to a fair fight; she had him outnumbered ten to one in available vocabulary.

"I'm not sure that's a wholly accurate description of May Wilson, Prentiss. That claim that she is not a fool is greatly diminished when you consider that Jerry is her nephew. That boy got his genetics from somewhere. Even if May had only a quarter of what Jerry has...well, those foolish genes could easily destroy ten times their weight in those non-foolish genes. I think May is at a big handicap in the *Not a Fool* contest, don't you, Prentiss?"

Prentiss either didn't want to answer, or he didn't understand the question, because he just glared at Jerry without looking at Mary. Mary just smiled. Likely Prentiss hadn't even realized there had been a question. She was enjoying herself and took another taste of strawberry ice cream.

"Know what I want to know?" asked Prentiss.

It was Mary's turn to wonder if there had been a question asked just now. She decided not to answer, and it took only a few more seconds to prove she'd been correct in her judgment.

"Where'd he get the money to open this place?" Prentiss said, answering his own question.

"Maybe he has a job?"

"Now that's a laugh," replied Prentiss, although he didn't laugh at all. He didn't look like he was going to laugh, either.

Mary smiled as Jerry returned with a full bowl of ice cream, some of which may have been mint chip root beer, but certainly not all of it. "Ran out of it, so I kinda mixed in a few more flavors for ya," he said, offering the bowl to Prentiss.

There was a tense moment until Mary nodded slightly and took the bowl from Jerry, and then placed it on the counter between them. "So, Jerry," she smiled. "Where'd you get the money to open this place?"

"Oh," said Jerry. "I've got a job out in California."

Jerry turned around and walked toward the side counter where the bowls were stacked. "Got an extra spoon here somewhere."

"I wonder what job that is?" said Prentiss under his breath.

Mary thought of suggesting that Prentiss ask Jerry the questions himself, but she was beginning to enjoy this even more. She was like an interpreter, and that was fun. Prentiss asked a question, and then she repeated the same question to Jerry. She wasn't at all sure why she was needed, since they were speaking the same language...well, basically the same language, but not exactly the same.

"What kind of job?" asked Mary.

Jerry returned with another plastic spoon, placing it in the bowl he'd brought a moment earlier. "In case you want to share," he smiled. "I sell grass in California."

Now the small towns in Nebraska differ from the towns in California, at least in some ways. Marijuana had been legalized in several areas of this country, but the people in small-town Nebraska had not accepted this decision. They were still debating the legalization of alcohol, after all.

First Mary and then Prentiss looked at the bowl in front of them, and those outside began to murmur uneasily. The murmurers were saying several things, but one word was contained within each phrase: *grass*.

"Did he say grass?"

"Isn't marijuana called grass?"

"In California, grass is sold everywhere, isn't it?"

"Would he put grass in ice cream?"

"Does this ice cream look like there's any grass in it?"

The crowd outside quickly divided itself into two distinct groups, and almost exclusively along a generational boundary. Those over thirty began to slowly deposit their free ice cream in whatever trash containers they could find, while those under thirty, but old enough to be here unattended, began to consume the ice cream with renewed enthusiasm. There were even, at this late hour, a few of the very young who began yelling as their ice cream was snatched from them by their parents.

Prentiss hesitated a few seconds and then picked up the plastic bowl of ice cream and crushed it. It was clearly a mistake, since he was now left with a handful of plastic pieces and messy ice cream.

"Oh," said Jerry. "You spilled it. Let me get you a wash cloth."

Prentiss waited not one second before wiping his hand on his tee shirt front and walking out of the shop. Mary surveyed the scene. At thirty-five she should clearly have been in the group that was discarding the ice cream they had so enthusiastically sought a few minutes earlier. She looked at her half-eaten bowl now and shrugged, taking a bite and savoring it. She then smiled at Jerry, who smiled back, and Mary began wondering if this recent revelation would improve business here, or improve it at her shop across town.

# Chapter 4

It was dark inside Jerry's shop, first because the shop was closed, and second because it was almost two in the morning. Things were in disarray, and Prentiss wondered how anyone could run a business who couldn't keep it organized better than this. He didn't wonder about that too much, because he tripped almost as soon as he started across the floor.

"Damn it," he cursed, and kicked at the lump over which he had tripped. That bastard Jerry had left a pile of...a pile of something long and soft, wearing clothes, and with blond hair and two arms and...Prentiss didn't finish counting as he got to his feet and ran from the shop. He had been a little careful not to touch anything on his way in, but exercised no such caution on his way out. Hand prints were on every surface that he could reach, in fact. The lump continued to lie there, unmoved by the trip of Prentiss or the noise that followed, or the scream that followed the noise and continued until it was replaced by the screech of tires leaving the parking lot.

***

It was a little after two when Mary's phone rang, and she almost didn't wake at all. When she did wake, she considered not answering it. Finally, she decided it might be important; and if it wasn't, she wanted the opportunity to curse long and loud at the caller for waking her at this ungodly hour, so...she answered. The caller had been persistent anyway.

"This...had...better...be...good," she said into the phone.

"Mary?"

"Not good yet. Who is this?"

"Mary, I got to talk to you."

"And the reason you have to talk to me at two in the morning and won't tell me who you are is what? Probably smart not to tell me who you are."

"This is Prentiss, Prentiss Forrest."

"So much for smart. And just to keep it all straight, how many people named Prentiss do you think I know?"

"Oh..."

"Have you been drinking, Prentiss?"

"Oh, no, but maybe I should be."

"Is that what you called about, Prentiss? You need advice as to whether you should be drinking at two in the morning?"

"No."

"Good." There was a pause, and Mary thought she should just hang up the phone, but she was wide awake now and was about to do the *curse long and loud* thing when Prentiss spoke again. What he said made her reconsider her decision to answer the phone in the first place. Maybe she could just pretend she was the answering machine?

"Mary, I think Jerry is dead."

"Jerry? Dead?" Mary managed to say. If it had been someone other than Prentiss she would be upset, but this man was more likely to be mistaken than anyone she knew, except Jerry maybe, and there was a rumor she had recently been made aware of that Jerry was dead. If it was true, it would move Prentiss into first place for sure.

"Why do you think that Jerry is dead, Prentiss?"

"Well, ya see, I was...well, kinda...well, in his shop...and..."

"When was this, Prentiss, and, oh yes, *why* was this?"

"Just a few minutes ago, and I thought I saw...well, what it really was, was that I think I tripped over him."

"Okay, Prentiss. We're doing just about perfect for a conversation with you at two in the morning. I've always wondered if you would make more sense at this time of night, and now you have answered that question."

"But what should I do, Mary?"

"I'm still a little unclear about what you already did, so advising you on future activities might be...oh, hell, Prentiss. Cut it short for God's sake. Why do you think Jerry is dead, and do we have to do something about it right now, or can we get a little more sleep first?"

"Like I said, I was kinda walkin' around in Jerry's shop an' I tripped over him and I think he was dead. I mean, I think I tripped over him."

"You're not sure whether you tripped or not, Prentiss?"

"Oh, I'm sure I tripped, an' I think it was over Jerry. It was a body with blond hair, an' it didn't move an'...well, I think—"

Mary interrupted him. She was fully awake and she was paying attention now. "But there was a body with blond hair and you think it was dead?"

"Yeah, I think so."

"In Jerry's shop, right?"

"Yeah. I was in there—"

"I'm hanging up now, Prentiss, to call the police. I will then drive over to the shop to see what they find, and if you're smart, you'll drive there too, to tell them what you found and what you were doing there and why you...never mind. I'm calling the police now, Prentiss."

Chapter 5

Mary was standing outside the shop thirty minutes later. The police had beaten her by a few of those minutes, but the flashers on the one cruiser this town had at night were not on. Carl, the one officer this town had at night, was waiting outside, and proceeded to berate Mary for bothering him at two in the morning. Carl then went inside Jerry's shop. It was unlocked and in fact, the door was wide open. Carl had been in there for ten minutes now. That meant that there was either a serious crime inside, or Carl was tasting the ice cream.

Mary wasn't sure, but was beginning to be inclined to give the latter possibility an edge when the sole ambulance the town had rolled up too. She began to think of what she was going to say when Carl did emerge. The ambulance had come to pick up something, and it probably wasn't ice cream. She quickly decided that what she would say would be the truth, since nothing else would work at all. Probably the truth wouldn't work very well either, but…

Her thoughts were interrupted by the arrival of the state police, and Mary decided that *the truth, the whole truth and nothing but the truth* was what she would say; and she quickly added *so help me God*. She wasn't sure that was still what they said when swearing in witnesses in court, but that was what she remembered from the old movies she watched, and from her own courtroom experiences. The new movies just shot 'em down where they stood, without too much boring courtroom drama anyway. Mary mused now that this might have been what happened here tonight.

"So help me God," she said softly, and hoped that there would be some help from God. Prentiss Forrest wasn't going to help, since he wasn't here. She didn't have his cell phone number, didn't even know if he had a cell phone, so she couldn't call him. It might be better that way. Prentiss was capable of confusing the most astute constabulary, and Carl wasn't even close to being an astute constabulary.

The state officer that emerged from the cruiser, which did have its flashers on, was astute. Captain Peter Morgan would be able to unravel this quickly, Mary hoped.

"Mornin', Mary," Captain Morgan said, as if they had just happened to meet outside this little ice cream shop.

"Good morning, Captain," replied Mary.

"Not sure," Peter replied. "That it's a 'good' morning, I mean."

"No," said Mary, wincing a little at her faux pas.

"You know what's going on here?"

"I know what Prentiss Forrest told me."

It was Peter Morgan's turn to wince. "Prentiss? Carl didn't say who had called."

"Prentiss called me, and when he told me what he saw...in there I mean, I called Carl and..." She was cut short by Carl as he exited the shop, looking scared and pale and motioning toward Peter.

Peter's frown grew deeper and he nodded first at Carl, and then at Mary. "Stick around if ya don't mind, so we can finish our conversation, I mean." He didn't wait for an answer, since he hadn't really asked a question, he'd just given instructions. He walked over to the door where Carl was waiting and they went back into the shop, reluctantly on Carl's part, it seemed to Mary.

So she stood there feeling lonely, but staying there as she had been asked to do. There were two men in the ambulance who were waiting as well, but they were waiting inside the ambulance, probably to take advantage of the air conditioning and to stay away from the mosquitoes. It was still a little muggy, even this early in the morning, and there were plenty of mosquitoes. Mary could have waited in her car as well, but somehow she preferred the outside, even though it was muggy and the mosquitoes were buzzing. She would be closer to what was going on, and she wanted to know what was going on.

What was going on right then was Peter Morgan emerging from the shop, followed by Carl. Peter looked at Carl and said something, but Mary couldn't hear what was said. He pointed to a spot outside the door, pointed toward it several times with considerable intensity, and then walked toward his cruiser, frowning and shaking his head.

Once at the cruiser, he pulled the microphone of his radio out and talked briefly. Then he pulled two pair of blue latex-free gloves from a box in the back seat. He put one pair on and walked back to where Carl stood.

He spoke to Carl, who looked at his feet, and then took the other pair of gloves from Peter. Next stop for the captain was the ambulance, and there a few words were spoken, and probably acknowledged, but there was no change in the position or demeanor of the men sitting inside.

Peter walked back to his cruiser, and Mary wondered briefly if these trips were part of a new exercise program Peter was doing now. He was a thin African-American of maybe forty years, and she didn't think he needed an exercise program, but she also didn't see why he needed to keep walking around the parking lot. She decided she was just tense. It had only been two trips to the cruiser.

While Mary was thinking, Peter had taken some yellow crime scene tape and what looked like a small camera out of his trunk, and was now walking to where Mary stood.

"Damned fool," he said when he reached her.

"Me?" asked Mary.

Peter looked at her and then chuckled a little. "No," he replied, looking over at Carl, who was still trying to get his gloves on his hands properly. It was an intense and complicated project, it seemed.

"So maybe we should go over what you know, Mary, since Carl may be too preoccupied to tell me what you told him."

"Okay," said Mary. "Do I just tell you, or do you ask questions like they do on TV, or should I ask for my lawyer? You'll have to tell me what I'm supposed to do."

"You kill anybody tonight, Mary?"

"No."

"Would the lawyer you call be your father?"

"Yes."

"I'll promise not to charge you with any crime if you promise not to call him. How's that?"

"Sounds good to me, although I can't understand why you don't want to call in Daddy Burke Esquire. All the other fruitcakes in town are involved in this already."

Peter cast another glance at Carl and nodded.

"And then there's Prentiss, Aunt May and her nephew Jerry, and...is Jerry in there dead, Peter?"

Peter looked at her. "Can't tell you who's in there, but you can tell me why you think it might be Jerry."

"Remember, you promised not to charge me, Peter. Prentiss Forrest called me, a little after two, to tell me he tripped over a body in that ice cream shop, and he thought it was Jerry. The only reason he thought it was Jerry was because the body had blond hair I think, and knowing Prentiss...well, we both know Prentiss.

"By the way, he didn't say why he was in the shop, and I did tell him to come over here himself to meet with the police. I don't know where he is now, or why he chose to call me, and that's about it."

"You and Jerry didn't get along, did you, Mary?"

"He was...well, he wasn't really trying to put me out of business, but he was giving away ice cream that people would have paid me for if he hadn't. No we didn't get along. It was just an ice cream war and I didn't kill him over that, for Christ's sake."

"Already told me you didn't kill anyone tonight, so that part is consistent. Know anyone else who mighta killed someone tonight?" asked Peter.

"Is there someone dead in there, Peter?"

"I don't watch too much TV, but aren't I the one that's supposed to ask the questions?"

"Well, yeah, I guess. Is this going to be on TV?"

Peter frowned. "Let's hope not, and let's get back to the questions. Do you know anyone who might've killed someone tonight, Mary?"

"Like Prentiss? No, I don't know anyone like Prentiss."

"You think he killed someone tonight?" asked Peter.

"Prentiss? Why?" Mary said.

"Why would Prentiss kill someone, or why am I asking you if you think he killed someone?"

"You're getting confusing, Peter."

"Just practicing for when I have to talk to Carl. So, you don't know what we found in there, and you don't know who left it there for us to find. That about it?"

"Yeah."

"Wish we could chat more, but it looks like Carl has finally got his gloves on, so I'd better get this crime scene tape put up, ya think? The crime scene boys'll be here soon and I want it to be ready for 'em. Might want to wait a bit in case I need to ask you a couple more questions."

"Don't take too long, or I'll call my father, Peter."

"Are you threatening an officer of the law? Calling John Burke at this time of the morning might even be a felony, ya think? Good thing I promised not to charge you tonight, but don't push it."

Peter walked away, and Mary was standing alone again, but that didn't last very long.

Chapter 6

"What's going on?" the voice behind her said.

Mary turned to see May Wilson standing behind her, dressed in a flannel nightgown, a bathrobe, pink slippers, and some sort of cap into which she had pushed most, but not all, of her hair. Stray pieces of rusty-colored hair were protruding in various directions, and Mary wondered if some hairdresser had purposely chosen a color that would make May look crazy. It was about the worst hair-coloring job she had ever seen.

"Who's in my shop?" asked May, looking at Mary.

"The police right now."

"Someone break in?"

"I'm not sure," Mary replied.

"Fool if they did. Only ice cream in there, and my fool of a nephew will likely be givin' it away for free again tonight." May shrugged.

"Maybe," said Mary. She winced, thinking that Jerry might never do anything again. Whoever was in that shop was not being rushed to the hospital or taken into custody, and Captain Morgan had come as close as he could have to saying there was someone dead in there. These dots were pretty easy to connect, but the picture they produced wasn't pretty at all.

"That nephew a mine'll be outta business in another week or two anyway, just like last year. Don't know why I let him use that shop, 'cept he's family."

Mary looked at the lady standing next to her. She was surely crazy, and maybe 'addled.' Her hair was solid proof of that, but she was still aware enough to care about her nephew and to remember that he was her nephew. Mary wondered how May would take the revelation that she feared was coming.

"Who broke in there anyways?" asked May, still staring at the shop.

Prentiss had been the only one Mary knew who had broken in there, and Prentiss had a logic all his own. Possibly no one would ever know why he had broken in there tonight. "I don't know," said Mary.

May had been talking to Mary but ignoring her otherwise, as if she was just talking to something that happened to be standing next to her, but not caring who or even what it was.

She looked intently at Mary now. "What're you doing here, anyways?"

Mary smiled slightly. It was a logical question that she had no answer for. Prentiss wasn't here, after all, so why was she? She could have just ignored his call. No, she couldn't have brought herself to do that with someone maybe hurt or dead, but maybe she could have called in "anonymously"? No, that wouldn't have worked either. She had to make sure that someone was doing something about whatever it was that was going on in this shop. Prentiss had said there was a dead body in there, but he might have been mistaken. There might have been an injured person. That didn't look like it was the case now, but she had thought that might have been the case when she called.

She was a little curious, too. It occurred to her that she didn't want it to be Jerry inside that shop, although she wasn't sure that was why she came over here tonight. Then again, she wasn't sure why she cared if it was Jerry in there, either.

"I wanted to see what was going on," she replied.

"Why're you here?" asked May again.

"I don't know, May."

"Fools, all a 'em. Shoulda opened the shop back up myself as soon as let that nephew a mine open it. I could be sellin' groceries outta there right now."

"Maybe you're right, May," said Mary. *Not selling groceries right now at two in the morning, and if you were then maybe you would be dead in there,* she thought.

Peter had finished with his chore. The yellow crime scene tape surrounded the building, and the camera was in his pocket. Carl returned to stand in the spot Peter had indicated earlier, as Peter walked over to his cruiser to deposit the camera and the remaining tape in the trunk. After he did, he started walking toward the two ladies.

"Well, I'll be going back to bed I guess," said May. "Don't like police," she added.

Mary thought of suggesting that like them or not, someone was probably dead in her shop, possibly her own nephew, and that maybe she should stay put and talk to the police. Then she decided May would probably not be able to give any real assistance to Peter, and he'd know where to find her himself if he needed her.

As if she had been reading Mary's mind she turned and said, "I'll get Jerry up an' send him down to talk to Peter. I'll tell him you're out here waitin' for him. That'll get him movin'." She chuckled at this, and turned to walk the thirty feet back to her house as Mary winced and shook her head, shutting her eyes as she did.

When she opened them, Peter was standing next to her. "Did May have anything to say?" he asked.

"Only that she should have opened the shop herself. Should have been selling groceries, she said."

"I heard that's what she was doing with the shop when her husband ran off. Before my time, though."

"That's what I heard too. Her husband, George, and his secretary ran off with all the money they could get a hold of, and have never been heard of again."

"Yeah, not that anyone was looking too hard for 'em," frowned Peter. His frown said that he at least thought a husband who ran off with his secretary and took all his wife's money should be looked for and looked for seriously, too, but he put none of that thought into words.

"I understand that was what really drove May over the edge," said Mary. "She has never recovered. Keeps this shop and keeps saying she's going to open it again, but of course she couldn't. Her family is anxious to get her money, and they wouldn't let her try to run a business and maybe lose a little of their inheritance, even if she could."

"That so?" asked Peter.

"Well, they are just rumors, Captain Morgan, but the rumor is that the family has been trying to get her declared incompetent. Pretty solid rumor, too. I'm a lawyer's daughter, and the lawyer in question says way more than he should about legal issues that come to his attention."

"That so?" said Captain Morgan again.

"That is so," smiled Mary. "May said she's going back to bed if you want to interview her before she's declared incompetent."

At that point an unmarked black car pulled up and two ladies got out, went to the trunk, and began getting boxes and bags out.

"May'll have to wait," said Peter. "Crime scene boys are here."

Mary looked again at the two ladies removing their tools from the trunk of their vehicle. They were in their late twenties, maybe, and neither would have been mistaken for a "boy," crime scene or otherwise. Peter's gaze was resting comfortably on them and he didn't appear to be mistaken about their gender either.

In another minute he shifted his gaze back to Mary, or to what seemed to be a spot somewhat behind her. "I've got to get them started right now, but we'll need to talk in a minute."

He looked back at the two ladies carrying the equipment toward the crime scene, and then looked back toward that spot behind Mary. "Mornin', Jerry," he said, and walked away.

Chapter 7

First Mary blinked, and then amazement spread across her face, all in the few milliseconds that elapsed before she spun around to look behind her. There stood Jerry, hair all at loose ends and in bare feet, dressed in a tee shirt and baggy shorts, the kind surfers wore, at least the kind they wore in the movies.

"Jerry!" said Mary.

"Oh, hi," replied Jerry. "Aunty May said you were out here. What's goin' on?"

"Jerry," said Mary. "You're not dead!"

Jerry looked at her and blinked a couple of times. "No, I'm not, but I already know that. What's goin' on here?"

Mary wanted to say something about the relief that was spreading over her, but she didn't. She was tempted, though. "I'm not sure, Jerry. I got this call an hour or so ago, and...well, never mind that. I think someone broke into your shop, and I think someone may be dead in there."

Jerry thought for only a few seconds. "And you thought it might be me, Mary? And you came all the way over here to find out? That's real nice." Jerry was smiling at her. Not the least bit of sarcasm was showing, even though Mary was thinking there should be. *You came over here hoping I was dead?* That's what she would have been thinking if it were her shop Jerry was standing in front of. This was also a faster and more logical thought progression than she thought Jerry would be capable of.

He was still smiling when Mary answered, "Yeah. I was kind of hoping it wasn't you in there."

"I'm kinda glad it isn't me in there too," said Jerry. So much for that flash of brilliance.

Peter was walking back to them now.

"So Jerry, is it? Wilson? May Wilson's nephew?" he asked, looking at Jerry.

Jerry paused, looking intensely at the ground. *Information overload*, thought Mary. *Two pieces of data that had to be addressed at the same time.*

Jerry looked up and smiled only a few seconds later, but long enough to raise a little anxiety in both Mary and Peter. "Yeah," he said.

"Do you have an ID I can see?" asked Peter.

"Oh, yeah, sure," replied Jerry, but he made no move at all.

After a few more seconds, Peter tried again. "Do you think I can see it?"

"Oh sure," said Jerry. "I don't have it on me, but I got one somewhere. Up in my room maybe." He patted his tee shirt and empty baggie short pockets to show they were empty.

Peter was shaking his head, and Mary was stifling a giggle. The ambulance *boys* had been galvanized into motion by now and were rolling their stretcher back to their vehicle with a body on it, covered with a sheet. Behind them were the two crime scene *girls*, casting mischievous glances and smiles at the *surfer boy*. Jerry didn't seem to notice.

"Maybe you can find that for me later, Mr. Wilson," said Peter. He looked at the stretcher as it approached the ambulance, and then turned back to look at Jerry. "Would you mind looking at her and telling me if you know her?"

Jerry shrugged. "Yeah, I guess."

Peter departed to speak to the crime scene personnel and then to the ambulance personnel, and finally motioned to Jerry to come over. Mary hesitated only a second before she started following closely behind him. She wasn't sure Peter had intended to have her look at the body, since Peter would likely have recognized anyone Mary would recognize. Small Nebraska towns are like that, but she was curious. Peter didn't indicate that she should leave when they did arrive beside the stretcher, so she stayed.

Peter looked at Jerry, who looked first at the sheet-covered body, and then at Peter. Peter nodded, and Jerry blinked and then nodded, too. Peter then cast a quick look at Mary, and pulled the sheet back to expose the face and upper torso of a twenty-five-or-so-year-old blond woman.

She still had her makeup on, of course, and it was heavy, but well done. None of the discoloration of death showed through it. She really did look like she was sleeping, lying there with her eyes closed peacefully. A heart necklace of thin gold was around her neck, and this added to the serenity of the scene.

Mary gasped a quick, soft gasp, but Jerry just looked at her.

After a few more seconds, Peter spoke. "Do you know her, Mr. Wilson?"

"Yeah," said Jerry. It seemed as if he wasn't going to say anything else at first, but he then looked up and said, "It's Angie." He then looked back at the face.

Mary was surprised, and maybe Peter was too, but none showed on his face. "Angie?" he asked.

"Yeah," said Jerry, and looked up. He seemed to gradually realize that he was supposed to say something more. "Poor kid."

"How do you know her, Mr. Wilson?"

"Oh," said Jerry. "Ya see, I have this apartment back in Huntington Beach, California. And, well, I had a roommate for a while."

"And the roommate was Angie?"

"Oh, no. Laura was the roommate. Angie was just a friend. Of Laura's, I mean. But she used to crash there every so often."

"Did you know she was here in Nebraska, Mr. Wilson?"

Jerry frowned. "No. Maybe she moved out here, ya think? I mean, I haven't seen her for months. I don't think she's from around here."

Peter frowned now too. "We'll find out. Do you know her last name?'

"No," said Jerry.

"But she was a friend of Laura's, did you say?"

"Yeah, Laura's friend."

"Maybe you can give me Laura's name and address and we can see if the Huntington police can give us some information. Is she still your roommate?"

"No, Laura moved out six months ago. Split just like that. Haven't seen either of them since. I thought Laura might come back. Been saving her mail for her." Jerry just shrugged.

"Do you know Laura's last name?"

"No, not really."

Peter cleared his throat. "She was just a roommate then, not a...you didn't have a relationship with her then?" asked Peter.

"No," said Jerry, absently looking at Angie on the stretcher.

Mary smiled a little. She knew she wasn't part of this interrogation, but she felt as if Peter was blowing it, and she was curious anyway. "Did you have sex with her, Jerry?" she asked. Peter looked at her with annoyance. He had just asked that question, hadn't he?

Jerry shrugged. "Not really. Two or three times a week is all."

Mary smiled a little triumphantly, and Peter frowned. "Two or three times a week? Sex I mean," she asked.

"Yeah," shrugged Jerry. "Just two, or maybe three."

"Times a week?" said Mary, smiling.

"Yeah."

"So you were lovers?" said Peter.

"Oh, no. Nothing that serious." When no one else could say anything, Jerry continued. "Ya see, Laura was supposed to share the rent, but she had trouble keepin' up with it. I didn't mind. It was a cheap apartment, ya know, an' she cooked some, but she felt like she had to...you know, make it up to me, so she would like insist on having sex. I didn't really want to, but well, it made her feel better, ya see, so I would just like, go along with it. I think she might have enjoyed having sex a little too. She used to tell everyone she did anyway." Jerry shrugged. He was the only one who was not embarrassed by this revelation.

Mary blushed a little as she looked at the blond, tanned man in front of her. Yeah, a woman might enjoy sex if she didn't have to talk to him.

"So Laura was...well, she was...but Angie?" asked Peter. "You didn't have a relationship with Angie, did you? I mean, you didn't have sex with Angie, right?"

"Well, no. Not with Angie," said Jerry, looking at the body again.

"Peter," said Mary, looking at him. "Let me help a little here." Peter should have looked annoyed, but instead he looked relieved, very relieved.

"Jerry. Did you ever have sex with Angie?"

"Not with Angie," he said.

"Not with Angie, but…?" said Mary.

"Well, it was with Laura...*and* Angie," said Jerry. "Ya see, Laura liked to, well, sometimes she liked to have, like, a threesome, and when Angie was around she would insist that we do it together. I never liked it that way, and sometimes I'd get one of my friends to...well, you know. Some guys like that sort of stuff." Even Jerry was beginning to look embarrassed.

Peter was totally embarrassed. "You were...well, they were...but you didn't know their last names?"

"Well, not really. I mean, Laura told me her last name was Jones."

"That will be a big help. Not too many Laura Jones in Huntington Beach, California, are there?" said Peter.

Mary shrugged. "But you don't think that was her name, right Jerry?"

"Well, her driver's license had a different name."

"And what was that?" asked Peter.

"Smith," said Jerry.

"Oh, that's different. We can get that one out of the phone book," Peter replied pointedly, shutting his notebook.

"But you have her mail, Jerry? Right?" asked Mary.

"Oh, yeah," said Jerry. "Been saving it for her in case she shows up again."

"And who is it addressed to?" asked Mary.

"That's real funny," Jerry replied. "Her mail is all addressed to Laura Stewart. Angie got some mail there too, and it was addressed to Angie Stewart. Kind of a weird coincidence, ya think?"

"Not," said Mary.

"Not at all a coincidence," said Peter, opening his notebook again, "but definitely weird."

Chapter 8

"Maybe we can finish this later, okay?" said Peter.

That's what Peter said, but Mary was on a roll now. "How'd she die, Peter?"

Peter frowned, but Jerry answered. "Might be drugs," he offered.

"Oh?" said Mary.

"Angie did a lotta drugs," Jerry said.

"Yes," said Peter. "We will be checking that. We'll be checking the shop too, particularly the ice cream. For marijuana. There's this rumor going around, ya know."

Mary winced, but Jerry didn't seem the least concerned. "Yeah," he said. "She did a lotta weed. Some coke and heroin too, but it was the bath salts that got me nervous."

"We'll be checking for all those, Mr. Wilson."

"Can't check for the bath salts unless ya know what's in 'em. Dealers keep changing the formula. Check with the cops in Huntington. They're usually up on what's going around." Jerry shrugged.

When Mary and Peter cast quizzical looks at him, Jerry shrugged and continued. "Most of the time there are amphetamines in them, and usually some sorta hallucinogen, ecstasy sometimes. Lotta herbal stuff too. No one can keep up with it. State can't even make it illegal before it changes, and a lot of it gets sold on the Internet anyway. Hard for anyone to make a livin' sellin' these days. I know a guy who's gettin' outta the business completely. Told me he wants to get a job in landscaping." Jerry shrugged again and looked back at Angie.

Mary shook her head. "So you think it was drugs, Peter? Angie comes all the way from California to overdose in Jerry's shop? Does that make sense?"

"No," said Peter. When both Mary and Jerry looked at him, he shrugged and said, "Oh, hell. Might as well see if you can make sense of this." He was looking at Mary, not Jerry.

"She was shot," said Peter. "Twice in the chest." The crime scene people were looking seriously and disapprovingly at him and he hesitated briefly, but then pulled the sheet back to show the chest of what had been Angie, maybe with a last name of Stewart.

There was a shirt, a man's shirt, with blood stains and holes that had been made by two bullets.

"Are those powder burns?" asked Mary.

"Jesus, Mary!" said Peter.

"...and Joseph," said Mary.

"What?" asked Peter.

"My Dad used to say that when he got mad. 'Jesus, Mary and Joseph.' I don't think it was because my name is Mary, though. It might be some sort of biblical reference, ya think? I always used to think it sounded silly when he said it. *'Jesus, Mary and Joseph, Mary.'*"

"It's Jesus and his mother and father, I think," offered Jerry.

"What?" asked Peter again, this time looking at Jerry.

"So Peter," began Mary again, "are those powder burns?"

"Am I supposed to answer that?" said Peter.

"I got myself out of a really comfortable bed at two in the morning, Peter. The least you can do is to answer a simple question without getting all testy and everything."

The two crime scene girls were smirking now, and one even giggled a little.

"They look like powder burns," said Jerry. Peter and Mary cast questioning glances at him, but he didn't look up from where his eyes seemed fixed on the bullet holes in Angie's chest.

When he did look up he said, "I had a friend who got shot that way. Angie must have been comfortable with whoever wasted her to let them get this close. It looks like a small caliber weapon, .22 maybe. Probably a small handgun. That was what they used on my friend. A lot a street workers like the small guns. Easy to carry, an' hide. Easy to ditch if ya need ta do that too. Looks like they're low velocity wounds. Not torn up too much I mean." He shrugged and looked back at the wounds. "Poor Angie. Would it be okay to cover her back up do ya suppose?"

Peter grimaced. "We call them flash burns. Not really any 'powder' in them."

"Yeah, I've heard 'em called that too," said Jerry. "There're some on her skin too, I think. Bastard who shot her was real close. Okay if I cover her, sir?"

The crime scene girls were looking at Jerry with renewed respect, and possibly a little admiration. One surreptitiously slipped a notebook out of her pocket and wrote something in it.

There was silence for a moment; crime scene girls writing, ambulance boys waiting, and Peter puzzling.

"Sir?" said Mary. "I think that would be you, Peter. Okay to cover up again, *sir*?"

"What? Oh, yeah, yeah, sure. And load her up, too," he said, turning toward the ambulance crew. Jerry pulled the sheet over the body of Angie, and the ambulance crew moved it to the back of their vehicle and began loading 'her' into the back.

"So can we leave now, Peter?" asked Mary.

"What? Oh, yeah. I'll need to talk to you both some more though."

"Of course," said Mary.

Peter turned to face Jerry. "Your shop will be closed for a few days, Mr. Wilson. Until the investigation is concluded."

"Yeah," said Jerry, looking around him.

"I have to find out who the victim was for sure, and I have to find Prentiss Forrest to find out what his story is. That last part could take a little work."

"Finding Prentiss won't be that hard. I don't think he knows how to hide," said Mary.

"Finding him is the easy part," smirked Peter. "Talking to him will be the most difficult thing I have done in quite a while."

"True," said Mary. "I talked to him this morning, and take a look at what happened to me."

"I hope the police in Huntington can help with the ID on Angie," said Peter.

"They'll know Angie," said Jerry.

"You sure?" asked Peter.

Jerry just shrugged. "She's been picked up a few times. Drug stuff, mostly. And soliciting, of course. Do you know that's still illegal in California?"

"I didn't know that," smiled Peter.

"Yeah," said Jerry. "Crazy, isn't it?"

"Crazy is a good word tonight," replied Peter. He smiled again and asked, "You think they would 'know' Laura, too?"

"Yeah," said Jerry. "She's been busted a couple times too."

Peter smiled a little more broadly. "And what about Jeremiah Wilson? Have the police picked him up for anything?"

"Naw," shrugged Jerry. "Got a few parking tickets, but they don't keep track of those. Parking can be really difficult in Huntington."

Peter nodded. "I learned another thing this morning. Doesn't sound like Huntington is a great place to move to, what do ya think, Mr. Wilson?"

"It's okay, but not great. Surf's awesome though."

Chapter 9

"Can I talk to you, Mary?" asked Peter, looking toward a bewildered Jerry. "Alone," he added.

Mary looked over at Jerry, standing in his tee shirt and surfer baggies and she smiled. "I think we may be 'functionally' alone already, but if you want to be sure, why don't we mosey on down the path a bit, pa'dner. Isn't that the way the people from Huntington Beach, California think we should talk?"

"Be serious, Mary."

"Why?"

"Look, right now Jerry is the only suspect in this thing."

"What?"

"His shop, his girlfriend, and the drugs; and he knows more about selling drugs and 'wasting' people than anyone else I know. Who's number one on your list?"

Mary looked at Jerry again, to confirm her last impression, formed just ten seconds ago. "She wasn't his girlfriend. Angie was his roommate's girlfriend, that's all. So they had sex a couple of times. That's nothing. Look at who we're talking about, Peter. Jerry killing someone? Get real."

"I don't think so either. Not unless he's the best actor in California, but...who else? Prentiss? May? Look, I've got to get some more information about this and quick, before the investigation is taken over by the big guys upstairs. So I'll get to work on that, and you watch Jerry, okay?"

"Why me?"

"Because you are the smartest person I know, that's why."

"Flattery will not work, Peter. Don't stop trying. I like it, but it will not work."

"I need someone to keep track of him, or I'll have to arrest him," said Peter. "You want I should do that?"

"Well, no," said Mary, looking back at Jerry. "Can we do a little more flattery before I agree though?"

"Mary, you're the smartest person I know, and I know you can solve this case easy, if you have the motivation. Having to hang around with Jerry could be that motivation."

Mary looked at her feet and shook her head.

"Mary," said Peter. "If you were to move out of this town it would drop the average IQ score here into the single digits. I need your help and if I have to put poor Jerry in jail to get it, I will."

"Okay, Peter. You've about got me flattered up enough. How about one more to clinch it before I agree?"

"Yeah, sure," said Peter. "You're pretty, too. How's that?"

"The obvious absence of sincerity diminishes that a bit, but I'll accept it." Mary turned to Jerry and yelled, "Hey, Jerry! How about I buy you breakfast?"

"Oh," said Jerry. "I was going to just have some ice cream, but…" He looked at the shop surrounded by crime scene tape. "I guess I can't do that."

"Come on," said Mary, "and I'll buy us breakfast." Mary looked at Jerry and frowned. "Maybe you ought to get some shoes though, and a shirt over that tee. No place in this town has a dress code, but I do. Shoes definitely, if Mary buys."

"Oh, sure," said Jerry. "I'll just run upstairs."

"To the room that Peter will be searching later today? Maybe he'll go with you and help you pick out a few days' worth of clothing, ya think, Peter?"

"Oh, I can wear these for a few more days," offered Jerry.

Mary looked at him. "No, you can't. Peter, go with him and tell me if he has a small .22 up there so I can cancel my too-hastily-made promise to you."

Peter nodded, and they went into the house to return a few minutes later with a knapsack, and shoes and a shirt on Jerry. The shirt was unbuttoned, and Jerry was smiling.

"Okay," said Mary. "You look presentable. At least for this town. Maybe a little overdressed for Huntington."

"Naw," shrugged Jerry. "I wear shoes in Huntington sometimes too. No one minds if ya do."

"Amazing," said Mary. "You didn't notice anything that would change my breakfast plans, did you, Peter?"

"Not the thorough search that will be done later, but I did look around and there was nothing that will relieve you of your commitment, Mary. I also made sure that Jerry packed only clothing, nothing else, in his knapsack. He even has his underwear packed."

"Yeah," said Jerry. "Both pairs." He smiled as if this were an amazing thing, that he had two pair of underwear. Mary thought it was amazing too, that he had *only* two pair. She hoped she wouldn't have to be with Jerry when he ran out of underwear.

"What else should I have packed?" asked Jerry.

"Nothing, Jerry. Get in my car, and we'll get some breakfast. It's too early to start drinking, isn't it?"

Jerry started for the car, and Peter looked at Mary. "Thanks," he said. "Way too early to start drinking. I owe ya."

"Can I ask you one more question, Peter?" said Mary.

"Guess so?"

"Do you drink at all, Captain Morgan?"

"Not a drop. Born-again Baptist is what you're lookin' at. Hell of a name isn't it? *Captain Morgan.*"

"Maybe if you solve this one, they'll promote you, ya think?"

"Maybe if *we* solve this one, ya mean. I'm countin' on you, Mary. *Major* Morgan sounds good to me."

Peter walked over to Carl and said, "You stand right here until someone comes to finish securing the scene, ya hear me? No one goes into the shop, or..." he looked back at Mary, "or the house."

"May's already in the house," said Carl.

"That won't matter much, but make sure no one else goes in. I'll put the tape on the house too when I get back."

Chapter 10

Mary walked over to her car. It was unlocked, of course, since this was Nebraska. Jerry was standing beside it looking as if he wasn't sure what to do.

"It's unlocked, Jerry."

"Oh," he said. "Just wondering where I should put my clothes. Ya think the back seat is okay, or should I put 'em in the trunk?"

Mary thought for a minute. "Maybe the trunk. I don't want people to think you're moving in with me."

Mary went to the trunk of her ten-year-old Japanese car and inserted the key to open it. She jiggled the key and tried to turn it, but nothing happened. "Damn thing won't open. Maybe in the back seat," she said, looking at the backpack.

"Mind if I try?" asked Jerry.

Mary looked sarcastically at him but nodded, offering him her keys. He didn't take them, but instead opened his backpack and after a few seconds pulled out a universal tool, the kind with twenty or so blades of various sorts on it. He opened one, and after looking at the uncooperative lock on the trunk, inserted the blade into the lock. He then shut his eyes and began to hum in a quiet monotone, but only for a moment. It was such a strange sight that Mary didn't even notice that he was manipulating the tool in his hand until the trunk popped open.

"Ya ought ta put some graphite in it," he said as he stood.

"You have any of that in your backpack?"

"I don't think so," he replied, as he looked at it. "I'll look."

"I'll buy some," said Mary. Jerry just stood there looking at the trunk, and then bent over to look inside.

"It's supposed to have a release from inside the car, but that hasn't worked for years."

"Yeah," said Jerry. "Wire's disconnected here." He pointed to a loose wire along the back of the trunk. "I thought maybe you had disconnected it on purpose."

"Yeah, that would be real logical," smirked Mary.

Jerry just nodded. "Yeah, people do that sometimes so if someone breaks into the car, like smashes in a window, they can't get into the trunk without prying it. Can't just pop it from inside I mean. I thought you might have done that." He shrugged.

Mary was slightly embarrassed. "No. It just broke and I haven't had time to get it fixed yet."

Jerry shrugged again. "Easy ta fix," he said. After a few seconds he looked up and smiled. "You want me to fix it? I'd feel better about breakfast if I did something for you."

Mary smiled. At least he hadn't "insisted" on having sex, as Laura had done when she couldn't come up with the rent. "Well, yeah. We can get something to eat and then you can fix the trunk while I open the shop."

"Oh," beamed Jerry. "This won't take but a few seconds." He didn't wait for an answer, but opened another blade on his universal tool. He took the loose wire, cleaned it of insulation, and then switched blades again to what looked like a screwdriver. He tried the screw on the small box next to the trunk release, but it didn't appear to move.

He stood and frowned, but only briefly. He bent and rummaged through his already open backpack and came out with two small cans, one of which was labeled "Penetrating Oil".

"Here it is," he said.

He then sprayed the stubborn screw, bent and jiggled it a few times with the screwdriver blade and then sprayed again, spraying some on the latch, too. When he tried the screw after the second spay, it was a serious effort, and the screw surrendered without a fight. Jerry smiled, pulled out the bottom of his tee shirt and wiped the oil and rust off the screw with it before wrapping the wire end around it. He then tightened the screw and turned to Mary.

"Want ta try the inside release?" he said as he shut the trunk.

"Pretty confident," said Mary.

"Should work now," Jerry replied.

Mary went around to the driver's door of her car, and pressed the button that hadn't worked in three years, and the trunk popped open. Mary was going to say that she'd had it to several mechanics who had offered to look at it for several hundred dollars, which she didn't have, but she decided not to get Jerry's ego too large this early in the morning.

Jerry shut the trunk again as Mary came around to the back of the car. "Your backpack, Jerry," she said.

"Yeah," said Jerry, but not to Mary. He put the universal tool and the oil spray into a canvas pouch in the backpack. He then took the second can he'd taken out and inserted the straw thing into the key slot. After a couple of sprays from this can, he looked up and said, "Can I borrow your key for a minute?"

Mary handed him her keys, and he fiddled several times with the lock until the trunk finally popped open again. He then shut it and fiddled several times again with the lock and key until the trunk opened easily each time he turned it. He took the key and wiped it off with the end of his tee shirt before handing it back.

He looked up at Mary and held up the small can, saying, "Couldn't remember if I still had any of the graphite." Having offered this explanation, he put it back in the canvas pouch and put the pouch into the backpack, closed it, and put it all into the trunk and then closed that too.

There they stood, Jerry smiling, with Mary standing next to him in puzzled admiration. Finally she said, "Well, let's get some breakfast."

"Yeah," said Jerry. "My treat."

"Your treat?" asked Mary. "I thought you were fixing my trunk in exchange for breakfast. You said it would make you feel better about breakfast, didn't you?"

"Well, yeah," shrugged Jerry. "That was so you would drive me to breakfast...and so you'd have breakfast with me too. I'd feel better about havin' breakfast with you if I fixed your car first."

Mary looked at him, but Jerry just walked around to the passenger's door and got in, and Mary did the same on the driver's side. She looked over at Carl, who had not moved from where Peter had told him to stand, and she waved. Carl looked as if he wasn't sure he was allowed to move enough to wave, but he finally took a chance and did. May was on the porch watching, and Peter had already left.

Chapter 11

So now Mary had a problem. She had planned to go to a local drive-through for breakfast since money, her money, was short. But now maybe a real sit-down place where they could talk a little would work better. If she was going to solve this case for Peter, maybe she should start investigating it first. The problem was that Jerry was paying, and while she hadn't earned any money last night because of Jerry, he hadn't earned any money either, for the same reason—his own fault. Everyone in town got ice cream without paying either of them for it.

As if he were reading her mind, Jerry looked over and said, "Let's go someplace where we can sit and talk a little. If that's okay, I mean."

"Good idea," said Mary, as she wondered if he really could read her mind. He was a strange one, and who knew what they were teaching people to do in California, beside surfing and "pharmacology"? She started the car and began driving towards the only good breakfast in this town, which also happened to be the only good lunch and supper. It was also the only decent bar, or "pub" as they preferred to be called: *Roses Pub*.

"So Jerry, that was moderately impressive back there," said Mary.

"What was?"

Mary thought for a moment. She had been talking about the car repair, but there had been a lot that was impressive, "back there" starting with a murder, the lecture on drug use and bath salts, and then the forensic evidence found on Angie. Mary frowned. The latter subjects were something any drug dealer would know, and maybe breaking into cars was a sideline that required a few skills that would be useful in repairing those cars as well. Still, her trunk now opened, which it hadn't done for three years, so…

"Do you always carry a car repair kit with you, Jerry?" she asked. *Is breaking and entering a second career choice on your resume?* she considered asking too.

"Yeah," he said, looking out the window. "Real bummer at the airports."

"Oh?" said Mary.

"Yeah. I don't fly too much, ya know. First time I'd flown in years was that last trip out here a year ago. Anyway, I just packed my backpack when Auntie May called an' asked me to come out an' help, but I didn't know ya couldn't bring a knife in your luggage."

"Yeah, can't do that anymore. What happened?"

"Oh, the security guys searched my backpack after they x-rayed it, and then told me I couldn't take my tool kit on the plane."

"So did you have to leave it there at the airport? They made me throw away my shampoo and conditioner one time 'cause the bottles were too big."

"Oh, it worked out. I just gave it to some guy getting off a plane an' asked him to get it to a friend a mine."

"And he did?"

"Well, yeah."

"Did you know him?"

"My friend? Sure. Known him for years."

"No," said Mary, shaking her head. "I mean the guy in the airport you gave your tool kit to?"

"Oh, him? No. Just a guy leavin' a plane. He looked honest. He talked to my friend a little when he dropped off the tools, an' when I got back we all went out to breakfast. Nice guy. I see him on the beach sometimes. I put my stuff in the check-in luggage now."

"You were lucky, Jerry."

"Ya think?"

"So, how do know about fixing locks, anyway?"

"I got a friend who showed me. He's not really a friend. Know him from the rehab center, but he showed me." Jerry just shrugged. "Not real hard. I can show you too if ya want." He looked at Mary and smiled.

"Maybe later."

They drove in quiet for a while, Mary thinking, and Jerry just looking out the window at the landscape rolling monotonously by.

"Too bad about your friend Angie," she said. She was truly sorry about that, and she hadn't even known her. She thought maybe Jerry wasn't as upset as she would have thought he should be. She looked quickly at him as she spoke, but somehow could not see him as Angie's killer.

"Yeah," he said. "She's been walkin' dead since I met her. Still too bad. And shot like that, too." He shook his head as the only sign that there was any emotion behind the words.

"Walking dead?" asked Mary.

"Drugs," he said. "First time I saw her I knew this would happen someday. She just couldn't see it comin'. Laura can't either. If she's still alive." Jerry shook his head again, and looked out the window at the few buildings that made up this town.

If this had been a friendly conversation, Mary would have let it end there, but this wasn't. She remembered Peter saying Jerry was the only suspect, and she needed to change the names on that list before someone further up the food chain than Peter was, got the case.

"Did you know she was here in Nebraska, Jerry?"

He looked at her before answering. Maybe he knew she was interrogating him, or maybe he was hiding something, or …

"No," he said. He sighed finally. "I heard she was asking about me a couple a times, but I never saw her after Laura split."

"Did she call you or anything?"

"No," he said, and became embarrassed. "I don't have a cell phone."

Now Mary began to feel as if she were entering another dimension in an upside down universe. Was she really riding next to the only person on this planet without a cell phone?

"You don't have a phone, Jerry?"

"No." He became more embarrassed now. "It's the microwaves. They affect your brain."

They might affect your brain if you had one, thought Mary.

Jerry must have sensed her surprise, which at this point wasn't requiring a great deal of observational skill. "They've done studies on it. Scans and everything. Besides, they can be addicting, too."

Mary really didn't know what to say at this point, but was glad to see Roses Pub right where it should be: where she had last seen it. If the world was entering a new dimension, at least they could have breakfast first.

Chapter 12

Mary had had a chance to think a little by the time they were seated by Sandy, the only server at Roses this early in the morning. It was almost six o'clock, and it would be picking up soon. Mary was ready to eat, and ready to ask a select few of the several hundred questions that were buzzing in her brain.

Sandy took their order: Coffee with bacon and scrambled eggs for Mary. A cheese and broccoli omelet for Jerry with only juice to drink. Mary hoped he wouldn't fall asleep in front of her. She knew she would be asleep unless she got coffee soon. Sandy might have been surprised there was no coffee included in Jerry's order (everyone here had coffee with breakfast), but she seemed more surprised at Jerry himself: blond hair, unbuttoned shirt over a dirty tee shirt, surfer baggies and shoes with no socks.

Mary was about to ask her first question, but Jerry beat her to it. "They serve alcohol here too?" he asked.

Mary looked at him nervously. "Yeah. It's a little early though. They could probably..." She let it dwindle to an end there.

When Jerry said nothing, she asked. "Do you want a drink, Jerry?"

"What? Oh, no. I don't drink," he said. "You can have one if you want," he added.

"Not this early in the morning, and not with the night I had last night."

"Oh," said Jerry.

Mary's first question had been pushed aside by this exchange. "So you don't drink, Jerry? At all?"

"No," he replied. "Bad karma."

Okay, thought Mary. *We are slipping back into that other dimension. I hope Sandy will be coming with us, because I'm not going to starve for Peter.*

The direct approach was the only option that would work, it seemed. "So, Jerry," Mary said. "Let me get this straight, if that's at all possible. You sell grass back in California, but you don't drink alcohol. Does that mean you don't use drugs either? Do you smoke the marijuana?"

"No," he said. "That stuff is bad for you, Mary. I hope you aren't into that stuff. Even the weed messes up your brain."

"Okay, Jerry, the part where this makes sense is missing to me. You sell it, but don't use it because you think it messes you up, is that right? But you sell it anyway?"

Jerry looked puzzled. "I sell grass," he said.

"Yeah," replied Mary. "That part I got. But you think it messes up your brain, so you don't use it yourself. Is this a study in hypocrisy or what?"

Jerry looked puzzled. "I sell grass, Mary."

"Yes?"

"I don't sell weed."

"You sell grass, but not...am I missing something?"

"Maybe. You're not making much sense right now. Do you smoke weed, Mary?"

"Of course not! Well, not for a long time."

"Good," smiled Jerry. He shrugged. "I used to smoke a little, back in high school."

"That's when I...we went to the same high school, Jerry. I didn't know you smoked. Okay, okay. High school reminiscences later. What am I missing here? What do you do back in beautiful, sunny California, Jerry?"

Jerry looked intently at her. "I sell grass." When Mary just stared, he continued. "You know, fescue, an' souza mostly. That's what the guys up country like for their lawns. Oh, I know what you're thinkin', Mary—that bluegrass is the best, and I think you're right, but people don't know how to take care of it."

Mary blinked a couple times. "You sell grass, not weed? Not marijuana?"

"Why'd you think I sold weed, Mary?"

"You said...but...You sell grass? Like, real grass, lawn and seeds and....What do you sell, Jerry? What do you do in the sunny country you live in?"

"I sell grass. Well, what it really is, is a landscaping service. Ya see, a bunch of my friends, mostly guys I surf with, set up this landscaping service. We all work, but each of us is like a specialist in something.

"George is really into the shrubs: topiary an' stuff, an' Paul, he's like the tree guy. I'm the grass guy. We all do mowing an' raking an' that stuff, but for the real landscaping, we specialize. It works better that way." He smiled and nodded at the bewildered face opposite him. "Nobody calls it 'grass' anymore anyway. That went out in the sixties."

Sandy arrived with the order and stayed, smiling at Jerry. When he smiled back she said, "So are you Jerry, May's nephew?"

"Yeah," smiled Jerry.

She looked around and lowered her voice. "I heard you might be able to get me some, you know—"

Mary cut her short. "He sells grass, Sandy. Real grass. If you want your lawn fixed up, keep talking, but if you want any weed, it's not going to be found here."

Sandy looked bewildered for a moment. "Real grass? Like a lawn?"

"Yeah," smiled Jerry. "It's tough this time of year here in Nebraska, 'cause it's dry, but if you get a hardy..."

Sandy had turned and was walking from the table by now.

"Poor Sandy," chuckled Mary. "But I'm still here, and you were telling me about landscaping."

"Yeah," said Jerry, taking a bite of the omelet. "It's a great job. Out in the sunshine and makin' things grow. God does the work, and I get the credit."

"Yeah," said Mary. She began to eat too, and to drink her coffee. Maybe it was the coffee, but she started to think about who this guy was, and not about his murdered friend as much.

"So how do you know so much about the drugs and the dealers and wasting people? Are you friends with the dealers or something?"

"Oh, I guess some of the people I know deal a little. I think Laura did, and maybe Angie, too. Not real friends." He shrugged and took a drink of the juice. He had asked for a mixture of orange and a little cranberry since there was no mango available.

"Mostly I pick it up at the rehab," he added, and took another bite of omelet.

"You go to a rehab? What are you rehabbing? Not that high school weed still?"

"Naw. I'm a counselor there."

"A counselor?"

"Yeah. I got a certificate and all that, so they could bill for it, but it really doesn't tell you what you need to know. The guys in recovery can teach ya more in half an hour than they can tell ya in a year in the classroom."

"So you work there too?"

"Not work, just volunteer."

"But you said they bill?"

"Everyone 'bills', Mary. I do it for the good it does for me and the guys I counsel. The rehab collects the money so they can stay open and give me a place to counsel the guys. It all works out."

When Mary just looked at him, he added, "Ya know, Mary, God put us here for a reason."

Mary smiled and said, "You mean it's not just about the surfing after all?"

"Ah, man. Ya got me there. The surfin's great. Out there on the water, under the sun. Sometimes I'll just lie there on the board and take it all in. Some days I paddle myself out there and then have to paddle myself back in. No surf to surf in on, even, but it's still great."

"Waiting for the perfect wave, right?"

Jerry smiled his most charming smile now. "There are no perfect waves, Mary. *People* are what it's about." He ate a little more before looking at her again.

"So the rehab. Is that where you met Laura and Angie?"

"No. Laura was gettin' evicted when I was renting my place, an' I told her she could stay for a few weeks 'til she got another place. She was still there three months later. Angie? Well, she was just Laura's friend."

"Did they go to…?"

"The rehab?" finished Jerry. "No. I tried, but they didn't think it was a problem. They thought I had the problem 'cause I didn't use."

Mary thought for a minute. She may as well finish her police work all at once. "How did your friend get shot? The one who got shot like Angie did?"

"Oh," said Jerry. "Not really a friend. A guy I was counseling. Back then I would tell people where I lived and how to get in touch with me. I had a cell phone then. Anyway, he called one night, said he was hurt, and needed help. I went and found him, but he was already dead. Shot just like Angie was.

"Cops showed up and I talked about it to them. I know a couple of 'em that surf with me. I talked to the guys at the rehab, too. The counselors and the guys in recovery.

"At the rehab they just said it happens that way. It's the truth, too. I was just starting there, but even I could see that was the truth. I would come in to see some guy for his regular session, and he wouldn't show. Somebody'd say: *Oh, Frank? He got busted, or, he overdosed an' is in the hospital, or, well...he got killed.* That's what happens if ya don't get clean and sober."

"Yeah," said Mary. "I guess it does. What do you do when it happens, though?"

Jerry shrugged. "I go surfing, an' then I go to work, 'cause I'm not the one that died. I don't have a cell phone anymore though."

"No surfing in Nebraska," Mary said.

Jerry shrugged again. "Maybe I'll walk around in the prairie. Lie on my board on the grass here. Maybe I can do some prairie surfing, ya think? Same God here."

"Yeah," said Mary. "Same devil, too."

Jerry sighed now and nodded. "Yeah. I got used to it. I got so I could see it coming. I cried after that guy got shot, and I'll cry about Angie too, but that's what happens. You try to help and sometimes you can, but.... One of the guys told me it has to happen that way.

"If everyone who uses lived forever, no one would ever stop using. Someone has to die so the rest can see they have to stop. I knew Angie was going to be one of the ones who would have to die."

He sighed again and looked close to those tears.

"You think it was drugs?"

"She didn't overdose, if that's what you mean. Bullet holes, not needle tracks; but it's not just about the drugs you use, it's about the lifestyle that goes with it."

"Yeah," said Mary. "I don't think I've ever heard a truer statement than that one, Jerry."

They were quiet for several minutes, eating and thinking. Jerry looked at Mary when he was finished his juice.

"I really like you, Mary," he finally said, and then just went back to his omelet.

Chapter 13

Mary stared now. *Oh shit*, she said to her numb brain. *This is not going the way Peter promised it would!*

Jerry smiled and looked out the window. "Ya know, Nebraska's kinda pretty, really. All open prairie and rolling landscape. Kinda like the ocean is. You can feel God here."

"Except they don't grow corn on the ocean, and they don't shoot people there either," observed Mary.

"They farm fish there a lot though," he said.

Mary thought this last statement might have been inserted just to emphasize the totally illogical nature of this conversation. She was going to ask if the fish farming was equivalent to growing corn or to killing people. The fish ended up dead, after all.

"It's okay for a nice, long, boring drive," said Mary.

Jerry looked at her. "You can't 'drive' through it, Mary. You have to walk through it. It would be like having someone take you out to surf in a boat. You have to paddle your way out there and wait for the wave to make it mean anything." He nodded and smiled again, as if this was the most logical thing in the world.

"Are you like, religious or something, Jerry? You talk a lot about God, but do you go to church? Or is your relationship with God through nature and surfing? Do you think Jesus surfed, by the way?"

"I don't think they surfed a lot back then. Yeah, I kind of go to church," he replied.

"Kind of?" asked Mary. "You mean you *kind of go*, or it's *kind of a church*? Do you just go down to the beach and talk to the seaweed or something?"

"Oh, it's a real church, but I just listen, I don't belong or anything. I sing in the choir sometimes and teach in the Sunday school if they need help, but I don't really belong to the church."

"It sounds like you...it's not a Baptist church, is it?"

"No," said Jerry. "I think it's Presbyterian or something. Is that the right name?"

"Probably," said Mary. "I don't think I could have breakfast with a Baptist, and of course a Baptist wouldn't be caught dead in a bar, even Roses. Peter maybe but not a good Baptist."

"Yeah. I went to the Baptist one once. They were really weird. Singing was cool though."

"It was weird, but you didn't like it? I'm surprised. Different kind of weird I guess, because you are not weird the way Baptists are weird. Actually, I don't think you are weird the same way anyone else is,"

Jerry just nodded and smiled.

Mary smiled too. She thought about Jerry from back in high school. Maybe he had a right to be weird. His mother died the year after Jerry graduated high school. Aunty May had sort of raised Jerry the rest of the way, until he moved away—to California. May had two brothers, younger than both she and her sister, and neither had ever married. Rufus and William were therefore free to devote all of their efforts to making sure that none of May's money was being squandered on such things as food or clothing for May, thereby ensuring that as much of it as possible would be left to be inherited by them. They were also trying to sell May's shop, it was rumored, and were trying to have her declared legally incompetent to accomplish this, and right now, they were walking over to the table where Mary and Jerry were sitting.

"Morning, Rufus. Billy," said Mary.

Jerry turned his smiling face toward the two frowning faces that had just joined them. "Oh, hi, Rufus, and you too, Billy."

Rufus was the older by a year or so, and the one that spoke for both. "Heard one a your friends got herself shot at that shop of May's last night, Jerry."

"Yeah, Angie."

Rufus wasn't much for subtlety, so it surprised Mary not at all that he cut to the chase. "That'll mean you won't be stayin' around I guess, Jerry."

"I thought I might. Until it gets settled."

"I think Peter Morgan, Captain Morgan I mean, kind of expects Jerry to stay around, Rufus," said Mary.

"You kill her, Jerry?" asked Rufus, ignoring Mary.

"No," Jerry said. Simple and straight.

"No need ta stay around then, Peter Morgan or not. If I was you I'd get outta here as quick as I could."

"I'll have to talk to Aunty May about that," smiled Jerry. If he realized he was being threatened, and Mary couldn't believe that he didn't realize that he was being threatened, he didn't seem concerned at all. Everyone else in Roses was aware of it, and watching it closely.

"May's got nothin' to do with this," snarled Rufus. "Crazy old bat, throwin' our money away."

Mary shrugged. "It's still her money right now, Rufus. Not your inheritance yet. All tied up in trusts. George, the runaway husband, did that, and there's his life insurance too, but it is May's money. Four years ago those trusts started working their way through the legal system and in another year, five years since George disappeared, the trusts will lapse. No one seems to know where George is, or has seen him, so he'll be legally dead then. Isn't that right, Rufus?"

"Fool," said Rufus, although it wasn't clear who he was speaking about. Mary had a couple of candidates standing right in front of her, but they were probably not the same ones Rufus was thinking of, especially since one of Mary's choices was Rufus.

"You'll be gone from this town by tomorrow if ya know what's good for ya, Jerry."

"I'll think about it, but I'm not sure I should leave just yet, Rufus."

Rufus scowled and looked as if he was about to speak, but then turned to his brother and said, "C'mon, Billy." They walked out of Roses, and there was a collective sigh of relief from all those still inside.

Sandy was at their table a nanosecond later with the check.

"I'll take that," said Jerry. He looked at the check and placed ten dollars on the table. Sandy didn't notice, since she was intently watching Rufus and Billy. Jerry looked at her and then at the check again and took out a five dollar bill to keep the ten company. He frowned and then placed a one with the fifteen.

"I could use another cup of coffee, Sandy," said Mary.

Sandy was still devoting her full attention to the Wilson boys and Jerry looked at Mary and said, "You really shouldn't drink so much coffee. The caffeine isn't good for you."

"Yeah, Mary," said Sandy, without moving her field of vision to include Mary. "That's a good idea."

"Thanks," Jerry said to the server, who was totally absorbed with other things at the moment.

"We better get over to your shop," he said to the only slightly less absorbed Mary, still staring at her empty coffee mug.

"Yeah, okay," said Mary, glaring first at Sandy and then at Jerry. "I can brew better coffee over there anyway."

Jerry walked out the door onto the street. Mary would have been right beside him except she wanted to look at the check that had caused Jerry so much consternation. When she did, she saw that the meal had cost a little more than eight dollars, which made a tip of almost eight dollars. Sandy was not worth anywhere near that much, especially since she hadn't produced any more coffee. Mary thought of removing some of the money Jerry had left, but she had just given a little lecture on avaricious behavior to the Wilson brothers, and it wasn't her money to take, so...your lucky day, Sandy.

If Mary had gone out with Jerry, she would have been there to hear the beginning of the conversation, but as it was, when she stepped onto the street, all that was left to be heard was Rufus saying, "...teach you a lesson."

Rufus had a baseball bat in his hand, while Billy had a tire iron, and both were coming straight toward Jerry with obvious malicious intent. Jerry for his part was standing almost motionless, facing the attack. His knees were slightly bent as if he were ready to move, but didn't know which way to move. His arms and hands were outstretched at his sides.

Mary was afraid that in two more seconds he would be lying on the ground, beaten to the proverbial pulp, as her father used to say.

"Jerry!" she yelled and started to run, but she was too far away to reach him in time.

Her yell brought the few people who were still seated inside Roses to the windows, and some were pulling out their cell phones. Most were preparing to video the event, but Mary vaguely hoped one or two were calling the police, who should arrive in time to take what was left of Jerry to the hospital, or maybe directly to the morgue.

What followed wasn't what was expected; not what anyone imagined even. It could have been a well-choreographed dance number for some music video, or even the trailer for the newest martial arts movie.

Billy reached Jerry first, his tire iron swinging down on Jerry, but Jerry leaned toward him, instead of away. The tire iron went over him, and Jerry had Billy's arm in his hands, pulling Billy over his back. Mary was close and could see that Jerry also was bending the hand that held the tire iron back at a very acute angle. Billy yelled and dropped the iron, which skidded across the sidewalk and Mary had to jump to avoid it.

Meanwhile, Jerry had flipped Billy over his back and sent him colliding into Rufus, and the two of them were entangled on the pavement.

"Be careful, Mary," said Jerry.

Rufus was up, bat in hand and swinging at Jerry, who again simply turned, and instead of trying to stop the blow, pulled it toward him, directing it to the side. This move put Rufus off balance and in a second he was on his back, on the pavement, as well. The bat spun toward Billy, striking him in the shin.

"Damn it, Rufus!" yelled Billy.

"Well, get him, for Christ's sakes!" replied Rufus.

Billy picked up the bat and looked at it and then at Jerry. He was standing as he had been before, with his knees slightly bent and his arms spread to the sides. Billy looked again at the bat, and raised it over his head as he took a few steps forward, almost as if he knew there was nothing he could do, but also knew he would have to do it anyway.

When he swung, Jerry again pulled the bat toward him, slipping it from Billy's grasp, and rolling him over his back and placing him on, not throwing him to, the ground. He stood over them with the bat in his right hand by his side, with the two Wilson brothers staring up at him.

"Sorry," said Jerry. "Hope I didn't hurt you." He then shifted the bat to his left hand and extended his right toward Billy. Mary could see this, although she could not yet believe it. It looked like Jerry was offering his hand to help Billy to his feet.

If Mary was having trouble, Billy couldn't believe it at all. He scuttled along on his back like some sort of crab trying to escape from Jerry until he ran into the outside wall of Roses. He only paused a moment before jumping to his feet and beginning to run for his pickup.

"C'mon!" he yelled to Rufus.

Rufus looked as if he thought one more attempt ought to be made, probably by Billy, but he quickly got up and started running as well.

"We shoulda—" he started to say.

"Shut up," said Billy. "Just shut the fuch up."

A few seconds later they were driving away as fast as they could.

Chapter 14

"You okay, Mary?" asked Jerry.

"In shock, amazed, scared shitless, and oh, yeah; I'm okay, too. What the hell was that?"

Jerry just shrugged. He then picked up the bat and tire iron and leaned them up against the outside of Roses. When he looked around again, Mary was looking down the street toward a state police car driving up the street, rollers flashing, with Peter behind the wheel.

Peter got out and looked around. "Someone called in that there was a brawl here?"

"You're going to have to drive faster than that, Peter," said Mary. "You missed the whole show."

Peter looked around again. "What'd I miss? Anyone hurt?"

"I don't think Rufus or Billy were hurt at all," said Jerry.

"Rufus and Billy?" asked Peter. "The Wilson boys? Who were they mixing it up with? They're probably the one's hurt."

"They were 'mixing it up' with Jerry, and it was a complete rout," smiled Mary, finding herself all of a sudden proud of her friend Jerry.

Mary might have been proud, but Peter was amazed. "With Jerry? This Jerry? You hurt at all?"

"What?" said Jerry. "Why would I be hurt?"

Peter looked at Mary. "Yeah, Peter. Why would Jerry be hurt with just the Wilson boys to deal with? They're just two of the toughest thugs in this town, that's all. Jerry is the grass specialist back in Huntington Beach, California. Not weed or marijuana, but *real* grass. Fescue and souza mostly, but he's really a dedicated bluegrass man, and the Wilson boys probably don't even know the difference. Oh, by the way, marijuana hasn't been called *grass* since the sixties."

"What are you talkin' about, Mary?" asked Peter.

"His only problem is that he doesn't answer questions. What the hell was that, Jerry?"

Jerry looked at Mary. "What?"

Peter shook his head. "Look, I gotta talk to you anyway. Can we go into Roses and talk over a cup of coffee maybe?"

"If Jerry will let you have one. How many have you had already this morning, Peter? Oh none at all, you said? I haven't had any either so we can all have our first cup of the day right here at Roses, and not get overdosed on caffeine," Mary said with her most winsome smile.

"You had a cup of coffee with breakfast, I think," said Jerry.

"Why were you paying attention to that, Jerry, when you're so oblivious to everything else?"

"I care about you, I guess," offered Jerry, and Mary rolled her eyes.

"And this will be my third," said Peter. "You know, you're not making much sense right now, Mary."

"Yes I am, and you'll be sorry, Peter. It was a perfectly good lie and it was working great until you decided to tell the truth. Anyhow...come on in and let's talk, before I pass out from lack of caffeine." She turned to re-enter the restaurant as Peter shook his head.

There were still a few people standing at the windows, and a few of these offered muted congratulations to Jerry. The police were here, and most appeared to be unsure whether they might get Jerry in trouble, or might get themselves in trouble, by acknowledging that they were witnesses to some sort of crime.

As they walked toward an empty table, they passed three workmen leaving, dressed as they did in Nebraska, contrasting with the California style Jerry was wearing. Their jeans and tees with baseball caps advertising various cars or tractor manufacturers and covering well-trimmed short haircuts would have seemed to place an unreachable divide between them. As they passed, however, each nodded to Jerry, who nodded back. The last in the line stopped and extended his hand.

"That was great," he said, as Jerry took the offered hand. He then reached with his left hand up to slap Jerry's shoulder. "Really great. Those boys have been cruisin' for a bruisin' for a long time. You're May's kin, aren't ya?"

"Yeah," said Jerry. "Jeremiah Wilson. May's sister Lucy's son." Mary had to marvel a little. This was exactly the proper thing to say, here in small-town Nebraska where whose kin you were was more important than who *you* were.

"Well I'm Bert, an' this here's Percy an' Homer," he said, nodding toward his companions.

"Glad ta meet ya," said Jerry, as he extended his hand toward the other two. They shook all around and as they left, Percy and Homer slapped Jerry's shoulder too.

"Hope ya stay a while, Jerry," said Bert as he left.

Peter turned to look at Jerry and asked, "What did happen here?"

Jerry just shrugged, but Peter only had to wait a few seconds before one of the younger patrons was at his side. "Ya want ta see? I got it on my cell." He then proceeded to show a video of the "brawl." The sounds of the brawl were missing since he had been safe inside when he had taken the video, but there were the sounds of astonished voices in the background which added to the drama.

"That's no good," said another young man as he approached pushing his cell phone in front of Peter. "You were too far away, fuzz brain."

Peter was looking intently at the recorded event. "How'd you get him to drop the tire iron so easily?" he asked of Jerry, but without looking up at all.

Jerry didn't have time to respond before a third person joined the group.

This one was a young lady, less than twenty years old, and Mary thought she was dressed suitably for California. Long blond hair, shorts that would have revealed any underwear larger than a thong, and a top that Mary would have been embarrassed to wear on the beach, if there were a beach here in this Nebraska town.

"You're a total loser, Dweeb," she said, smiling at him and tossing back her hair. She was still watching him as she pushed her cell phone in front of Peter with her pink nails. "And mine's already posted on the Net."

Peter was looking intently at the new offering. "Nice," he said. "Good close-up." She had obviously been outside, too, since the sounds of the brawl were recorded on her offering.

When it had finished, she closed the phone and shook her hair and her hips. "Losers," she said again and walked away, her long blond hair and her body swaying as she did. Mary was watching with just a little envy, and Peter was watching with obvious admiration. Even Jerry cast a glance after her, but neither of her friends paid any attention at all.

"How'd she get the close-up?" one asked.

"I don't know," the other said with incredible dejection in his voice.

"I'm going ta post mine anyway," the first said.

"Why bother, Dweeb?"

They walked away shaking their heads. Mary was tired, and that might have explained her thoughts, but Jerry didn't have a cell phone, she remembered. Was that why he was getting sex from Laura and Angie, and these two weren't even paying any attention at all to the opportunities that presented themselves, presented themselves within easy reach, because the cell phone was too important? Maybe Jerry could fix car trunks and handily mix it up with the Wilson boys because he didn't waste his time with a cell phone; or maybe Mary needed another cup of coffee before she philosophized herself into a coma.

"You think we can sit down now, boys?" she asked.

"What?" Peter said, as he tore his attention away from the retreating figure and back to Mary.

"I think we can find..." began Jerry, but hadn't finished before Sandy was at his side.

"Sit anywhere you want," she said, probably to everyone, but Jerry was the only one she was looking at. "Mr. Wilson," she added with a smile and a toss of her shorter, but also blond hair. It was not as blond as Jerry's hair, but then again the "loser's" friend wasn't as blond as Jerry either.

They did seat themselves where they wanted. All the options were pretty much the same anyway. Jerry kept looking back at Sandy for some sort of guidance, but she provided none except her smiling face. Once seated Peter asked, "So what did happen here?"

"You saw it, three times in fact, Peter. What do you want? Do you want to know why it happened or something?" said Mary.

Before Peter could answer, Sandy was at the table. "What can I get for you, Mr. Wilson?"

Mary took an extraordinary leap of logic and assumed that Sandy intended to "get" something for everyone else at the table too. "Coffee for me."

Sandy looked pensive. "Is it okay for her to have another cup of coffee, Mr. Wilson? You said she shouldn't be drinking so much coffee, didn't you?"

"Sandy," Mary said. "I do not need Jerry's permission to have a cup of coffee, for Christ's sake."

Sandy looked quickly at her and then turned back to look at Jerry. "Do you think it's all right?" She paused and then added, "Jerry?"

"Well, yeah, I guess so," he smiled.

"And if it's all right with Jerry, I'll have coffee too, Sandy," said Peter.

"Yeah, sure," said Sandy, but didn't turn her attention from Jerry. "I'm afraid we still don't have any mango juice…Jerry. Is orange juice with a little cranberry in it all right?"

"Oh, yeah, sure," he said.

"I'll mix it myself," she said. "To make sure it's perfect...for you."

She smiled and when Jerry smiled back, she added quickly, "But I'll make sure we have mango the next time you come in...and I hope you come in often...real often."

Jerry smiled, and Sandy looked as if she might swoon right there in front of everyone. Peter and Mary passed incredulous glances at each other, and then Sandy just walked away.

Jerry looked after her briefly and turned back toward Mary. "You see, even Sandy is concerned that you drink too much coffee, Mary."

"Sandy?" said Mary. "Sandy doesn't even know there's anyone else at this table, Jerry."

"Besides you, you mean?"

"No, that's not what I mean."

"Maybe we can get back to the police stuff," said Peter.

Chapter 15

"Okay, so what do you want to talk about, Peter?" asked Mary.

"Well," said Peter. "We can start with you, or we can start with me. Matter much to you who goes first, Mary?"

"I can be quick," Mary said. "First of all, Jerry sells grass for a landscaping outfit he and his friends run, sort of as a sideline to pay for their surfing, He does not sell marijuana or any other drugs; doesn't even drink. Being a Baptist, that will impress you, Peter.

"He does work; or rather, he volunteers as a counselor at a rehab, which is how he came to know so much about the drugs on the streets of Huntington, and the forensics of death by small caliber, low-velocity weapons. I'm not bad for an amateur, wouldn't you say, Peter?"

Peter smiled. "Not too bad. Don't want you to get a big ego thing going though. I called the police out in Huntington Beach and they did know you, Jerry."

Jerry looked at him, but seemed unperturbed. Mary was feeling a little nervous, and embarrassed that she had accepted Jerry's word for it all.

"Guy I spoke to knew you pretty well, in fact. Said he surfed with you, that right?"

"That would be Stan," Jerry said. "Yeah, he's pretty good on the board, an' he can do the comeback better than anyone." There was clearly respect in his voice.

"Yeah," smiled Peter. "He said you were good, too. Placed high in the ISA, he said. Could have gone pro, he said. That right too?"

Jerry shrugged. "Maybe, but that was a while back."

"The ISA?" asked Mary.

"International Surfing Association," said Jerry nonchalantly.

Peter grinned, and Mary giggled a little. "So your stuff is more interesting than mine, but does any of it help with any crimes we've seen here in Nebraska recently?"

"I almost forgot that part," smiled Peter, "but you had done all the work there, Mary. Stan said just about what you said. Jerry never had a single finger on a drug as long as Stan has known him. Works with a group of guys who do landscaping, pretty good landscaping, Zen Landscaping, is that right? That's the name of the company, isn't it?"

Jerry nodded.

"He didn't tell me the name, Peter," said Mary.

"The name is kind of embarrassing," Jerry offered.

"Stan said you worked—he called it work, not volunteering—at a place called West Side, a drug rehab center. He did mention that he didn't think you got paid though. I didn't think to ask him how he knew, or about how working without getting paid was different from volunteering."

Sandy returned with two coffees and the perfect orange juice and a little cranberry juice. "I hope I got it right, Jerry," she said. She smiled, and then left the table.

"So," said Mary, shaking her head as she looked after her.

"We talked about some other stuff, too. About Angie and Laura Stewart." Peter was looking at Jerry, but there was no anxiety at all on Jerry's face.

Peter considered this for a moment before he continued. "They are sisters, and are heavily into the drug scene and into prostitution, which he seemed to think had not been legalized since you left California, Jerry. He said you were friends, but not at all involved with either of them. Not involved at all, he said, and that everyone in the Huntington Beach Police Department would not have believed that was possible if...if it had been anyone except you. But everyone did believe you had a friendship and concern, but no relationship with either of them."

Jerry nodded, and Peter looked at Mary. When he continued it was Mary he was looking at. "He said there were rumors that you had a sexual relationship with at least Laura, but he was not inclined to give that too much credibility. He said it was mostly Laura who said you were...well, I forget the exact word he used, but he wasn't sure Laura was telling it exactly as it was."

Jerry sighed. "She talked a lot sometimes."

"That's what Stan said. He also said they were both on probation, and both had missed their recent appointments and would be doing some jail time when they showed up again. When I told him I thought Angie had finally made it to a place where even the law couldn't get her, he wasn't surprised. He said he had expected that would happen eventually." After a pause, Peter continued.

"He said that he knew it because you had said it first, Jerry. He said that after you said it, he could see it too, but that you had said it first."

Jerry just nodded.

"I had to ask him, Jerry, so don't take this wrong, but I had to ask if he thought you could have killed Angie."

Mary's gaze shifted quickly from one to the other, but Jerry just looked at Peter.

"*No way in fuckin' hell* was his answer."

Mary sighed a sigh of relief and Peter said, "Sorry about the language, Mary. Didn't know you knew any of those kinds of words, but that's what Stan said. I think he meant it, too."

Jerry smiled. "Yeah, that's Stan. Great surfer, but he has a mouth you couldn't kiss your mother with."

There was a chuckle now from Mary and Peter and a smile from Jerry.

"So," said Peter, "Stan said he had a cell number for Laura, but she wasn't answering his calls. Not sure I can reach her."

"She won't," said Jerry.

"Won't?" asked Peter.

"Well, yeah. I mean, she's not going to answer if she doesn't know who it is. If it's a blocked number, she lets it leave a message...maybe. She'll recognize the official police numbers, and Stan won't call her with his personal number, 'cause then she would have it, and he sure doesn't want Laura to have that."

"So we can't reach her if she won't answer."

Jerry just looked at him until Mary said, "Or is there a way you could reach her, Jerry?"

"Well, if you have the cell number and you're the police, you could probably get the company to tell you what cell she's in, but that won't help much. She'll answer her cell if she knows the number that's calling, particularly if she wants to talk to that person."

"Okay, I'm guessing that's not Peter or me, and you don't have a cell phone, so I'm making a guess here again, but you probably don't have a cell phone number either. Most of the time the companies require that you have a phone before they'll give you a number."

"Yeah," said Jerry. "I always thought that was strange too."

"But," said Peter, "we don't have a number that she'll answer, so we can't reach her."

Jerry just looked at them, first one and then the other, not saying a thing until Mary could stand it no longer.

"Say something, Jerry."

"About what?"

Peter looked at Mary, and then at Jerry. "About how we can reach Laura, maybe? That's kind of where the conversation is right now, at least for Mary and me. I'm not sure about you, Jerry."

"Well, ya can reach her if ya want to, but...well, I thought you didn't want to do it that way for some reason that I didn't understand. I mean, I didn't want to say something that would make me look stupid."

"No, of course not," said Peter. "Actually, I don't think anything you say, Jerry, could change my already formed opinion of your intelligence. You've established your credentials in that area so well already."

Peter smiled at his joke; more eloquence than was his usual language. Mary was growing embarrassed for Jerry, and Jerry was looking pensively at Peter. Mary hoped that Jerry didn't understand what Peter had said, and soon Peter looked as if he was regretting his abuse of Jerry too.

"So," said Mary. "You think we can reach Laura, Jerry?"

"Yeah, of course you can."

Peter rolled his eyes.

"On her cell phone, I'm guessing," offered Mary tentatively.

"Well, yeah, of course. I just don't understand why you don't want to do it. Must be some police thing." Jerry looked over at Peter.

"Well, Jerry, let's get all the stupid out in the open and I'll go first," said Mary. "I don't have any idea how to reach Laura on her cell phone if she won't answer any number she doesn't recognize."

Jerry blinked. "Well, Mary. She'll answer Angie, I think."

Jerry was still thinking as the light began to dawn on the stupid people at the table.

"She had a cell phone, but there were no numbers in the speed dial or the calls or messages or anywhere," said Peter, with a little amazement on his face. "We were going to call the numbers in her phone, but there weren't any."

"Company can probably get 'em for ya if ya really want 'em," said Jerry. "Lots a people erase everything from the phone so if they get busted they won't have any contacts that can get picked up too."

"Nice of them," offered Mary. "Not to want their friends picked up, I mean."

"Not really," said Jerry. "Most of their friends would rat 'em out in a second."

"Oh," said Mary.

"Of course, you don't need Laura's number. You have that," Jerry continued. "But I guess you don't want me to call. Is that what it is?"

Peter was looking embarrassed now, and was clearly not following the logic at all. He looked at Mary, who didn't have any idea what Jerry was talking about either, but she wasn't supposed to understand, not being a smart police captain. She was allowed to be stupid. She had also not accused anyone sitting at this table of being stupid; not recently, at least. Finally pity swept away her more malicious inclinations; pity for Peter.

"I don't quite understand what your...your brilliant plan to contact Laura is, Jerry," she said, looking at Peter more than Jerry.

"Oh," said Jerry. He looked at Peter too. "Captain Morgan can call Laura on Angie's cell and she'll probably answer. Even if she already knows Angie is dead, she'll take a chance that someone she wants to talk to has Angie's phone. I don't think she'll know about Angie yet. California is a long way from here. Of course now that Stan knows, the word will get around quickly, so—"

Mary held up her hand. "So Peter should just call Laura on Angie's phone, right?"

Jerry cast an indulgent smile at Mary. "It has to be someone Laura knows and trusts on the other end when she answers or she'll hang up in a second. She's not going to trust a police officer, even one as nice as Peter."

The dawn was finally complete, although the glow of embarrassment was providing a great deal of light as well.

"And she knows you, Jerry," said Mary. "If it's you that calls, she'll recognize the voice and stay on the line long enough for you to tell her what happened, and she'll believe you when you tell her, too."

"Well, yeah, but I guess Captain Morgan doesn't want to do that," said Jerry, shrugging.

Mary let her malicious smile spread to its fullest before she asked, "Why don't you want to have Jerry call Laura on Angie's cell phone, Peter?"

Peter cleared his throat. "Am I going to have to tell the truth here?"

"Might work best, Peter," said Mary.

Peter cleared his throat again. "I didn't think of it."

# Chapter 16

Mary smiled. "Well, now you have...thought of it, that is."

Jerry shrugged. "I think he knew it all along, Mary. He's pretty smart. He just wanted to think about it first. But ya know, Laura will hear soon that Angie is dead, even though you warned Stan not to let it get out too quickly, Captain Morgan. Maybe we should call as soon as we can, ya think?"

Mary was getting her malicious devils back in their cages, but they were still capable of one more attack before they were subdued. "You did remember to tell Stan not to let it get out too quickly, didn't you, Peter?"

Peter ignored the assault. "Let me call and make sure the cell phone is still at the station," he said, and got up to make his call in private. Maybe a couple of calls, Mary thought, and anyway, he would be able to get away from this suddenly very embarrassing table.

Mary looked at Jerry, "That was..." she began, but was interrupted when one of the young video makers from earlier approached. Long, unwashed hair, tee shirt and ragged jeans with a couple days' growth of beard. No wonder Sandy was falling over Jerry if this was his competition.

"Hey. Jerry is it?" he asked.

"Yeah," said Jerry. "Dweeb, right?" Jerry put out his fist and they traded the punch greeting common among the young.

"Yeah, how'd ya know?"

"Heard one of your friends call you that," Jerry replied.

Mary was again impressed, as she had been so often with this surfer today. When the young lady had called this man "Dweeb" she had thought it might be an insult, not a name; but Jerry had picked up the subtle nuance and realized it was his name she was saying. He also seemed to instinctively know that Dweeb would greet with a fist punch, while Bert, an hour earlier, would shake hands.

"So how ya doin', man?" asked Jerry.

"Okay. Say, is your ice cream shop really closed?"

"For a while," said Jerry.

Dweeb looked dejected. "Bummer, man."

"Mary's shop is open though."

"Yeah," Dweeb said, but his dejection didn't clear at all.

Mary was wondering, but only a little, what was the cause of this gloom. She smiled and said, "Jerry will be helping out at my shop until his opens up again, isn't that right, Jerry?"

Jerry looked surprised.

Mary looked at him and said, "Let me do Jerry's line. too. *'Sure I will, Mary,' said Jerry.* That was Jerry talking, Dweeb."

Dweeb and Jerry shared a confused exchange of looks before either spoke.

"Sure I will," said Jerry.

"*'Sure I will, Mary'*," she corrected. "Ya have to pay attention, Jerry. First rule of drama."

"Oh, yeah. Sure...I will...Mary." Jerry smiled at her, but not as big a smile as Dweeb put on.

"Really? I'll be by this after', man."

"Look for ya," said Jerry. "By the way, who was that with you just now?"

"Dexter, ya mean?"

"No. I meant the woman with the video," explained Jerry.

"Oh, that's Jasmine. She's...well, she's always beatin' me up."

"The babes are like that, Dweeb," said Jerry.

"Yeah," said Dweeb. "Later, man." They fist punched, and Dweeb departed as Peter returned.

"They still have Angie's cell phone at the station," said Peter. "Would you mind coming down and helping us contact Laura, Jerry?"

"Not at all," said Mary. When Peter looked at her she added, "That was Jerry talking, Peter. He's having trouble with his lines today."

Jerry just smiled and said, "Yeah, that was me talking."

Mary took a sip of her coffee, only about a third down, and Peter finished his in one last swallow. Jerry drank his juice, and Sandy was at the table as he put down the glass.

"Was it okay, Jerry?" she asked.

"Yeah," said Jerry. "Perfect."

"Oh, thanks," gushed Sandy. When Jerry reached into his pocket, Sandy stopped his hand with a light touch of hers, lingering a tantalizing few seconds. "Oh, no, I'll take care of this. You left a big tip earlier this morning."

When Peter looked on in amazement, Mary said, "He did leave a big tip. Not all that you deserved, and certainly not what you had hoped for, Sandy."

"Oh,...thanks," said Sandy, shifting to Mary for the briefest of moments before returning her adoring gaze to Jerry.

"Well, yeah," said Jerry. "Guess we better be going. See you later, Sandy."

There was another near swoon moment as they departed. It was a close call, but they made it out without having to lift a collapsed Sandy to her feet again.

"Why don't you follow me to the station, okay?" said Peter.

"There are a few reasons, the first being that I know how to get to the station and don't really need to follow you," Mary replied.

Peter shook his head and got into the cruiser as Jerry and Mary got into her car. They did follow Peter since they were going to the same place and he started first, but it was just a coincidence, Mary told herself.

"So, what shall we talk about on the way, Jerry?" said Mary, with a little exasperation in her voice.

Jerry shrugged.

"What about Sandy?" Mary said. "Shall we talk about her?" She was feeling a little jealous, but she didn't know exactly why. Maybe it was that all the guys were watching the young and beautiful and they were not—

"She's a nice kid," said Jerry.

Yeah, thought Mary. A nice...well, she had to be old enough to handle alcohol in order to work at Roses, so she was above the age of consent. She was also a pretty, and a sexy, and an *I would jump into bed with Jerry without a second thought* kind of kid.

"She's more than a kid," Mary said.

Jerry seemed to be thinking, not listening. "It's Jasmine I was thinking I should talk to."

"Jasmine? You mean half-naked Jasmine, friend of Dweeb's Jasmine? Do you...?" Mary could feel jealousy rising along with disgust at this thirty-five-year-old chasing the twenty-year-olds, and wished now she had never started this conversation.

Jerry looked over at her. "She has to dress that way," he said. "She's not beautiful, so she has to dress that way."

"She's not beautiful?"

"Not really," said Jerry. When Mary said nothing, partly because she was in shock, Jerry looked at her and continued. "When you're beautiful, you can dress any way you want. You'll still be beautiful. Jasmine is just pretty, so she has to dress the way she does. I think she likes Dweeb though, and I want to talk to her about that."

"We can talk about Dweeb in a minute. You don't think Jasmine is beautiful, is that what you said, Jerry?"

"Well, I don't think she is." He shrugged. Mary was silent, and this seemed to make Jerry feel he had to explain what he was saying. "A really beautiful woman doesn't have to...to advertise. She's just beautiful. It must be hard for a beautiful woman to understand why other women dress the way Jasmine does, since they don't need to do that."

Mary remained silent, trying to grasp even a little of what Jerry was saying, and trying to figure out if he really believed what he was saying. After a brief pause he continued. "You see, Mary, for a really beautiful woman like you, it probably doesn't seem logical. But for people like Jasmine...well, she has to dress like that to get anyone to pay attention to her. Even so, Dweeb doesn't notice her, and he's the one she wants to notice her."

Mary's shock was complete. She wanted to turn and stare at Jerry but she was driving and...she must have misunderstood him. Had he just casually slipped into this bizarre conversation that she was beautiful?

Had he done that while discussing two, well, two young, pretty and sexy women, one of whom was fawning all over him? Was he really worried about Dweeb and Jasmine? Maybe they were in that other dimension again and nothing was real. That had to be it. She would wake up soon and—

"I think Dweeb might like her too," Jerry said.

Right now, Mary wasn't too concerned about Dweeb. She wanted to know if Jerry really thought she was beautiful, but that was also the last thing she wanted to ask right now. If he was right about the beautiful dressing any way they wanted, without regard to how they appeared, she qualified there for sure. No makeup today, of course. The rush and the hour that had begun this day, being in the middle of the night, had made that seem unnecessary.

She was wearing jeans, not fashionably torn, and a flannel shirt that was beginning to make her perspire since it was getting hot and the shirt was buttoned up well above the modest cleavage she possessed and...well, she was a little nervous now, too. Okay, she was really a lot nervous right now. Maybe it was her pheromones that were causing Jerry to become delusional. She suddenly became aware of just how strong the scent of those pheromones was, or as those less-educated in the science of denial called the odor: sweat.

"Do you think he likes her?" Jerry asked.

Okay, if this was going to be bizarre, Mary could do bizarre. "Why do you think they even notice each other, Jerry?"

"Well, it's obvious that she likes him," he said.

"It is not obvious," Mary said. "In fact, I don't know why you think it is even possible. His hair is long and dirty, and he dresses like a slob, and doesn't shave and...why do you think she likes him?"

"Well," said Jerry. "She was really only talking to Dweeb and ignoring Dexter. Dweeb was the one she called by his name. She looked at him and smiled at him and walked away so that he would see her, and...well, she wanted him to see her. She just doesn't understand."

"Understand what? That Dweeb is a moron who can't see a...well, can't see how...how *pretty* Jasmine is?"

Jerry frowned. "I think Dweeb can see Jasmine, but Jasmine thinks that this is a contest. Love isn't a contest, Mary. It's not a competitive sport like...like football. It's more like...like surfing." He smiled and nodded.

"Yeah, that's it! It's like surfing," he continued. "Ya know, one wave is perfect for this guy, but a total downer for this other guy. You have to ride the right wave, not try to make the wave right."

Mary was tempted to tell Jerry that he was making no sense at all right now, but she wasn't sure it would make any difference. *He's on a roll, so let him ride the wave*, she decided.

"Jasmine's trying to get Dweeb to notice her by showing off, by competing with him and with all the other women, too. Like she dresses sexier or her video is better, but no one wants that. Woulda been easy for her to say like: 'Your video is great, Dweeb. Wanna look at mine?'."

"Well, maybe," ventured Mary. She wasn't at all sure Jerry was correct, but he was getting closer anyway.

"That's what you would have done, right? You don't have to prove you're smarter than everyone else, because you know you are, and everyone else knows you are. Same as you don't have to prove that you're more beautiful than all the other women because you already know you are, and they know that too. So...well, it's not a contest for you." He shrugged as Mary remained speechless in her amazement.

"Yeah, for you it's like surfing, not like football," Jerry added.

Mary shook her head and looked up. "We're at the police station, Jerry, but this conversation is not over yet."

"Yeah," said Jerry. "I think you're right. I should talk to Jasmine."

Chapter 17

They entered the police station like this; Jerry pondering the proper metaphor for love, and Mary hoping that she could get back to the planet earth from where she had been sent by the twisted fates.

"We have Angie's phone in the office, Jerry," said Peter.

"Yeah," said Jerry. "Better to be in a quiet background. What should I say to her?"

"Well," said Peter. "We would like to talk to her, to see if she has any information that could be helpful."

"Of course," Jerry nodded. "It might be better if she came here. Maybe I can suggest that she come here, like maybe that she should come to identify Angie or something, ya think?"

"Will she come here?"

"She might." Jerry shrugged. "She's probably worried that you'll pick her up for skipping out on her probation."

Peter was silent and Jerry looked at him.

"Will you do that, Peter?" asked Mary.

Peter sighed. "I don't have a warrant from Huntington yet so I can't really hold her here. If I get a warrant I'll have to."

"But you don't have a warrant. You have no jurisdiction. All you have is a verbal assertion from Stan that there may be a violation of her probation, and that's not a justification for detaining her."

Peter smiled and shook his head. "Are you going to represent her, or just prosecute me?"

"Maybe both, Captain Morgan."

Jerry shrugged. "Can I tell her you don't have a...what did you call it, Mary?"

"A warrant or jurisdiction."

"Yeah," said Jerry. "Can I tell her that? I mean, are you going to hold her here until you get the paper from Huntington Beach?"

"I'll not exceed the scope of my jurisdiction," said Peter. "Is that the right way to say it, Mary?"

"Close."

"But if I get a warrant I'll have to enforce it."

"I'll talk to her," said Jerry. "She might want to come to see Angie even if it is a chance. They were pretty tight. Well, yeah, I guess maybe they were sisters." He shrugged.

"Yes, they were sisters," said Peter, and Jerry just shrugged again.

"You'll want to be there when I call her, of course. Are you going to record her conversation too?"

Peter looked uneasy, but it was Mary who spoke. "Unless either Laura or Jerry agrees, Peter can't really record that without a court order. Law's pretty clear on that, isn't it, Peter?"

Peter glared a little at her, but said, "Mary is correct. We're not allowed to record anything without informing at least one of the persons being recorded. Or if we can get a court order, and..."

"And you haven't had time to do that," smiled Mary. "He can record you though, Jerry, if he tells you he is recording you, and Laura too if you put the phone on speaker ..."

"Laura won't let me do that," said Jerry. "She'll just hang up."

Mary shrugged. "He can video us here, but ...It's a strange law."

Peter cast another glare at Mary, who smiled back. Jerry looked mystified by this exchange, mostly because he was in fact mystified by it.

"Shall we make our call?" said Mary.

They went into a small office in the back of the station. There were three chairs around a rectangular table, with three more against the back wall. There was a cell phone on the table, and a note pad and pen. Mary sat at one end and smiled.

"Would you like to stay too, Mary?" asked Peter sarcastically.

"Why yes, I guess I would," Mary replied with equal sarcasm. "Thank you for asking."

Mary looked around the room and finally settled on the camera in the ceiling.

"You're not really supposed to be here, Mary," Peter said.

"But Jerry wants me to be here, don't you, Jerry?"

"Well, yeah, of course," he replied, somewhat surprised to be pulled into a conversation to which he had just been an audience a second ago.

"And he probably won't make the call at all without my presents," said Mary.

"You're not..." began Peter.

Mary just smiled. At least one of the people in this room had just said she was smarter the everyone else, and she thought she could convince the other person, too. "I may be of help, Peter. You seem to think that, or at least you used to think that. I can't help if I don't know what's going on. Shall we make the call?"

Peter sighed. "Yeah. Let's make the call."

Mary smiled, and then turned to the camera, scrunching her face and sticking out her tongue. "Since it's only a video recording I thought I ought to make sure the substance, if not the exact words of the conversation, were being accurately recorded."

Jerry had been watching the exchange with interest and a little amazement, but now turned his attention to the phone. He looked at it and then said, "Plenty of bars here, reception I mean, and the battery has still got plenty of charge too."

He looked up with a puzzled expression. "Did you charge it, Captain?"

"I...ah, I don't think so."

"I wonder why it's still charged. Lot of roaming out here. Uses up the battery pretty quick."

Mary was puzzled too. "That's true," she said.

Jerry was puzzled as well. He turned the phone over and looked at the back. When he looked up he asked, "Did she have it turned off, or did she pull the battery out?"

Peter cleared his throat. "The battery was out. We thought she was trying to keep the charge in it, but..."

Jerry just shrugged. "Might be, but you can't locate the phone with the battery out." He looked up to see puzzled stares. "The company can track the phone if the battery is in it. Tell what cell it's in. With the battery out they can't do that. I wonder why she didn't want her phone tracked."

He looked up and then looked at Peter. "You got a court order to track Laura's phone, right, Captain?"

Peter cleared his throat and was about to answer, but Jerry shrugged and continued. "I'm sure Stan is doing that, and you'll impress him if you're doing it too. That way he'll know you're on top of this and savvy on the way these things move. He'll be likely to feed you information if he thinks you're good at the job, I mean."

"And you want to look savvy, don't you, *Major* Morgan?" smiled Mary.

Peter cast her a quick look of disapproval before he pulled the note paper over to him and wrote on it.

"Do you have one of those for me too, Peter?" asked Mary.

Peter smiled and said, "Let me run out and get one, okay? Please don't make the call without me." He stood and went out of the office and Jerry turned to Mary.

"You know of a lot of legal stuff, Mary."

"I'll tell you about that some time." She smirked and shook her head.

Peter returned after a few minutes, more time than was probably necessary to find a pad and pen for Mary, but sufficient time to ask that a cell phone be tracked. He did have another pad of note paper and a pen which he put in front of Mary. "So, are you all ready now?" he asked her. Mary just nodded and smiled.

Peter turned to Jerry. "Are you all ready?"

"Yeah," said Jerry, and picked up the phone and began to dial. Peter had been pulling a small notebook out of his pocket but stopped when he saw Jerry dialing.

"You know her number, Jerry?" asked Mary.

"Yeah," said Jerry. "When ya don't have a cell ya got to remember the numbers. No speed dial in your brain. That's the trouble with cell phones. Nobody has to remember anything since the phone does it for 'em, so their memory just atrophies like..."

He turned his attention to the phone now. "Oh, hi, Laura," he said. "This is Jerry."

Mary and Peter watched him, but could only hear his side of the conversation.

"Yeah, I'm usin' her phone."

"No she's not, but Laura, I have to tell you something."

"I know, but Laura..."

Laura was talking loud now, loud enough to be heard although not understood. She sounded angry. Jerry looked at Peter and Mary and waited. When the sound of Laura's voice stopped he said, "Laura, Angie is dead. She died yesterday."

There was silence and finally Jerry said, "You okay, Laura?"

"Yeah."

"In the little shop my aunt has out here in..."

"That's right, out here in Nebraska."

"No, I hadn't even seen her since you split back six..."

"No, not even talked to her."

There was a long pause and finally Jerry said, "Yeah, I'm still here."

"I don't think it was an overdose, but I'm..."

"Look, Laura. I thought maybe you would want to see her. They kind of need an ID and..."

"No, I don't think the police know about that yet, and..."

"Well, she has some jewelry an' I thought you might want it to, you know, to remember her by, or something. They won't release it to me, but maybe to family they would."

"Well, maybe."

"Yeah, I know, but it looks like it might be really valuable, too. Shame to let the state of Nebraska keep..."

"Yeah, the locket is here."

"Okay then."

"Tomorrow morning?"

"Can I pick you up, or..."

"Oh, yeah, sure, if you got a ride already."

"Yeah, I'll be here. At the police station. The state police. Let me get you an address."

Peter pulled his pad toward him and began to scribble on it, but Jerry continued. "Okay, if you're sure you can find it."

"You've got a friend who...?"

"Yeah, okay. Nine o'clock."

"I'll be here."

Jerry looked up and then pressed the button on the phone to hang it up.

"She said she'll be here at nine tomorrow morning."

"Better write that down, Peter," said Mary. "The one note on your pad is getting lonesome."

Peter began to write but stopped and looked at Mary. "Can I copy your notes?" he asked, looking at Mary's blank page.

"Wouldn't that be cheating, Peter? What if the principal catches us?"

Peter frowned and then chuckled. "Okay, I won't tell." He turned to face Jerry. "What did she say, and do you really think she'll be here?"

"And where is this valuable jewelry?" added Mary.

Jerry blushed and said, "Oh, I just made up the stuff about the jewelry. She didn't sound like she was going to come, so I figured if she thought there was...well, I thought Laura would come if there was money here."

"Will she be disappointed when there is none?"

Jerry shrugged. "Angie had a necklace, and...well, maybe you can release that, or maybe just tell her you can't release anything yet. I don't think she'll stick around waiting for it." He frowned now.

"I can go through my extensive jewelry boxes, note that the *boxes* are plural, please, and find a few trinkets to give the poor, grieving sister," said Mary.

"I bet you have a lot of jewelry, don't you, Mary?" said Jerry.

Mary thought he was being sarcastic, but the look on his face said he was serious, and this made her blush. She owned very little jewelry, and what she did have had no value at all.

Peter smiled and said, "So what else did she say?"

Jerry frowned. "She said that she was pissed that Angie was out here. She thought she was out here with me, I think."

"Oh?" said Peter.

"And that upset her, Jerry?" asked Mary.

"Yeah," said Jerry. "I wonder why?"

"But she will be here?" asked Peter. "Maybe we can ask her why when we see her."

Jerry was silent.

"She will be here?" Peter asked again.

"I think she will," said Mary. "I'm not sure who she'll be coming here to see though."

Peter looked puzzled, but Jerry just nodded.

Chapter 18

Peter looked at Jerry and then at Mary and shook his head. "So there are a couple of other questions I had. Maybe I can ask those now?"

"I have to open the shop sometime today, Peter. Now that, thanks to you, I'm the sole provider of ice cream for the citizens of this fine community."

"Same as you were two days ago?"

"Two days ago, when I was able to open my shop. What are the questions, Peter?"

Peter smiled. He kind of enjoyed this sassiness in Mary. He wasn't sure, but thought it was more than her usual. He wondered why, and then he looked at Jerry. "Jerry. We didn't find any evidence of a break-in at the shop at all. Was it locked?"

"I didn't lock it," said Jerry. "I didn't, like you know, think it was necessary."

"Since the ice cream was free anyway," said Mary.

Jerry was obviously embarrassed, by this. "Well, I just..."

"So anyone could have gotten into the shop. The house is not all that close, so...would you have heard a shot? Two shots?"

"Well, I sleep pretty soundly and my room is—"

"In back," said Peter.

"May sleeps in the front room," offered Jerry. "Maybe she heard something?"

"Your aunt May, ya mean? If she's the only witness then I'll never solve this." Peter paused as if he was considering something, and then he shrugged and continued.

"The coroner hasn't had time to look over anything, so we don't have any tox or time of death. We don't even know the cause for sure and no ID, except Jerry's."

Jerry looked at his feet and Mary said, "Cause of death is pretty obvious, and I don't think it was suicide."

"No," shrugged Peter. "So Prentiss said he was in the shop and tripped over Angie. Is that right, Mary?"

"Said he tripped over a body. He didn't know it was Angie. He thought it was Jerry, in fact."

Jerry looked up, and Mary realized that Jerry probably hadn't heard this part before. "He called all in a panic and said he was in the shop, but never did say why. Then he said he tripped over a body and he thought it might be Jerry because it had blond hair. I hung up after telling him to go back to the shop so he could tell you what he found, although I kind of thought he was mistaken. Anyway, then I called Carl, and then I went over and then you came, and then...well, you know the rest." Mary finished with a sigh as the enormity of what had happened finally settled in on her. A young woman had been killed, and there was no clue as to why she had been killed or by whom she had been killed, or why she had been in that shop, or even why she had been in Nebraska at all.

"I'm going to have to talk to Prentiss," sighed Peter. "The crime scene boys have done the first sweep, but they'll have to go through it more thoroughly, and through the house as well. Maybe they'll find something, if Carl doesn't destroy it all first. What was going on with the Wilson boys?"

Mary had forgotten that, even though it had been only an hour or so earlier. "Well, Rufus and Billy came by. I'm not sure how they knew Jerry and I were at Roses, but they stopped by to say hi, and chat, and oh, yes, they threatened Jerry if he didn't leave town by sundown, partner."

"Try to be serious about this, will you, Mary?" Peter replied.

"You keep asking me to do that, but you never say why I should, Peter."

Jerry shrugged. "Somebody killed Angie," he said. It sounded like it was a response to Mary's question at first, but it was clear in a minute that he was just talking about what had happened. "I don't think Rufus or Billy would do that."

"They tried pretty hard to kill you, Jerry," said Mary.

Jerry thought for a moment. "You really think they were trying to kill me?"

Peter smiled. "It looked like they would not have minded if you ended up dead from what I saw on those videos, Jerry."

"Why would they do that?" asked Jerry.

Mary frowned. "Now that's a question. Not that the Wilson boys need a reason to try to kill people, but could it be money? That seems to be what moves their souls the most, and they did suggest that was their reason when they talked to you, Jerry."

"What was their reason?" asked Peter.

"They said they wanted to sell the shop and...well, somehow Jerry was interfering with that plan."

"How is he interfering?" asked Peter, looking at Mary, not Jerry.

"I don't know. Maybe by just being there and running an ice cream shop. Maybe they think May would let them sell, or they could force her to sell, if Jerry wasn't using it?"

Peter frowned.

"Look, Peter, May Wilson is crazy, right? As in not rational, right? Her hair is proof of that. She slipped over the edge of sanity when her husband, George, ran off with the money they had saved, *May* had saved, ran off with his secretary, who was younger by twenty years. May was the one who saved the family fortune by running that shop and then...well, it's all gone in one night.

"So she's crazy now, and she keeps talking about opening the shop again," continued Mary. "And then Jerry opens the shop again and the brothers are pissed because they think that as long as Jerry is running the shop they can't sell it. Does that make sense, or am I just too tired to know what I'm saying?"

Peter frowned and then nodded. "But would they kill Angie? What good would that do?"

"I have no idea," said Mary.

"Would they hurt their own family just for money?" asked Jerry.

Peter and Mary looked at his astonished face. Finally Mary said, "Laura's coming here tomorrow to get the family jewels, not to see the remains of her beloved sister."

"Wow," was all Jerry could say.

"I'm going to try to find Prentiss now," said Peter.

"And I'm going to try to sell some ice cream," said Mary. "Come on, Jerry."

Jerry looked up and then stood up.

"One more problem, Mary," said Peter.

"Oh?" said Mary.

"Yeah. Where do you suppose Jerry will sleep tonight?"

"At May's house?"

Peter shook his head. "Won't be finished for a couple of days probably. It's definitely not going to be ready by tonight."

"Oh, shit," said Mary.

"I can find someplace," said Jerry.

"There's always Sandy," smiled Peter. "'Course, she still lives with her parents. Do you think that will be a problem?"

"Shit," said Mary again.

Chapter 19

They walked out of the police station, Peter to go around the corner to his cruiser to start the search for Prentiss, and Mary and Jerry to her car to head for the ice cream shop. They would have had plenty of time if they hadn't driven by the drug store. In the parking lot was the local police cruiser, and Mary recognized it as the one Carl had been driving. There were three in this town during the day, but all different.

Could someone else have picked up Carl's cruiser? No, that wasn't the solution. Carl was emerging from the cruiser. He then went around to the passenger's side to help May Wilson out. She didn't appear to want any help, shooing him away. Maybe Carl had been released from the duty of guarding the crime scene? Maybe Carl was a screw-up? The latter was definitely true, at least in Mary's experience, but the question was, whether he was screwing up at this very moment. Mary pulled into the drug store parking lot.

"I have to pick up some stuff," she said. "Just be a minute."

"I better pick up some stuff too," said Jerry, and they both got out. Mary wondered what Jerry was picking up, but she was too preoccupied to think much about this.

Once inside, Jerry began wandering around, and Mary headed after Carl and May, who were heading for the prescription end of the store. Drug stores were really small department stores, and department stores usually had pharmacies in them, so the distinction was blurred and based more on size than on what one could buy in the establishment in question. This one had the usual medications, greeting cards, toiletries and rows of cosmetics and shampoos, and then further in were rows of toys and nick-nacks and cheap jewelry and finally at the very back, next to the small section selling food, was the pharmacy.

By the time Mary reached the counter, there was already a heated discussion in progress.

"But I'll die if I don't get my medicine!" May was saying. Carl was a police officer, Mary thought, but he was just standing by with hopelessness on his face.

The pharmacist didn't even bother to try to recruit assistance from Carl. "Your prescriptions were filled a week ago, May. I can't give you a refill so soon. Your insurance won't cover it."

"You must be mistaken," she insisted.

The pharmacist looked past Carl to rest his gaze on Mary.

"You've heard, I'm sure, about the incident out at May's, Jeff," Mary said to the pharmacist. "May won't be able to get into the house to get her meds for a couple of days. Not until the crime scene boys have finished."

Carl decided this was the perfect time for him to enter the conversation, which in Mary's opinion was of course the worst time. Carl proceeded to validate her opinion. "She could get into her house, Mary," he said.

Mary looked at him in exasperation. May was going to argue with poor Jeff until she left with her medication, and it was the simplest solution to just convince Jeff he should give her a few pills and send her on her way.

"No, she can't," said Mary. When Carl looked as if he might be preparing to speak again Mary added, "It would constitute a statutory violation of a female's right to...to...fornicate. Or something like that."

Jeff was smiling, but Carl was clearly confused. "I hadn't thought of that," he said.

Mary was pretty sure this last statement was true, since she was pretty sure Carl had not thought at all today. She was sure he had not thought of "that" this early in the morning.

She turned to the pharmacist and said, "Could you let May have a couple days' supply until she can get back into her house, Jeff?"

"Sure, I can do that, Mary. Wouldn't want to do any of that statutory violation stuff." He grinned broadly now and added, "The fornication, on the other hand...but not May. Be right back, okay?"

"Sure," said Mary, turning to face Carl.

He began to speak as soon as she turned. "I'd forgotten about the sta———...that thing you said, and the forn———...fornic———..."

"Fornication?" offered Mary.

"Screwing," offered May.

Carl looked at her, and then shrugged and said, "You're a crazy old bat, May."

"What are you doing here, Carl, and who is watching the crime scene?" asked Mary.

"Oh, it's okay, Mary," said Carl. "No one's there right now, and May said she needed her medicine, so I had to drive her over here. I'll be back before anyone gets there."

"Oh," said Mary. "Just so I get this straight, Carl. No one is watching the crime scene, is that right?"

"Nope," said Carl, "'cause no one is there."

"And," added Mary, "no one will be there when you're back there."

Carl thought for a moment, his first of the day maybe. "Tryin' to trick me, aren't ya, Mary. When I get back there, *I'll* be there, won't I?"

"I'll have to think about that one, Carl."

Jeff had returned to give May three bottles. "No charge for just these few, May. I'll take them out of your next refill. And Mary, you'll let me know about that fornication stuff. If you want to practice I mean." He grinned broadly now.

"Jeff!" replied Mary. "You're over seventy!"

"And I have several bottles of—"

"Never mind," said Mary, walking away. She was on her cell phone less than a minute later.

"Peter," she said. "Just got done having a conversation with Carl...in the pharmacy, of all places. Is anyone watching your crime scene tape to make sure it isn't stolen or something, to be used in the next reality TV show? Oh, and then there's the evidence that's being tampered with too."

She listened for a few seconds as noise of increasing volume issued from her phone.

"Peter," said Mary finally. "I didn't know a good Baptist boy like you knew those kinds of words."

She listened again and then looked at her phone. "He hung up on me," she said.

"Who did?" asked Jerry, standing beside her.

"Peter," said Mary. "What did you buy, Jerry?"

"Nothing," he said, holding up a bag.

Mary continued to look until finally Jerry said, "Some razors and shampoo."

The bag looked too large for that, but Mary was a little afraid to ask why he needed razors and shampoo.

"Ya think ya have some conditioner I could borrow?" he asked. "I didn't like the ones they have here."

Mary closed her eyes for a moment. May as well just accept it, she decided. Jerry was going to be her roommate for a day or two.

"What makes you think that the one conditioner I have, will by some miracle be the one you like, when this place must have twenty and you can't find one you like here?" Mary asked.

"Well," said Jerry. "Your hair looks so good."

Mary looked at him and he smiled at her.

"Oh, come on, and let me see if I can at least sell a little ice cream today," she said.

Chapter 20

They arrived at the ice cream shop which Mary had named "The Ice Cream Shop". It hadn't been a very inspirational moment.

"Nice sign," said Jerry.

"Yeah," Mary replied. "I spell-checked it before I put it up."

"I guess I should have done that too."

They got out of the car and walked over to the door, which was locked. As Mary unlocked it, Jerry asked, "So, do you always lock the door?"

"Yes," said Mary. "I do it to protect the public from overdosing on my delicious ice cream. You should do that too, as a community service, Jerry."

"Ya think?"

Mary didn't answer.

Once inside, she began to turn on lights and straighten things up.

"Can I help?" Jerry asked.

"There wasn't much traffic last night so...but if you want something to do, you can mop the floor."

"Where're your mops and buckets?" he asked.

"Closet in back," she said, motioning toward the back of the shop.

Jerry went to the back of the shop and was soon cleaning the floor, and the counters, tables and chairs. It was a small shop with a counter, behind which were the freezers for the ice cream and shelves for bowls, cups, spoons, straws and all the other things that went with serving ice cream. There were also some heaters for fudge, and the dispensers for nuts and jimmies and all the rest. She served drinks, too, but no food. By the time Mary had everything turned on that needed to be turned on, Jerry was busy cleaning. He was doing it differently than Mary did, but he was doing it, so why not let him do it his own way? thought Mary. He had a mop and bucket with a small amount of soap in it, and also a pan with soapy water and another with clean water. He would wipe down the counters and the tables in a small area with soapy water, and then wipe them down with the clean water.

The shop had only five tables inside with two chairs each. There were another six stools along a counter in the back, and six more along the counter in the front where the ice cream was served. After the tables, counters, and chairs in an area were cleaned, Jerry mopped that section of floor. He then took the clean water that he had used to rinse the counters, tables and chairs to the back and disposed of that, replacing it with fresh, clean water. It was a good and efficiently done job, and the only thing at all unusual was that he was doing all this in his bare feet.

Mary had to ask him why.

"My feet are clean," he said. "Shoes are dirty."

When Mary asked if his feet were really cleaner than his shoes he shrugged and said, "I washed 'em in the back."

It took only a little time before the floor, counters, tables and chairs were as clean as they had ever been. "Shall I turn the sign to OPEN?" Jerry asked.

"May as well. A little early, but who knows who will want ice cream early today."

He did, and then came around to sit behind the counter with Mary.

The sign on the door said "OPEN," but beneath it was the sign that said the shop opened at 10:00, and the clock on the wall said it lacked a few minutes until it would be 9:00. It might be a slow start.

Jerry looked around him and finally said, "It's fun doing this with someone else."

Mary looked at him and thought, *That depends on who you're doing it with.*

Then she thought that maybe it was fun to do it with Jerry, just a little. Then she decided that if those were the only two available responses, maybe they should talk about something else.

"It's sort of like—" began Jerry.

"Surfing, right?" said Mary.

"Surfing?" asked Jerry.

"Well, that's what you always say, Jerry. Love is like surfing, and...there was something else you said was like surfing."

Jerry thought for a minute. "Surfing is like surfing," he offered.

"For other people maybe, but for Jerry Wilson it's like lying on a board in the middle of the ocean."

"But I was thinking that this is kind of like landscaping."

"You're not going to sell any grass here are you?"

"No," he replied. "I mean, like, you clean up the ice cream place, and I clean up the sitting place and...we work together. We're each specializing."

Mary frowned and shook her head. "New topic, okay? What was that martial arts stuff you pulled out on Rufus and Billy?"

"Oh. That was Aikido."

Jerry remained silent, looking about him as Mary waited, waited almost patiently. "Well, are you going to tell me what that is?"

"Oh," said Jerry. "I didn't know you were interested in it."

"Yeah, I can see why you're confused. I always ask about things I'm not interested in. It confuses people, but I'm not sure I needed to go to that much effort, since confusion seems to be pretty easily had right now. What is Aikido, Jerry?"

"Well, it's this non-violent martial art."

"It looked a little violent to me, and I think the Wilson brothers might think so too."

"But you're wrong. You see, the violence came from Rufus and Billy. I just redirected it. It's really neat." He was becoming animated now. "This guy in Japan, Morihei Ueshiba, developed it back in the 1920's. When someone attacks you violently, you take their violence and redirect it. You don't oppose it, you turn it away. You pull the bat towards you, not push it away from you."

"Toward them, you mean?"

"No, you can't do that. The practitioner of Aikido has to be concerned about the attacker as well as himself. If you try to hurt the attacker, you become the attacker, and the Aikido won't work. You'll end up hurting yourself."

"You're serious, right? You're not just making this up are you?"

"No, of course not. I wouldn't lie to you, Mary. Remember that last time Billy attacked me? He wasn't really attacking me at all, just...well, pretending to attack me. Because he wasn't really violent, I was able to just pick him up and put him on the ground. When Rufus attacked, he was trying to hurt me, and he ended up hurting himself. I didn't hurt him, he hurt himself."

Mary thought of that moment earlier and remembered that the last time Billy attacked Jerry, Jerry just put him on the ground. He didn't throw him. "Maybe?" she said.

"Mary," Jerry said, with an earnestness she had not seen before. "Violence always hurts the attacker. Always."

"Angie got hurt by the violence and she wasn't the attacker, Jerry."

Jerry was silent for a moment, and Mary thought maybe she shouldn't have brought Angie into this conversation. Finally Jerry looked at her and said, "Angie lived a violent life. She used people and hurt people, and she was finally consumed by the life she led. That's what happened to Angie. That's what will happen to the person who killed her, too."

Chapter 21

There they sat, each in his own thoughts. They were not allowed much time to think though, because Dweeb and Dexter came in a minute later.

"Hey, dude," said Dweeb. "You know Dex, don't ya?"

"From Roses," said Jerry. "Whazzup, guys?"

They traded fist punches and Dexter leaned forward a little. "Can ya get us some *ice cream*?"

"Sure," said Mary. "What do you want?"

Dexter looked around and then settled his sights on Jerry. "You got any *ice cream*, Jerry?"

"Well, sure," said Jerry. "What flavor do ya want?"

"Whatever flavor you think we want, man," Dexter replied and winked, and then chuckled.

"Oh," said Jerry. "Mint chip root beer. Do we have any—"

"No," said Mary. "Fresh out."

Jerry turned back to the two and said, "I bet you guys would like some strawberry. What do ya think, Mary?"

"I think—" began Mary, but was interrupted by a new arrival. He was thirty or a little older, jeans, tee shirt and a baseball cap.

"Hey, Mary," he said. "Didn't know you were open. Got some ice cream for a fella what missed breakfast this mornin'?"

"Sure, Mort," said Mary. "Jerry, I think—"

"Yeah, sure," said Jerry. "I'll get Dex and Dweeb some strawberry, an' you can get something for Mort."

"No, Jerry. I mean, I'm not sure Dexter and Dweeb want—"

She was again cut short by another new arrival, and one more concerning than any of the others. Before her stood Prentiss Forrest, wearing a baseball cap and sunglasses and looking like...well, looking like Prentiss Forrest wearing a baseball cap and sunglasses.

"Prentiss?" said Mary. "Peter is seriously looking for you."

"How'd you recognize me?"

Mary shook her head. "You look like Prentiss, Prentiss. You're still wearing the same tee shirt with the same ice cream on it from last night, for Christ's sake."

Prentiss looked at his tee shirt and wiped his hands across it, as if this would erase the ice cream stain from it.

Mary looked at the hands and asked, "Did you wash your hands since last night, Prentiss?"

Prentiss looked at his hands now and quickly put them behind his back. "I got ta talk to you, Mary."

"You have to talk to Peter, Prentiss."

"But what do I say?"

"The truth, or some really good lie," said Mary. "No, I take that back, Prentiss. You couldn't carry a lie in a bucket. Just go with the truth."

"But what should I say, Mary?"

"Prentiss. Okay, I'll drive you over to the station to talk to Peter. I can tell you what to say while we drive over there."

"Will you stay with me, Mary?"

"Prentiss!"

"Please."

"Prentiss! Let me explain what that means." She looked over at Jerry, who was putting two bowls of strawberry on the counter as Dexter and Dweeb were pushing twenty dollar bills at him.

"Oh, no, guys. This one is—" began Jerry.

"Jerry!"

"What, Mary?" said Jerry. "You want me to get Mort, too?"

"Strawberry looks good," said Mort.

Mary turned back. "Prentiss," she said, as disaster flooded over her. "Prentiss. Look. Take your truck and park it out back and I'll drive you over to talk to Peter."

"We can take—" began Prentiss.

"Now, Prentiss. Now!"

"Okay, Mary," he said.

As he went out of the shop, Mort waved. "Catch you later, Prentiss."

At this Prentiss turned back and said, "Don't tell Peter ya saw me in here, Mort."

"Sure, Prentiss."

"Please don't tell Peter you saw him in here, Mort," said Mary.

"Let me get you that strawberry, Mort," Jerry said.

"No!" said Mary, and everyone looked at her. "No," she said, trying to maintain a calm exterior, even as her life passed before her eyes. "Let me talk to you first, Jerry."

"Sure," he said.

"Back here. Away from...back here, Jerry."

They were at the back of the shop before Mary started to speak again. She had hoped the time would give her inspiration, but it had not. "You can't do this, Jerry."

"Do what?"

"Give away ice cream."

"But they like it and—"

Mary shut her eyes. "Jerry. Serving ice cream is...it's like..." Her eyes widened and she turned to stare at Jerry, straight into his face. "It's like surfing."

"What?" said Jerry.

"Serving ice cream is like surfing, Jerry. They both begin with 'S' and they both have 'R' in them."

"What?" said Jerry again.

"Jerry. You can't just take someone out in a boat and put them in the water to ride a wave. That's not surfing, is it? They have to paddle out there themselves or they'll never really appreciate it. Never love it. Never grow."

Jerry was looking at her intensely.

"Jerry. You have to earn the wave to really enjoy the wave. If you don't earn it, it's just...just a bunch of water."

"Yeah," said Jerry slowly.

"Ice cream is the same thing. You can't just give it to people. They have to earn it to really enjoy it. It isn't fair to people to just give it to them. It's cruel if you do that. They won't grow if you do that, and they'll spend their whole life never really enjoying, never even really *tasting* ice cream. Don't do that to people, Jerry," Mary finished, with a shake of her head.

Jerry nodded slowly and turned back to the counter. "Yeah, guys," he said. "Let me get your change."

"Oh, that's okay, man," said Dexter. "Worth it, right?"

"Okay," Jerry said. "Strawberry for you too, Mort? How many scoops?"

"It's not goin' ta be a twenty, is it?" Mort asked.

Jerry looked at the sign where the prices were listed. "Three bills and ninety cents for you, Mort. If ya only want one scoop, that is."

"Okay, Jerry," said Mary. "I'll be back as soon as I can, and Jerry..."

"Yeah?"

"Try to keep our little conversation in mind."

"Sure," he said. "So, Mort my man, was that one scoop or two? Two might be better for a guy what missed his breakfast, ya think?"

"Yeah, ya might be right."

"Only a buck more," Jerry said. "An' the tip would be the same for either one."

Mary shook her head and left, not knowing if her shop would still be there when she got back, and not knowing whether the police would seize all her ice cream to test it for drugs, and not knowing if Prentiss had parked his truck or just split again. If she was lucky...but she wasn't. Prentiss was waiting by her car.

Chapter 22

"Okay," said Mary. "Let's get this over with."

"We don't have ta go right over there, do we?" asked Prentiss.

"Yes," said Mary. "I'm not giving you any chance to back out, and I have to get back to the shop before Jerry starts giving away the furniture."

They climbed into the car, Mary driving, and Prentiss sitting and fidgeting nervously next to her.

"First, buckle your seat belt, Prentiss, and then tell me why you were in Jerry's shop at two in the morning. And then tell me what you saw and then...just start with the why, okay?"

"Well ya see—" began Prentiss.

"No, I don't see, Prentiss," interrupted Mary, as she started to drive toward the state police headquarters and Peter Morgan. "So just say it and make it fast, and make it simple." She cast a quick look at the man sitting next to her and added, "Simple should be easy."

"I was lookin' for the money."

"Okay," said Mary. "That one was a little too simple. What money? Jerry was giving away the ice cream so there was no money to steal, and even Jerry would have taken any money he did make with him." Mary wasn't sure that Jerry would have thought to take any money he had with him, but Prentiss...well, he was beginning to speak again.

"Not Jerry's money. I wouldn't a stolen any money from Jerry."

"Of course not, Prentiss. Jerry is a perfect stranger, and you had sort of been angry with him and it was his.... Who the hell else would you steal money from, and why would that person have any money in Jerry's shop?"

"May," he said.

"May?" said Mary. "But she doesn't have any money, Prentiss."

"Well..."

"Well what, Prentiss? Are you the only one who doesn't know that May has no money of her own? It's all tied up in trusts and insurance, and her brothers make sure not one penny goes to her that's not necessary to keep her barely alive. I'm not sure why they're even doing that much, since they really wish she would die, and soon." Mary shrugged and wondered why she had added that last comment.

"Not that money," said Prentiss.

"Okay," said Mary, shaking her head. She wasn't sure why she had expected this to be a simple, direct conversation anyway. "What money are we talking about?"

"Well," said Prentiss. "May's husband, George, left with Jessica, his secretary, with all the money he could get. She was a lot younger than George, and she wanted to live wild on that money, and—"

"Got that part, Prentiss."

"Yeah, well George, he couldn't get Jessica to run off with him without the money, an' he couldn't get at the money in their savin' and stuff 'cause May was watchin' that real close. George was pissed she was doin' that. Said she shoulda trusted him."

"He was planning to run away with a secretary who was the poster child for 'Gold Digger, Inc.', taking all their money with him, and George thought May should be more trusting? Did he also expect she would take out a second mortgage on the house so he could be sure he had adequate funds to keep Jessica happy? How do you know all this, Prentiss?"

"George asked May about the loan on the house, the shop really; house was already pretty well mortgaged up. But she wouldn't do it."

"Damned inconsiderate of her."

"George thought so. Anyway, he found out where May kept the money she made at the store she ran. May was real suspicious an' she kept that in the store, locked up in one of the refrigerators, I think," Prentiss said. "George said she let it slip out, an' he knew where it was hid."

"Oh," said Mary.

"But I figured maybe May had some that George didn't find."

"That's still lying around in the shop for four years?" said Mary. "You realize this is not making any sense, don't you, Prentiss? Why would you think George left any money behind, and why would May keep it in her old, unused, unguarded—that last part is important, Prentiss, so I'll repeat it—her unguarded store?"

"Where else would she keep it?"

"In her house, under her mattress, in a bank; should I keep going?"

"Couldn't put it in a bank. Her brothers woulda found out she had it if she did that."

Mary had to grudgingly acknowledge that was probably true. Even if May could have found a bank that her brothers couldn't find, she wasn't really mobile enough to use it. She didn't drive anymore, and what bank would even open an account for crazy, demented May?

"She wouldn't have kept it in her house. Rufus and Billy are always over there checkin' up on her and probably goin' through all her stuff, too."

"Probably," said Mary. "Making sure they haven't overlooked something of value they could be selling. But why do you think she has any money in the first place? Didn't George take it all?"

"Said he was goin' to, but..."

"But what, Prentiss?"

"Well, May is spendin' more than her brothers is givin' her."

"Why do you think she's spending more than her brothers are giving her? It sure isn't on her wardrobe or hair care."

"Well, ya see—"

"No, I don't see, and we're about to arrive at the police station so you'd better make it so I can see pretty quickly."

Prentiss looked at her with fear in his eyes. "Dexter told me."

"Dexter? You're not making it clear, Prentiss. Why did Dexter think May was spending money, and why did he tell you about it? There are two questions there, Prentiss, and I need them both answered."

"Well..." began Prentiss.

Mary stopped the car by the side of the road about a block from the police station and looked at him. "I need to know, Prentiss. Why did George tell you about his plans to fulfill Jessica's dreams? Why did Dexter think May was spending money? And why did...just say it."

"Well, ya see..." Prentiss began, and was stopped immediately by Mary's glaring face.

"My brother told me the whole thing. What he had planned, an' how he was goin' ta do it, an' everything."

"Your brother?"

"George," said Prentiss.

"George is your brother?"

"Half-brother," said Prentiss. "Same ma."

Mary shook her head. "I didn't know that. So you knew what was going on, right?"

"Sort of. I knew he was thinkin' about it, and then he said he was leavin' an' he'd be in touch when he got settled."

"But he never did?"

"I got a postcard from him. Florida some place. Just said 'Wish you were here' an' his signature. Nothin' after that."

"Nothing about leaving any money behind though?"

"No. That was Dexter told me that."

"Dexter? Now why would Dexter know about May's money, and why would he tell you?"

"Well he's my...well, I guess he's my cousin-in-law, seein' as George is still married to May. He is, isn't he?"

"Yes, I guess on a technical basis at least." Mary shrugged, struggling to get it all straight in her mind. "So Dexter is what? George's nephew or something?"

"No. He's a Prentiss, not a Forrest."

"What are you saying? Prentiss is your first name, right?"

"Oh, yeah, but you see, my ma named me Prentiss after my pa." Prentiss was growing chatty now. "Ya see, my ma wanted my pa ta marry her, so she got pregnant thinkin' that would push him into it. When I was born, she didn't know what my first name was goin' ta be, but she wanted my pa's last name on my birth certificate, so I was named Baby Prentiss-Forrest.

"By the time my pa finally said there was no way he was marryin' her, she decided she liked Prentiss, so she just named me that. Prentiss Forrest. She just took the hyfoon out from between the two names. The hyfoon is that little tiny line between the names ya know, Mary. Anyway, Dexter's my cousin on the Prentiss side. Or maybe cousin-in-law, ya think?"

"Not related to George, but to whom? One of your father's relatives?"

"His brother's kid."

"That would make him your cousin, and May's nephew, too, by marriage."

"That'd explain it."

"Explain what?'

"Why May paid Dexter the five hundred dollars."

"May paid Dexter five hundred dollars? For what?"

"Well ya see—"

"Prentiss!"

"Rufus had done somethin' got May really pissed, so she paid Dexter to flat all the tires on his truck."

"And Dexter told you this? Isn't he afraid Rufus will find out? Isn't he trying to be a little secretive about it?"

"Well, yeah, but...ya see, Dexter is in Roses one night buyin' everybody rounds a' drinks an' he was blabbing around an'...well, he was pretty drunk. I talked to him a while an' then I left. He'd run outta money by then."

"And he told you this story right there in Roses? Why haven't I heard about it then? Why haven't I been invited to Dexter's funeral? That's what happens to people who are stupid enough to flat Rufus' tires and brag about it. Nothing is kept secret that gets said by a drunk in Roses."

"Well, ya see.... Well, Dexter didn't say nothing in Roses, but he thought he did, so the next day he comes ta me an' asks what he said, and then tells me what he thought he said, and then I told him he didn't say anything and then...well, then he asked me not ta say anything to anybody, so don't tell him I told ya, Mary."

Mary waved a dismissive hand. "Okay. Okay. Time for a reality check here. May paid Dexter five hundred dollars to flat the tires on Rufus' truck? Are you sure?"

"Rufus' tires was flat, Dexter had a whole lotta money, an' he said May gave it to him to flat the tires," deduced Prentiss.

"Yes, that would seem to indicate...but, Prentiss. If you thought May had the money in her shop all along, why did you go last night? What were you waiting for?"

"Shop's usually locked. May never left it unlocked—but Jerry did. At least he did the last time he was here."

"Yes," said Mary. "That's our Jerry."

"Yeah," said Prentiss. "Everybody knew that shop'd be unlocked last night."

Chapter 23

Mary called to make sure Peter would be there and he was. She didn't want anyone else interviewing Prentiss, particularly someone who might not be patient enough to listen to the meandering tales that Prentiss would tell. She also wanted to find out what Carl had left unguarded and for how long, and if anything had shown up, and yes...she was being a nosey bitch. She realized just how involved she was in this case when she considered that her shop was being destroyed at that moment by Jerry. It was probably too late anyway.

Peter greeted them. "Been looking for you, Prentiss," he said. Prentiss looked at his feet.

"Shall we interview him now, Peter?" asked Mary.

"We?" asked Peter in return. "Why would you be interviewing him?"

Prentiss' head shot up. "If'n Mary ain't there, then—"

Mary silenced Prentiss with the raising of her hand. "This would be for your own good, Peter."

"I appreciate your concern for my well-being, but there are procedures."

"And there is Prentiss. Prentiss is the black hole in the middle of the intelligent universe. All logical or rational thought that comes near him is sucked in, never to escape again. If that's the fate you wish for yourself, then I can do no more than to mourn your passing, or at least the passing of your brain.

"Besides, I have talked to him all the way over here from my shop, and I know what he knows, and I can tell all of it to you in less than a month, which is what it will take you to get him to tell it to you." Mary finished her argument with a winsome smile and a nod of her winsome head.

"Why do you think it will take me a month to extract the information that it took you only thirty minutes to gather?" asked Peter.

"Because I'm smarter than you are."

Peter frowned, and Prentiss nodded, and finally Peter said, "Okay. Just wanted to make sure that was it. Let's go, Prentiss, and you too, Mary, but just remember—"

Mary raised her hand again. "I know, Peter."

"What do you know?" Peter asked.

"Whatever you were going to tell me, Peter. Now let's go."

They sat in the same office in the back of the station that they had used earlier. There were only two chairs at the table, but Peter quickly moved one of the ones against the wall to provide seating for three. He then left briefly to get a second pad of paper and a pen for Mary.

There then followed the "questions," and after each answer Peter would write on his pad, and Mary would just look on quietly. The next question would again give Peter cause to address his pad of paper, first to cross out the previous answer he had written, and then to write a new one down, which was almost always crossed out in its turn.

"Why were you in Jerry's shop?" --- *"Lookin' for something'."*

"What were you looking for?" --- *"Not sure, it mighta been money."*

"Why did you think there was money there?" --- *"I wasn't sure there was any money."*

"But you went there looking for money, is that right?" --- *"But I didn't find any, so maybe it wasn't there."*

"But you did find a body?" --- *"Maybe."*

"Maybe you found a body?" --- *"Wasn't sure that was what I found."*

"But you thought...oh, hell," said Peter. There had been more questions than these and more answers too, but there had been no information at all. Mary was actually impressed that Peter lasted as long as he did.

"We'll have to talk to you some more, Prentiss," Peter said.

"I have a question, Peter," said Mary.

"Sure. Enter at your own risk."

"Did you kill anybody last night, Prentiss?"

"What? Me? You think I killed that...?" Prentiss was horrified.

"No," said Mary. "I didn't think so."

After a moment, Peter recovered enough to continue, even if Prentiss had not. "We'll need to contact you, Prentiss. I'll get a sergeant to take down your information, your cell phone—"

"But I don't have one," pleaded Prentiss.

"Then your home phone will do."

"Don't have one of those, neither. I can get one if ya give me a day or two, Captain Morgan. I didn't know I was supposed to have a phone. Will I get sent to jail for not having one?"

Peter shook his head. "You have a house, don't you?"

"Where I live, ya mean?"

"Yes, that will do. We'll need to fingerprint you too. There are some ice cream fingerprints in that shop and we need to match them."

Prentiss quickly put his hands behind his back, and Peter called for the sergeant, who in a few minutes would hate Peter more than anyone else on the force. Prentiss could make people do that.

When they were alone Peter said, "I'd call him dumber than dirt except I would be insulting the dirt. How on earth can he—"

Mary interrupted. "I'm prepared to bargain, Peter. I'll tell you what Prentiss knows if you'll tell me about Carl and the crime scene. You go first."

Peter shrugged in defeat. "Nothing much to say that you don't already know. May started wailing that she would die without her medication, so Carl decided to drive her to the pharmacy. He seemed to think that because no one was at the shop at the time, it didn't need to be guarded."

"So it was unguarded for as long as it took Carl to leave and come back?"

"That took a while. May forgot which pharmacy she used, so Carl went to both of the ones in town. Wrong one first, of course. I guess I'm lucky he didn't cruise over to the city to start the search."

Mary winced. "Oh," she said.

"Yeah, it was probably more than an hour, but the house at least wasn't unattended that whole time."

"Well that's good," said Mary.

"Or maybe not," Peter replied. "I called Carl and told him to get his ass back over there, but I also took one of my own people over to 'relieve' Carl of the arduous responsibility, and—"

Peter shrugged. "When I got there, before Carl got there, by the way, Rufus was coming out of the house."

"Oh," said Mary again.

"Yes," said Peter. "Rufus said he had been looking for May, all over the house and the shop, and so—"

"Oh, again," said Mary.

"Rufus said he had looked everywhere, and curiously enough, asked me if it was Jerry who was using that back bedroom."

"Ya think that means he was looking in there, too?" asked Mary. "Making sure May wasn't back there cleaning up for her nephew?"

"I wouldn't be surprised if that was the only place he was looking," said Peter.

"So Rufus pretty much destroyed any evidence that might have been there," sighed Mary.

"Not as much of a loss as you think, Mary."

"Oh, for a fourth time," Mary looked at him with a little surprise.

"I think that may be only the third time that you said that, but I'm not keeping track or anything. Seems Carl thought he might avoid the long trip to multiple pharmacies if he found May's medication, so he looked everywhere for it."

Mary shrugged. "At least he wouldn't have gone into Jerry's—" Mary was stopped by the slowly shaking head of Captain Morgan.

"He said he looked in there specifically. May apparently thought Jerry might have taken her medication for some reason." Peter was shaking his head.

"Carl has more fingerprints in that house than everyone else combined. We might find something he overlooked though."

"Not admissible in court though," said Mary.

"No," said Peter. "But it might point to someone, and right now nothing is pointing to anyone, but a deal's a deal. Explain the unexplainable. Tell me what, if anything, Prentiss Forrest knows."

Chapter 24

Mary shook her head. "Actually, you had a lot of information that I didn't know, Peter, so I'm not sure I'm obliged. Since you lied to me when you said you didn't have much information, I mean."

"I'm surprised, Mary. Surprised that you hadn't figured out all of it yourself, I mean. All you would have had to do is to think of everything that Carl could possibly have done that would be wrong, and then just assume he had done it."

"True, but that would involve pushing some of what Prentiss told me out of my mind, and you wouldn't have wanted me to do that."

"Interesting?"

"Very."

"I can hardly wait to hear."

Mary smiled now. "I'm going to rearrange the order that it was told to me, so as to make it a little more understandable."

"Prentiss told you this? Better to rearrange then."

Mary nodded. "First of all: Prentiss was a half-brother to George, May's disappeared husband, and a cousin to Dexter Prentiss."

"Didn't realize that."

"Neither did I. But Prentiss apparently knew that George and his secretary, Jessica, were planning to run off with all the money George could get his hands on. Trouble was that apparently May was suspicious that George was up to something, and she was watching the saving accounts and all that pretty closely. George couldn't get at that."

"I'm not sure there isn't more to it than that, but Prentiss said the only money George could get was the money May made in her store."

"Really?" frowned Peter. "He couldn't get at the community property, but he could get at May's money?"

"Not sure; it is Prentiss, after all. But that's what he said. He also said that George found out where May was hiding her money, locked in a freezer at the store or something, and told Prentiss he was leaving and that he would be in touch when he got settled."

"Did he?" asked Peter. "Get in touch, I mean?"

"He did, once, Prentiss said. A postcard from someplace in Florida saying he wished Prentiss was there. Probably not really the truth, but Prentiss said that's what it said. He didn't mention any other contact, but I didn't really press that point.

"So, Prentiss knew George and Jessica were leaving and taking all of May's money with them, knew they were leaving, and apparently knew when," smiled Mary.

"Curious," said Peter. "One postcard and then nothing? You think maybe Jessica took the money after they got to Florida?"

"And George is what: dead in Florida? That would explain why he sent only the one postcard."

"Curious," said Peter again.

"I thought so, but it gets curiouser. Curiouser and curiouser. Prentiss is convinced that George didn't get all of May's money. Maybe she was on to him and hid the money in different places or something, I don't know, but this next part is a major feat of logic, and Prentiss seems to have done it all by himself."

"Now that's curious," smiled Peter.

Mary nodded. "Yes. Apparently May's brother, Rufus, did something that got May really angry, because she paid Dexter to flatten all four of Rufus' truck tires. Prentiss was in Roses when Dexter was buying drinks for everyone to celebrate his newfound money and...well, Dexter got pretty drunk and thought he might have said something that would prompt Rufus to kill him."

"Rufus would have, if he found out, I suspect." Peter shook his head.

"Yes, and I was surprised that he didn't find out. I guess from what Prentiss said, Dexter didn't actually say anything at the bar, but he was worried that he had. So the next day, he went to talk to his cousin, Prentiss, to find out what he had said, and ended up telling the whole story."

"Now I knew Rufus' tires were flattened about six months ago, but I never heard anyone blamed for it," said Peter. "He reported it to the local cops and they passed it along to us. I expected there would be someone that got the shit beat out of him over it, but nothing came up."

"And Dexter told Prentiss he did it, and told him May paid him to do it. Prentiss thinks that last part is significant."

Peter looked at Mary and she continued, "This is the part Prentiss figured out himself. May has more money than what is in the banks, and insurance, and is all tied up in the trusts, and under her brothers' control. She paid Dexter five hundred dollars."

Peter raised his eyebrows. "Five hundred?"

"That's what Prentiss says Dexter told him, and he was spending it at Roses, so that part is probably true. What Prentiss thought was that May had money, and that he could find it in the shop. He pointed out that May wouldn't keep the money in the house since Rufus and Billy looked in there all the time, and she couldn't have put it in a bank. Her brothers would probably have found out about that, and she doesn't drive, so she couldn't have gotten to a bank anyway, or to anywhere else that she couldn't walk to from her house. That could really only be the shop.

"She also kept that shop locked, but Jerry didn't. Burglary isn't as much of a problem in California as it is in Nebraska, I guess. So Prentiss thinks May has money stashed in the shop, but May has it locked. Jerry comes along and leaves it unlocked; he did that when he was here last year too, so Prentiss knew it would be unlocked, and he went over there looking for the money and he finds Angie instead. Pretty simple, ya think?"

"Finds Angie, but he didn't kill Angie?" asked Peter.

Mary shrugged. "I don't think so."

"Neither do I. How much of this do you think is real? Does May have money stashed somewhere? Did Dexter really get five hundred dollars from May? Why did George leave the money behind anyway? Was May really clever enough to have hidden it from him?"

Mary shrugged. "I'm only guessing, Peter. It looks like May had some money, enough to give five hundred to Dexter, anyway. I don't know why George left that money behind, but...what else is possible? May went over the edge when her husband left, and rumor has it that it was the money that he took that bothered her, not the loss of meaningful companionship.

"Whatever it was, she closed the shop and has never reopened it. There has been no income coming to May except what she gets from her loving brothers. They do not give her enough for her to save up five hundred and still stay alive."

"I wasn't here when that happened. Didn't know George, and didn't know May before she became batty. I always thought it should have been investigated a little more than it was. I even wondered if George was still alive."

"I wondered about that too," said Mary. "He was alive enough to mail a postcard from Florida, but since then...nothing."

"What about George?" asked Peter. "Was he clever enough to pull this off? Steal May's money and run with it and then disappear? He would have to come up with a new identity and all."

"He was a lawyer," smiled Mary.

"Well, he was probably smart enough to know how to disappear then."

"Not necessarily," Mary smiled. "He was the law partner of John Burke, Esquire."

"Your father?"

Mary nodded. "Yup. The very one. So much for smart. Daddy was really upset when George ran out on him. I think he really misses Jessica."

Peter just nodded.

Chapter 25

They parted now. Peter was prepared to look into Prentiss' story, at his great trepidation, but had to admit that it was worth the effort to do so. He promised to contact Mary if anything came of this line of investigation. What he said was that he would come by the shop if anything came of it, and since he would undoubtedly get ice cream if such a journey was made, Mary suspected he would find some reason to get in touch with her.

Mary had the more onerous task. She had to see what, if anything, was left of her business. It was with increasing anxiety that she drove the thirty minutes to get there. If she had been capable of cognitive thought when she arrived, she would have noticed that the parking lot was full to overflowing; but all she did see was an empty space in front, and she took it.

Inside she was greeted by Jasmine, the half-naked friend of Dweeb, and she was still half-naked. "You have to get a number..." she began. "Oh, it's you, Mary." With this she turned her attention back to the table in front of her. On it was a glass of soda of some sort and a stack of index cards. She was laboriously writing a number on the card in front of her, and then with even more effort drawing smiley faces and hearts on it. There was a stack of blank cards in front of her, and next to it a smaller stack of cards, the top one showing a number and some sketches of flowers and a heart. Beside these was a small notebook.

Mary was going to ask what was going on when a young lady came in behind her. Jasmine looked up immediately and said, "You have to get a number from me."

The woman looked around, but then took a card from Jasmine, number one hundred twenty-two, it said. "How long is the wait?" she asked.

"Just a few minutes," said Jasmine. "He's real quick."

She looked over toward the counter where the ice cream was served and waved at Jerry, who said, "Oh, hi, Mary," but went right back to the three-deep line of customers. Mary stared as her worst nightmare seemed to be unfolding before her. She had never had this many customers in her shop before noon, but she had seen this many in Jerry's shop last night. Jerry had to be giving it away, she concluded.

Jerry continued as she stared, placing three covered dishes of ice cream in front of the nearest customer. "Three to go," he said. "That's eight eighty-five."

The man pushed a ten-dollar bill at him and said, "Thanks, Jerry. Keep the change, okay?"

"Sure thing, Joe. Who's up in the box next?" he asked.

A woman raised her hand as Jasmine looked up. "It's number one eleven, Jerry. I think you're number one twelve, Mrs. Snyder."

"Oh, so I am," said Mrs. Snyder. "Sorry."

"No prob," said a young man next to her. "I'm gonna be quick."

He approached the counter and said, "Hey, man."

"I'm Jerry. Whazzup?"

"Oh, hey, Jerry, I'm Phil," he replied, and they traded fist punches. "Look, man, I need a banana split with vanilla, cookie dough an' chocolate."

"Strawberries and pineapple?" asked Jerry,

"Yeah, and nuts and chocolate jimmies, too."

Jerry was looking at him, but also at the young lady with him. Mary couldn't see the face of that lady, but Jerry clearly could, and when Phil said he wanted jimmies, Jerry raised his eyebrows. "But not on both ends of the split, right?"

"Oh. Not both ends."

"So let me guess," said Jerry. "Which end will get the jimmies?" He put his index finger to his brow and looked, not at Phil, but at the lady.

Before Phil could speak, Jerry said, "The chocolate end, right?"

Mary winced. How could Jerry think that anyone would want more chocolate on chocolate ice cream?

"Wow," said Phil. "How'd ya know?"

"It's your karma," smiled Jerry and winked, not at Phil, but at the lady.

"You're like, awesome, man!" said Phil. He turned to the lady with him and said, "Isn't he awesome, Cissie?"

"Awesome," said Cissie, and winked at Jerry.

Mary looked at him and smiled. "Can I help, Jerry?"

"Sure," he said. "I think Mrs. Snyder is next."

"Oh, I'll wait for you, Jerry, if that's okay," said Mrs. Snyder.

"Then it's number one thirteen," said Jasmine. "Is that you, Bill?"

"Yeah," said a middle-aged man in a tee and jeans as Mary came around the counter. "Got a list here," said Bill. "Four bowls to go, is that okay?"

"Sure," said Mary.

Jerry looked up from the freezer where he was scooping and pointed at him with the scooper in his hand. "Bet one of 'em is strawberry."

Bill looked at the list and then at Jerry. "How'd ya know?" he asked in amazement.

"I could tell you're a strawberry kind a guy, Bill."

Bill's list was finished at the same time as the split was, and both were therefore paying up at the same time too.

"I've been putting the big bills in this can," said Jerry, indicting an empty gallon chocolate syrup can under the counter, "and keeping enough to make change in the register." He put a ten-dollar bill from Phil in the can, almost overflowing, and pushed it down.

"We've got enough tens in the register," he added, taking two dollars and twenty-five cents out and handing it to Phil. Phil began to pocket the change when Cissie nudged him.

"What?" he said.

Cissie nodded toward Jerry, but Phil remained oblivious. Finally she took the change and put it on the counter.

Phil was enlightened. "Oh, yeah. The tip, right? Thanks, Jerry."

Cissie smiled, and when they turned to leave Phil said to her, "I was going to do that."

"Of course you were," said Cissie.

The day continued like this. Jerry did get some of the younger patrons that requested him. Mary thought this was in hopes that the rumor of "grass" in the ice cream was true. She thought to tell them it wasn't, maybe even put up a sign, but then thought that maybe that would just reinforce the rumor, not dispense with it. Word should be getting around when it was realized that no one was getting a high from what was served at her shop.

When they reached number one hundred forty-four, it began to slow, and Mary was able to ask Jerry what the hell was going on.

"Well," he said, "I've been doing just what you told me to do. Selling ice cream is like surfing. You talk to people; give 'em what they want, and they pay for it. Isn't it great? I never knew it could be so much fun."

Mary was looking at him seriously now.

"It's more fun now that you're here, Mary," he added.

Mary looked at the table where Jasmine sat, still numbering and decorating her index cards. "You had a hundred and forty-four people through here today?"

"Oh, no," said Jerry. He nodded toward Jasmine and said, "We just started the numbers about ten o'clock. Jazz came by looking for Dweeb, and she was going to wait here for him since she thought he was coming back, so I had her get some index cards and make up some numbers, and—"

"Okay, Jerry," interrupted Mary. "I got that part; but how did you get so many people in here?"

"Oh, just being friendly. I didn't do anything special."

Mary frowned at him. "Friendly? How did you know the jimmies went on the chocolate ice cream?"

"Aw, that was easy. You shoulda seen the look on Cissie's face when Phil asked for jimmies. I knew they were going to share, and that she didn't want jimmies, and Phil had asked, so it was just a matter of figuring—"

"Which end to put them on," said Mary.

"Right," said Jerry.

When he said no more about it, Mary had to ask. "So how did you know it was the chocolate end?"

"Oh, Cissie kinda mouthed that to me. I was looking at her and she knew what I was thinking, so..." He just shrugged.

"And the strawberry for Bill?"

"Kinda telepathy, I guess. It's one of the favorites today. That's all."

"And you knew everyone's name by telepathy too?"

"Oh, no," said Jerry. "That's Jazz."

"Jazz?" asked Mary, looking over at Jasmine and her index cards.

"Yeah. Ya see, when I started having her make up the numbers to keep everything in order for people, and mostly to give her something to do while she waited for Dweeb, I asked her to make a list of people in a notebook, and kinda call out their names when it was their turn. Ya know, like she was reminding them it was their turn, but really it was so I would know their names." He turned serious now. "People like it when you know their name, Mary."

"Yeah," said Mary. "So Jasmine had index cards with her? Where did she keep them? There are no pockets in that outfit of hers."

"I sent her out for them," said Jerry. "And I had her pick up these little notebooks too." He produced several small notebooks. "She has one to write down the people's names and numbers, and I got some for us."

"For us?"

"Yeah, you know, so we can write down people's orders."

"I can usually remember the orders, Jerry."

"Of course, but when we're working together, we can write down the orders to give to each other to make." Jerry smiled at her.

"We're not going to be—" she began, but was interrupted by Peter as he came in.

# Chapter 26

"Afternoon, Mary," he said.

"You have to get a number from me, Captain Morgan," said Jasmine.

"He's the only one in the shop, Jasmine," said Mary.

"But Jerry said to give everyone a number."

"But it isn't Jerry's—" Mary started to say, but Jasmine was already walking over, and Peter looked as if he was going to do whatever she asked him to do. All she asked him to do was take an index card with hearts and flowers on it surrounding the number 145. Peter didn't look at the card. He was busy watching the woman who had delivered it as she walked back to her table.

"So, what number are we up to, Jerry?" asked Mary.

Peter looked up and then at his index card, and Jerry began to say something, but it was Jasmine who answered. "Number one hundred and forty-five...Captain Morgan," she said, and winked at Jerry.

Jerry smiled. "See how well it works, Mary?"

"Jerry, you already know who Peter is."

"Ah," said Peter, "but do you know what Peter wants? I've heard a rumor you're practicing telepathy without a license here."

Jerry smiled and placed his index finger on his forehead. He looked at Peter, and then past him at Jasmine. When Mary looked at Jasmine she was mouthing words.

"Not vanilla," said Jerry. Peter just smiled.

"Chocolate," said Jerry, and Peter smiled a little more, "would not be the flavor," Jerry continued.

Mary was shifting her gaze between the three when Jerry said, "Raspberry...in a dish."

Peter's eyes widened and Jerry said, "With rainbow sprinkles. One scoop."

"How did you...?"

"Let me get that for you, Captain Morgan," said Jerry, and went behind the counter.

Peter turned to Mary and asked, "Did you tell him?"

"Is your ego always this big, Peter? Do you think I have the time...or the inclination, to tell Jerry about your culinary preferences? Your incredible deductive powers should have established that I didn't tell him after you arrived, and you usually have two scoops anyway."

"Well, I intended to have two scoops, but I'm supposed to be on a diet. Michelle thinks...how did he know?'"

"About the diet?" asked Mary. "Maybe Jerry has been talking to your wife, ya think? Or maybe you're overweight?"

"Michelle's visiting her sister, and..." Peter shook his head.

"So, did you come all the way over here for the ice cream, or the telepathy demonstration, Peter?"

"What? Oh, not...well, I do have some information for you, as the co-investigator on this case."

"Before I ask what the information is, maybe I should establish that you'll be paying for the raspberry with sprinkles."

"Well," began Peter. The sternness on Mary's face silenced any further efforts at gaining free ice cream.

"The information is worth a single scoop at least, even if you're not willing to compensate me for it. The initial coroner's report is back: Cause of death is the bullets in her, .22 into the heart and aorta. She died very quickly, if not immediately."

"Shot at close range too?"

"Yes," said Peter. "Tox stuff is preliminary, but her blood showed cocaine and some sort of amphetamine they can't characterize yet. Bath salts they're suggesting."

They both looked over at Jerry who was sculpting, not scooping, a dish of raspberry ice cream.

"Yes?" said Mary.

"Yes," said Peter. "She had a plastic packet in her purse with what the crime scene boys think might be bath salts too."

"Maybe they should show them to Jerry and see what he thinks," Mary said.

Peter smiled. "I'll suggest that. Fingerprints are all preliminary too, but behind the counter of the shop, they almost all look like they're from just two people, and it looks like those two people are going to be May and Jerry. In front of the counter where she was found there are hundreds of prints, but that was where all the customers were."

"Were any of Prentiss' prints behind the counter?"

"Preliminary still, but it looks like he didn't get that far into the shop. There don't seem to be any recent prints from someone who might be Rufus or Billy, either. Some they think are old, but no recent ones that are unidentified. All preliminary still."

"Anything on the house?" Mary asked.

"The crime scene boys are just starting there," smiled Peter. "It won't be ready for Jerry to move back into tonight. I even told Rufus he had to take May over to his place tonight."

"Is it really necessary to move May?" asked Mary.

"No, but I wanted to torture Rufus a little. Make him earn his inheritance."

Jerry came over and handed Peter a dish of raspberry ice cream shaped like a snow man.

"We don't get snow in Huntington Beach, but I think I remember what it should look like," said Jerry.

"Pretty good, except for the color," Peter replied.

"So, what are you and Mary planning for tonight?" asked Peter tasting the snow man.

"Watch TV, I think," said Mary. "In separate rooms."

Jerry looked at her, but said nothing because at that moment, Dweeb came in. The first to see him was Jasmine, and she immediately straightened and turned to cross her legs, her naked legs, in front of her. She took a deep breath and her chest expanded, and then she bowed her back forward. Mary noticed and Peter certainly noticed, even Jerry seemed to notice; but Dweeb was oblivious to it all.

"Oh, man, that ice cream was so great, man!" he said to Jerry.

Jerry shrugged. "Strawberry is my favorite."

Dweeb weaved and wobbled and smiled inanely. "Awesome, man."

Peter just looked at him and Jerry seemed a little surprised, but Mary wasn't at all. "There was no grass in the ice cream, Dweeb."

"What?" said Dweeb. "But Dexter said—"

"Oh," said Jerry. "Is that what you thought?"

"Well, Dexter said...and last night..."

Peter was beginning to grin. "Ah, last night. At Jerry's ice cream shop, you mean? I have verified information, officially verified information, that no marijuana or any other mind-altering drug was present in any ice cream sold there last night."

Mary smiled. The expansive statement just uttered by Captain Peter Morgan was of course beyond the scope of the testing that had been done on Jerry's ice cream. There could not possibly have been testing done on all the ice cream, particularly all the ice cream "sold" last night, since the ice cream "sold" wasn't available to be tested. Only the unsold stuff was still around. Of course, technically, none of it was "sold," since it was given away by Jerry last night. Also true was that all the known drugs could not have been tested for. Mary thought of pointing out these obvious flaws in Peter's statement, but the essence of what he had said was true. Also true was that a large part of the crowd that had mobbed her shop today would probably not be back, but it was better to have it gone.

"There's nothing but good ice cream sold here, Dweeb," said Mary. "Sorry," she added, although she wasn't sorry at all. Peter took a taste of raspberry, non-drug containing ice cream, as if to prove she was correct.

Jasmine was relaxing a little now. Even the young could hold their breath for only so long. She still wanted to be noticed though, and made one final try. "Can someone get me another diet soda, please?" she said.

Mary smiled, since she knew what Jasmine really wanted, and Peter looked as if he were considering providing the service requested, although not the service wanted. Dweeb was totally sober, and more than totally deflated.

It was Jerry who spoke, "Sure, Jazz," he said and went to the table, picking up her empty glass. Defeat was complete.

Dweeb shook his head. "But Dexter said..."

By now Jerry had rinsed the glass, filled it and was bringing it back to place it in front of Jasmine. Rather than leave, however, he sat and began talking softly to her.

Peter was eating his raspberry and giving his lecture on the dangers of drug use to a totally dejected Dweeb, who of course had to listen to the lecture even though he had not used any drugs; he just thought he had. Peter had given the lecture before, several times, and he was dividing his attention three ways; lecture, ice cream and Jasmine.

Mary had not used any drugs, at least not in the past decade or so, and she had also heard the lecture before, so her attention could be focused on Jerry and Jasmine.

Jerry was talking softly, with occasional movements of his hands to emphasize a point, but Mary could hear none of what was said; only the actions gave a clue to any of the content. While Jerry talked, Jasmine seemed to be trying to deal with the only male who was showing any interest, in the only way she knew to deal with any male. She turned to display her legs to Jerry, took the deep breath again, and bent her back to push her chest forward as much as was possible, which was quite a considerable effort, and produced quite an astounding chest. Jerry ignored the effort completely. Jasmine made one more attempt, reaching with her pink finger-nailed hand to the inside of her top and running it down the inside, pulling it slightly aside as she did to expose a little more of the breast beneath.

Mary was impressed. She realized she could not compete in this league, not with Jasmine, and probably could not have competed when she was nineteen or twenty, as Jasmine was now. She looked at Peter, who was still lecturing but watching, and his facial expression confirmed her suspicion. Jasmine, not Mary or Dweeb, had his full attention.

But Jerry ignored it all and just continued to talk quietly and earnestly, and finally Jasmine acknowledged defeat. Either her failure to impress him, or possibly what Jerry was saying, caused the effort to collapse, and Jasmine looked as if she had lost three bra sizes in a few seconds...if she had been wearing a bra, that is.

The look on her face said she was listening, and then that what she was hearing was upsetting. She looked quickly at Dweeb and then back at Jerry, who was silent now. She was speaking, and spread her hands before her in dismay. She shook her head and looked as if she might begin to cry.

Jerry said something and she looked at him, shook her head, and then buried her face in her hands. Jerry reached toward her with his hand, but didn't touch her, simply motioning with his hand as if he were counseling her to calm herself. When he began to talk again it was a dialog, each speaking in turn. After a few exchanges, Jasmine reached for the pen and an index card and wrote, looking up at Jerry frequently. At one point he motioned toward the card, and she crossed out something and wrote again.

Jasmine shook her head again, and Jerry said something and nodded toward the other three, a dozen steps away. Jasmine shook her head, and Jerry raised his hand in the calming gesture. Finally Jasmine rose and faced the others. Her chest began to swell, but she stopped her breath and looked at Jerry, who shook his head once, and her chest returned to its normal size; still adequate, Mary noted.

Jasmine looked at the card she held in her hand and mouthed some words, shot a quick look at Jerry, who smiled, and then she walked the steps between them to stand next to Dweeb. Another quick look at the card, and then she seemed ready.

"You're so silly sometimes, Dweeb," she said, and smiled.

Dweeb looked up. "Oh, hi, Jazz," he said, but there was apprehension in his look.

Jasmine looked quickly back at Jerry and then at the card at her side before she spoke. It seemed to Mary that she was as scared as Dweeb appeared to be.

"You're so cute when you're silly, too," she said.

Mary was surprised, and Peter looked as if he was in shock. Jerry smiled, and Dweeb stared, and smiled, and then shrugged. No word came from him, however, and Jasmine looked back at Jerry, who just nodded again.

One more look at the card, and Jasmine reached her arms across her chest, placing each hand on the opposite shoulders, thus minimizing the view and said, "I…I mean…it's so cold…no, I mean, it's so cool in here." Her confidence seemed to return. "Do you have a jacket I could borrow, Dweeb?"

Dweeb looked as if he was in shock now too, and Jasmine was looking a little frightened. She looked back at Jerry, who sat at the table, calmly watching. He mouthed a word Mary couldn't quite get, and Jasmine turned back to Dweeb and said, "I mean, Francis."

Dweeb, now named Francis, finally managed to speak. "Oh, yeah. Sure. I have one in my car. I can run and get it. Get it for you, I mean…Jazz…Jasmine."

Francis was waiting, not moving, and Jasmine seemed hesitant and looked one more time at Jerry, who nodded toward the doorway to the parking lot.

"I can come with you, Francis," she said.

"Oh, yeah. Sure, Jasmine. It's just outside."

They seemed to hesitate, but finally Jasmine started toward the door, and Francis rushed to get there first to open it for her. By the time they managed to get outside, Jerry was standing next to Mary and Peter, holding a bag and a purse at his side.

"Jasmine and Dweeb?" asked Peter.

"Dweeb and anyone?" said Mary.

"His real name is Francis," said Jerry.

"Dweeb by any other name is still Dweeb," Mary said. Jerry just shrugged.

"Really, Jerry! Dweeb didn't get that name by accident. It wasn't given out in a lottery, you know. There are no romantic novels whose male lead is named Dweeb. There are no Dweebs walking down the red carpet to accept the best actor at the Oscars. He's still Dweeb."

"Francis," said Jerry.

Mary began to speak, but was interrupted as Jasmine ran back into the shop, with a nylon windbreaker on.

"He's so dreamy," she said, and sighed. "I forgot my purse. You were awesome, Papa Wilson."

Jerry smiled and handed her the purse he had in his hand and said, "Most people call me Jerry."

"Thanks, Papa Jerry," Jasmine said. She frowned and then said, "Papa J? That's it! Thanks, Papa J. Oh, and I'd better zip this up," she added, handing her purse back to Jerry in order to zip the windbreaker up. "Francis likes it better that way."

She looked puzzled for a moment and then shrugged. "You said most men like it when a woman covers herself up a little. I would never have believed it. My ma always told me not to cover up, but you were right, Papa J. You're so awesome, and so smart." Jasmine then reached up and kissed Jerry on the cheek, took her purse, and was out the door.

"Papa J?" asked Mary.

"She never knew her father. I was just kind of substituting."

"But you're only thirty-five, like me. You couldn't be old enough to be her father, Jerry. You would have had to be fifteen or sixteen when she was born," said Mary.

Peter smiled. "Were you still a virgin when you were sixteen?"

Mary blushed. "Well, kind of...not completely, but..."

Peter cleared his throat. "I was actually asking Jerry, but thanks for sharing, Mary."

Mary blushed again. "Oh, I was actually answering for Jerry. He was sort of a virgin when he was sixteen, isn't that right, Jerry?"

"Well, yeah," said Jerry, with no hint of embarrassment. "I was kind of a late bloomer."

"I guess," said a totally mystified Peter. "Maybe still not fully bloomed. Did you really tell Jasmine that most men like women to cover up?"

"Well, yeah," said Jerry. "They do."

Mary looked at him, but Peter spoke. "I don't know about most men, but I like it when..." He cleared his troublesome throat as embarrassment stopped his speech.

Jerry looked at him. "You mean, like Michelle?"

"What?" said Peter.

"Do you like it when your wife, Michelle, dresses like Jasmine? In front of other men I mean?"

Mary began to giggle, and Peter's embarrassment grew. "Well, no, not..."

"Maybe at home, but not here in my shop," said Mary.

Peter could only stammer, but Jerry was looking as if he expected an answer. "Most men don't really like women who dress and act like Jasmine did. They like to pretend that they do, but they really want beauty, not sexy."

"I could start dressing like Jasmine, Peter. Might improve business, ya think?" offered Mary.

Jerry looked at her. "You don't have to do that, Mary. You're more beautiful than Jasmine is, no matter what you're wearing."

Mary shook her head and looked at Peter. "You'd better agree, Peter."

Chapter 27

Another customer came in, and Jerry went behind the counter. "How ya doin?" he said. "I'm Jerry, and I'm helping Mary for a little while. You Joe's brother?"

Jerry extended a handshake and the man took it. "No, I'm Bill's brother, Louis."

"Oh, yeah. I think he was in here earlier today. What can I get you, Louis?"

Peter looked at Mary and spoke in a low voice, "How did he know?"

"Jerry you mean?"

"Yeah."

"Know about what? About your diet? That Dweeb was really named Francis? That Jasmine thinks he's '*dreamy*'? That men don't really like half-naked women, they just pretend they like them? Or were you wondering how he knew what you like Michelle to wear around the house? You'll have to be more specific, Peter. He doesn't know everything. He didn't know that Louis was Bill's brother."

Peter smiled. "Oh, those are simple. How'd he know my favorite ice cream?" He chuckled now.

"Probably the stains on your uniform," said Mary.

"There are no stains on my uniform…are there?"

Mary walked away as Peter examined his uniform. "I'll see you tomorrow at the station at nine, right? To meet with Laura Stewart," he said as he left the shop.

"Nine sharp," said Mary. "And put on a clean uniform."

"I didn't see anything on his uniform," said Jerry.

"Neither did I," Mary replied.

There were several more that came in, more than Mary thought her evening would bring, but maybe there was still a little anticipation that there might be "grass" in anything that Jerry was serving.

Several of the younger patrons asked to have Jerry serve them. A few asked for "special" ice cream, and Jerry just shrugged and said all ice cream was special. Most of the young people just wanted to meet the new guy in town, and some talked to him about California. A few even asked about surfing. Jerry enjoyed talking to all of them, but especially about surfing.

Mary was fairly busy too, which meant the shop was busier than usual, since she could usually handle it herself. Jerry would occasionally write down an order and give it to her to fill, more because he thought it was "neat" to do so. If he had trouble filling an order because he didn't know what was being asked for, he would just ask her, or sometimes ask the customer. There were some pretty unusual ice creams being served up tonight, but everyone paid.

It began to slow around eight, and Mary thought of having Jerry take a break, but when she did, and before she suggested it, Jerry suggested she start cleaning up, since she knew how she wanted it done, and then that she count the money. He handed her the nearly overflowing chocolate syrup can.

She cleaned and counted, and by nine the last customer was out the door and half an hour later they were turning the sign to say "CLOSED."

"Almost twenty-two hundred," said Mary, as they exited and went to her car.

"Is that good?" asked Jerry.

"Damn right that's good. Let me buy you supper at Roses."

"I can—"

"No, you can't. You paid this morning, so it's my turn."

"Okay," said Jerry. "This is sort of like a date, isn't it?"

"No, it is not like a date, Jerry. It's like two people who have worked hard going out to get something to eat."

"But you don't usually take your co-workers out to supper, do you?"

"I don't have any co-workers, Jerry. You're the only one who has ever worked in my shop besides me."

Jerry thought for a minute. "So it's really like going out together, right?"

"Jerry, just stop it, okay? You can think of it any way you want, just don't talk about it, and don't start telling everyone we went out on a date tonight."

"Okay." Jerry shrugged. "Who would I tell, anyway? I don't really know that many people here."

"Good," said Mary.

"Oh," said Jerry. "I forgot to tell you. Your father came by looking for you this morning."

"My father?"

"Yeah. He seems like a nice guy. It wasn't busy, so we chatted for a while."

"Chatted?"

"Yeah, he wanted to know where I was from, and how long I was going to be around."

"Oh, no," said Mary, shaking her head.

"And if I was married, or had a girlfriend, and if I like you. Stuff like that."

Mary stopped. "And what did you tell him?"

"No, no, and yes."

"What?"

Jerry shrugged. "Not married, no girlfriend, and of course I like you."

"You didn't tell him you were staying at my place did you?"

"No," said Jerry.

"Good. At least that's—"

"He'd already heard about that."

"Oh, great," said Mary. "We may as well go out on a 'date' to Roses then. I've known you for twenty-four hours already, so what are we waiting for? You're the longest relationship I've had with a man in a decade anyway, I think."

Jerry seemed pleased, and Mary was resigned to it. She dropped him off in front, saying it could be crowded because the supper crowd was still eating, and the bar crowd was arriving. "Get us a nice table while I deposit the cash," she said.

When the deposit was done, she entered the restaurant to find Jerry chatting with Sandy. When she approached the table Sandy turned and asked, "Coffee, Mary?"

"If Jerry will allow it."

"Oh, coffee is perfectly safe, for crying out loud," said Sandy.

"You want some coffee, Jerry?"

"No. Maybe some juice?"

"Look, Jerry, we don't have any mango, and probably never will, so get over it. And I don't have time to be mixing up something special for you every time you come in. I've been here twelve hours, with only four hours off in the middle, for Pete's sake."

"Maybe ginger ale then."

"You got it," said Sandy, and was on her way.

Mary sat and looked after her. "Quite a transformation. What happened?"

"Oh, she's just a kid. I got to thinking about what you said in the car, and I thought it would be better if she understood."

"Understood what, Jerry?"

"That I'm older than her."

"And so how did that go?"

"Okay."

"You didn't tell her we're dating, did you?"

"I didn't think of that. Maybe I should have, ya think?"

"NO, Jerry. What did you tell her?"

"I asked her what kind of music she liked, and then I told her I liked the Beatles."

"And she doesn't?"

"Doesn't even know who they are. I was going to mention Benny Goodman if the Beatles didn't work."

"Yeah," said Mary. "That would have made things clear to Sandy. I actually like Benny."

"So do I," beamed Jerry. "One of my favorites."

"I knew it would be," said Mary, shaking her head.

They ate and chatted. Nothing special. Mary got around to saying that she really did appreciate Jerry's help, and that he was a natural at the shop. Jerry said he didn't think he was, partly because it didn't involve any sun or seawater, but that he enjoyed it. He suggested that it was more fun when it was organized the "way it should be."

He ended by saying that Mary was really "rad," and when she asked if that was a compliment, Jerry said of course. All the surfers say that.

Mary paid and left a generous tip. Sandy had brought her coffee and a refill, and they were both back to their normal selves. Jerry had left a generous tip that morning, too, and...well, Mary had had a good day. And while she wasn't really competing with Jerry, she didn't mind beating him once in a while.

They were leaving Roses and heading for Mary's apartment by eleven o'clock.

Chapter 28

They arrived shortly at the place Mary called her home. It was an apartment in a residential area of town, and when they entered it was into a sitting area with a TV, two chairs, and, Mary pointed out, a sofa that would be a bed tonight.

"I have a bedroom," she said, hoping Jerry was clear on the sleeping arrangements. He seemed to be.

"There's only one bathroom and shower, so I'll try to be quick in the morning to give you a chance after I'm finished," she added, hoping to make the bathroom arrangements equally clear. This was her home and he was a guest, with no privileges at all.

When he nodded she felt inhospitable, and pointed to the small kitchen at one end of the room. "There are some sodas and snacks you can help yourself to, but I'm afraid I have no mango juice."

"That's okay," said Jerry. "I don't really like mango juice anyway."

"Why did you ask for it at Roses, then?"

"Oh, just to tease Sandy, I guess. People sometimes think surfers are all weird or something."

Mary shook her head. "People are sometimes right, too."

It was late, but she wasn't really tired, and Jerry wasn't moving quickly to get to sleep either, so she decided to chat a little. The topics were limited; not Laura or Angie, that would suggest an interest in his sexual activity, and that wasn't what she wanted at all. The murder was...well, time enough for that later. *Ah, yes, surfing.* Why had she thought there could be anything else?

"So, you really like surfing?" she asked, realizing how totally unoriginal she was being, but only realizing this after she had asked.

"Yeah," he said, looking around.

If there was going to be "chat" she'd better get it moving. She had expected Jerry to start "chatting" with enthusiasm at the opportunity to tell her how great he was, or surfing was. Maybe if she could sound a little more interested in it?

"So you were pretty good, Peter said?"

"Yeah. Back a while ago."

All right, Jerry, let's go for the jugular of the male ego. "You could have gone pro?"

"Not really."

What was wrong? She hadn't really cared about the "chat" until Jerry hadn't really cared about the "chat," but now she was going to get him to "chat" even if she had to strip...no, she didn't want to chat that badly. Besides, if she stripped, they might not ever get to the chat.

"Peter said, that Stan said, you were really good."

"That's different."

"Okay, Jerry. I realize I'm a woman from Nebraska and this is sports from California we're discussing, or at least I'm discussing, and women are at a disadvantage when it comes to discussing sports, but what is different?"

"Oh," said Jerry. "Being a good surfer is different from being a professional surfer."

"The professionals aren't good, or the good guys aren't professional?"

Jerry frowned. "I'm not sure."

"Okay, Jerry. I could just let this go, but I'm stubborn, and you're not going to beat me. Please explain why Stan thinks you're good and you don't."

Jerry looked a little bewildered now. "I'm not sure why Stan thinks I'm good."

"Jerry! Sorry, sorry, I promise to stay calm, okay? Jerry, are you a good surfer?"

"Well, yeah. Pretty good."

"So that would explain why Stan thinks you're good, because you are a good surfer, right? Stan said you could have gone pro, right?"

"Well, yeah, but that was back—"

Mary held up her hand. "But you didn't, right?"

"Well, no."

"Okay. Big finish. Why didn't you go pro?"

"I didn't want to."

"Not finished. One more chance, Jerry. Why didn't you want to?"

Jerry shrugged. "I don't think you would understand."

Mary looked, and thought, and then she spoke, and what she said was surprising to her. She hadn't realized what she said, not until she said it anyway, but once she had said it, she realized how true it was.

"But I want to understand, Jerry."

Jerry looked at her and seemed to accept what she had said, even if Mary was so surprised that she'd said it that she couldn't have said another word right now.

"It was after the ISA meet at Huntington," he replied. "I did really well. Waves were good and I was ready for them. Then this guy asked if I'd come to Hawaii for a couple demo events. The hotel would pay to get me there and let me stay there free if I'd like, mingle with the other surfers. I would be a *drawing card* he called it, to get people to stay at their hotel. He said they would even set me up to give a few private lessons if I wanted."

"And you didn't like that?"

"Well, I thought about that, but then this other guy came over with an article he wanted me to write. About surfing or something."

"You could write an article, Jerry. I'm sure you could."

Jerry shook his head. "He didn't want me to write an article. He already had the article. He just wanted to put my name on it. He was surprised I even wanted to read it first."

"Oh," said Mary.

Jerry shrugged. "I learned that day that surfers are supposed to be dumb, at least the pros, and I didn't want to be dumb. I didn't think you would understand. You've probably never screwed up in your whole life."

"Wrong, Jerry," laughed Mary. "Is this going to be the night of the confessions? Do you really want to know how screwed up I am?"

"Well, you don't have to..." he began.

"But what if I want to? What if...what if it will make me a better person to be honest? Will you listen then?"

"Well, if you want..."

"And I do. Are you ready? I went to law school."

"Really!?" said Jerry. "You're a lawyer?"

"No. I run an ice cream shop, but I went to law school, and I graduated, and then...then I never took the bar exam. I got a degree, but I can't practice because I never took...well, I...no, it's not that. I was just afraid to practice. I interviewed at a couple firms in the city. They were interested, once I passed the bar exam, but I didn't think I could make it there. My dad would have...well, that would have been worse, if I let him down. My mother had died, and he was really depressed, and I didn't want to..."

She was close to tears now. This was her biggest secret, and she had told it to Jerry of all people. She deserved whatever he said or thought for being stupid enough to tell him. He didn't say anything though, just came over and hugged her. Hugged her for a long time it seemed, and when they finally parted she felt better, and Jerry said, "I went to law school too, ya know?"

"What?" she asked.

"Yup," he smiled. "Berkeley."

"Really? You went to Berkeley?"

"Yup." He was laughing now. "They have these courses for the law students on the different drugs and counseling people, and how to talk to people so you could understand the street language and all that."

Mary laughed too. "And you took the course. Is that where you learned all the drug stuff that impressed Peter?"

"Wsll, no." Jerry blushed. "I kinda taught the course."

Mary smiled. "That's better. I would never have believed you could be dumb enough to take a law course."

"But you're really smart, Mary."

"No," she said. "Going to law school and then being too scared to even try to practice is not smart."

"Sure it is. Smart enough to go to law school and even smarter to know you didn't want to be a lawyer. Most people aren't anywhere near that smart."

"Well, I guess that means I'm not most people," she smiled. He was at least easy to talk to. "I suppose you think you're going to have sex now," she laughed.

"With who?"

Mary continued to laugh as she shook her head. "Never mind."

Jerry thought for a minute as Mary calmed herself and began to look at him.

"I guess I should be honest with you, too. You probably figured it out already anyway," he said.

"That you're really a lawyer? I won't believe that."

"No," said Jerry. "It's about Laura and Angie."

"Oh," said Mary, turning serious now. She hoped he wasn't about to admit that he had killed Angie, hoped that very sincerely, since she was alone in her apartment with him right now. "What about Laura and Angie?"

"It's about the sex," he said.

"Yes?" she replied. Good so far. Not about the murder.

"I really didn't have sex very often with either of them."

"Oh," said Mary, with a mixture of surprise and disbelief. "Just bragging to Peter I guess."

"No," said Jerry. "Ya see, I figured with Angie dead, Peter was going to talk to Laura sooner or later, and...well, she was going to tell him we had sex all the time."

"And she would, what...be lying?"

"Yeah," he said, looking up at Mary as if this was a relief to him. That she had understood what she didn't believe.

"Why would she lie, Jerry?"

"She always did. She was always telling everybody we had sex all the time, all morning, all afternoon, and stuff like that. Bragging about it, I think. So I just figured if that was what she was going to tell Peter, I'd better say that too, or Peter would think I was lying to him.

"I mean, if she said we did it all the time, and I said we hardly ever did, who was Peter going to believe? Then he would think that I was lying about other stuff too. So I..."

Mary shook her head. "You really...you didn't...well, what the hell did you do, Jerry?"

"Laura was always after me, like it was some sort of a conquest thing and...well, I wasn't interested. I mean, I didn't love her or anything."

"And you didn't want to do it just for the sex, I suppose?" Mary said, and she thought it sounded pretty sarcastic, too.

"Yeah," said Jerry. "That's right. You do understand. You're really great, Mary. I had to a couple of times, but she was drunk or high so much."

"And she would brag about it? You didn't brag about it though, right, Jerry? You would never brag about a conquest, like most men do?"

"No." He shrugged. "With Laura it wasn't anything special. When she wasn't selling it, she was giving it away. But she liked to brag about...well, she thought we had sex more often than we did, anyway."

"She thought? How could she think she had sex if she didn't?"

"Like she would be drunk and say she wanted to do it and then pass out and like I would tell her we had sex when she came to, and she was so out of it she thought we did."

"But you didn't, right?"

"No. Of course not. That would be like rape or something, wouldn't it?"

"Maybe. I'm not sure. You know, Jerry, a lot of guys here in Nebraska get the women drunk so they can get sex, not so they can tell the woman they did when they didn't."

"Really?"

"Really, Jerry. As a matter of fact, if it weren't for alcohol, a lot of guys would only be able to have *meaningful relationships* with farm animals. Didn't your mother talk to you about this, Jerry?"

"She was pretty sick, and then she died when I was still a kid."

Mary shrugged. "Yeah, I knew that, sorry. So like...well, assuming I'll believe you...how often did you...you know...with Laura and Angie." Mary consoled herself by thinking that this was part of the *investigatio*n and not just curiosity.

"Only three or four times."

"A week? A day? With Laura or with Angie or with both of them?"

"With Laura. She was in the apartment for about three months and...maybe three times during that. With Angie it was only once."

"So only three times with Laura, and once with Angie?"

"Once with Angie and Laura. They insisted on doing it together. After that, I left when Angie stayed in the apartment."

"You left your apartment? And left Laura and Angie there even though they weren't paying any rent? Or at least not any money." Mary was having a little trouble with this whole conversation.

"Well, yeah. I stayed over with Stan, but that didn't work out too well."

"Stan from the Huntington Beach Police? I'm afraid to ask why that didn't work out," said Mary.

"Stan's gay." Jerry shrugged.

"I didn't really ask that, Jerry," Mary replied.

"He thought I moved over there because he was gay, and when I told him I didn't want to have sex with Laura and Angie, he kind of assumed it was because I wanted to have sex with..."

"Enough, Jerry. In fact, it's way more than I needed to know. Was Stan right? Are you gay, Jerry?"

"I don't think so."

"Don't you know? I mean, the guys in Nebraska usually know when they are...never mind."

"Well, it's just that I never had sex with another guy. I haven't had sex with any farm animals either."

"It's all right, Jerry. Neither have I. I mean, I've never had sex with farm animals. I have had sex with some guys."

Jerry looked at her until finally she said. "No, I have not had sex with any women, but I'm pretty sure I'm not a lesbian."

"I'm glad," he smiled. "About the farm animals, I mean."

Mary's phone rang just then to save them from any further embarrassment.

# Chapter 29

Mary shook her head, but it was no clearer when she looked at the caller ID. When she answered, she said, "Dad? Why are you calling me now? It's after midnight."

"What?"

"Oh, yeah. Right here, why?"

"Sure."

She looked at the phone and then handed it to Jerry. "It's for you, Jerry. It's my father."

Jerry put the phone to his ear and said, "Hi, John. How ya doin'?"

"Oh, no problem at all, man. We were just talking."

"About stuff, you know."

"What?"

"Oh, yeah. I've got to be at the police station in the morning, but I'll be at the shop after that." He looked at Mary and smiled as she spread her hands and mouthed the word "Why?"

"Mary? I think she'll be at the shop too, won't you, Mary?"

"It's my shop," Mary said.

"Yeah, she said she'll be there."

"What?"

"No. We were talking about that though."

"Okay, see ya tomorrow, John," Jerry said, and handed the phone back to Mary.

Mary put the phone to her ear and said, "Dad?"

"I think he hung up already. You could call him back though."

"What was he calling you for at this time of night, and on my phone?"

"He said he wanted to talk to me about something. Tomorrow at the shop. He knew I didn't have a phone."

"And so he assumed he could reach you on my phone?" asked Mary.

"He knew I'd be staying here for a few days."

"One day, Jerry. You're only staying for one day. What did you tell him we were talking about?"

"Oh, he asked if he was disturbing us or anything, and...well, I told him...we were like talking about…"

"We were not talking about...did he ask you if I'd had sex with you, Jerry?"

"Well...I'm not sure what he said exactly."

"Well next time he asks, tell him that you do not have sex with someone unless you love them. That will shut him up."

"Okay, but..."

"But what?"

"That wouldn't be a problem with you, Mary."

Mary closed her eyes and shook her head again, but with no better results than had been the case earlier.

When she opened her eyes she said, "You'll sleep on the couch, Jerry. I'll sleep in the bedroom, with furniture piled against the door, but I'll bring you some bedding. I get the bathroom first in the morning, and I'll let you know when I'm done, so don't try to sneak in early, okay?"

"Sure," said Jerry. "Can I use your conditioner?"

"My what? Oh, the hair conditioner? I guess so."

"Thanks," Jerry said.

Mary had calmed herself by the time she brought the bedding out. "Don't pay any attention to my father, Jerry. He's certifiably crazy."

"Yeah, I know. But he's a nice guy and he has a nice daughter, too."

Mary shook her head again and retreated to her bedroom. "Shit," she said to herself, but she decided that piling furniture against the door wasn't really necessary.

She set her alarm for seven to make sure she got through the bathroom in time for Jerry to use it. It was a courtesy and a precaution, too. And it was a failure. When she emerged from her bedroom, he was already dressed wearing the same clothes as he had worn yesterday. The only evidence he had prepared for the day was that he was shaved and his hair was washed, but not yet dry.

Jerry was cooking something on her two-burner stove, and looked up when she entered.

"You only had a couple of eggs, so I made French toast instead of scrambled, is that all right?"

"I was supposed to get the bathroom first, Jerry."

"Sorry." He shrugged. "Ya wanta eat first or shower first. Coffee's almost ready."

"What are you drinking?" she asked, and realized she was being irritable for no good reason. She was supposed to get the bathroom first, but it was available for her, and she wouldn't have to hurry to let Jerry use it since he was already done with it. He was cooking breakfast, which she wouldn't have done, probably couldn't have done with what she had in her kitchen, and he had made her coffee. *He's the best houseguest you've had in a while, so stop acting like an ass, Mary!* she said to herself.

"I thought I'd try coffee this morning. You like it, and so maybe I'll like it, too," Jerry replied.

"Maybe you will. I don't have any mango juice, either. I think there's some orange juice if you would rather that."

Jerry frowned. "I think it might be sour, but I can run out and get some if you want it."

"My orange juice is not...well, it was fresh a couple weeks...or a month...or two...ago. Mary sighed. "Coffee is fine for me."

"So you take coffee with milk and sugar, right?"

"Yes, but I'm afraid the milk is sour, too. You see, I don't really cook here too often, Jerry."

"Oh, no prob. I ran out for some fresh this morning."

"Oh."

He placed the coffee on the table in two mugs and a sugar bowl and spoon, and several small containers of half and half together on the table. "You had sugar," he smiled.

"Yeah, well...thanks," said Mary. "Where did you get the half and half?"

"From the fast food place at the corner. I just picked 'em up there by their coffee refill counter."

"Didn't you buy anything?"

"Well, no. I didn't need anything except these," he said, pointing to the half and half containers.

"You could have picked up breakfast, too, I suppose. And saved yourself all this work, I mean."

"No trouble, and I like to cook. When it's for someone I like, that is." He smiled and Mary felt like an ass again.

They sat, and Jerry watched Mary as she poured some half and half into the coffee and added sugar. When she looked up, Jerry was still watching her. "Something wrong?"

"I just wanted to see if you liked it. I don't usually make coffee so...you know. How is it?"

Mary tasted and smiled. "It's pretty good."

"Great," said Jerry. "If I have to make coffee for you again I know how to do it."

Mary began to speak, but Jerry got up and brought two plates, forks, and butter to the table. "No syrup," he said.

"No," sighed Mary. Her housekeeping failures were mounting quickly.

"I could have bought some, but I didn't have a car. I think if you sprinkle sugar on them they'll taste okay."

He brought a plate of French toast to the table and Mary looked at it. "You made them in different shapes, Jerry?"

On the plate were six pieces of French toast: two in the shape of a heart, one that looked like a flower or something, and three that were round with smiley faces cut in them.

"Yeah," he said, and offered Mary first pick. She took a heart, the flower and a smiley face. Jerry took the other three.

They sprinkled them with sugar after spreading them with butter, and Mary had to admit they tasted pretty good.

"So, are you dressed for the day, Jerry? You're wearing the same clothes as yesterday, aren't you?"

"Not really," said Jerry, finishing his last bite. "I changed my tee shirt. Just the shirt and the shorts are the same."

"And the underwear, too," she said.

"Well...I don't usually..." he began.

"Oh," nodded Mary. There was no point in making an issue of it. She was almost sad to think he would be gone tomorrow morning, and she didn't want to be too critical.

"That was a lot of trouble to cut the French toast into shapes like that."

Jerry shrugged. "Not that much trouble. I had to cut the bread anyway. It was a little moldy."

Mary looked at her empty plate and then at Jerry as he cleared away the dishes.

"I'm going to the shower now, Jerry," she said.

"We maybe ought to do some shopping for food for tomorrow, ya think?"

"No...well, maybe," said Mary. "I'll be ready in a few minutes." *If I don't decide to vomit up breakfast while I'm in the bathroom, that is.*

# Chapter 30

She was ready in a few minutes and of course Jerry was ready, too. The kitchen was cleaner than it had been when he arrived the night before; dishes from the breakfast washed, and it looked like Jerry had been washing other things, too. Mary wondered if he had emptied her cabinets and washed her "clean" dishes, but they weren't stacked to dry as the breakfast dishes were.

Soon they were driving in her car, slowly since they were early, and Mary decided that she was going to give advice.

"Okay, Jerry," she said. "We need to get back to the murder of Angie now. Laura will be here, and she'll tell us about her sister. She may be able to tell us why she was here, and who might have killed her, and…. Well, she's the one person who can tell us what the hell makes any sense in this whole thing."

"She can," said Jerry. It was a statement not a question.

"She can, but…?"

Jerry shrugged. "I'm not sure Laura will tell us what she knows unless it's what she wants us to know too, and I'm not sure what she wants us to believe will be what she really knows. I don't think it will be the truth."

"Her sister was murdered," said Mary. "She'll want to punish the person who killed her sister."

"I'm not sure she'll care about Angie's murder that much."

"But...her own sister?"

"I'm not sure. We'll see," said Jerry.

So much for the giving of advice. Mary looked quickly at the man riding next to her and wondered how much he cared about Angie's death, or how much she really cared, or anybody cared about the death of a drug-using prostitute from Huntington Beach, California. She cared. Angie may have been all that Mary had just said, but she was still a person, with a sister, who might not give a shit about her, but she was still a person.

"We have to find out who killed her, Jerry. We have to find them and see that they are punished."

Jerry looked over at her. "We will, Mary."

They rode in silence now, and in a few more minutes they arrived at the state police station. Peter was waiting outside to greet them, and they parked and got out to walk over to where he stood. Mary had her purse, and Jerry was carrying a plastic bag. Peter greeted them, and then mentioned that after Jerry greeted Laura, he needed to talk to him a little more. The request didn't seem to be a request exactly, but an order. Peter seemed to be more official than a request would warrant.

Laura was late, but only by fifteen minutes. Not enough time to raise serious concern that she might not show up. They had waited outside because Peter thought that Laura should see Jerry first, to reassure her that she had not come here under any subterfuge.

When she arrived it was in the front seat of a pick-up truck which was driven by a bearded man of about fifty. He smiled and leaned toward her as if he intended to kiss her, but Laura was opening the door of the truck almost before it had stopped.

She was on the sidewalk, striding away in an instant, and had not bothered to shut the door as she did so.

"Hey, babe," the driver said. "When shall I pick ya up?"

"Never, Luther," replied Laura. She turned to face him and added. "I have a better ride. A way better ride than you."

The astonishment on Luther's face was clearly visible from the dozen or so feet that separated him from the party waiting for Laura.

"But ya said..."

"Don't be an asshole," said Laura. "If that's possible."

"But what about all yur clothes? They're still at the house."

"Give 'em to your wife, Luther." With this Laura walked over to Jerry, put a hand on either side of his head, pulled him to her and gave him one of the most pornographic kisses Mary had even seen. Jerry seemed only a little surprised, and wasn't nearly as surprised as Mary or Peter, but the most surprised person of them all was Luther.

Laura looked back at him and then turned to face Jerry again, and as she did, she struck a seductive pose. Mary could see her clearly now; bleached-blond hair, far too much makeup, a tight shirt that barely covered an enormous cleavage, and stopped well above her miniscule miniskirt and bare legs. Even Jasmine would have been eclipsed easily.

For some reason, Mary thought of Jerry, and how he had said men don't like women who dress like this. She almost smiled as she wondered if Peter liked Laura and the way she was dressed. Trouble with liking the way Laura was dressed was that you would have to take Laura with her body, and right now Luther was demonstrating how dangerous that could be.

Before she could speak, Luther yelled, "You goddamned..." He stopped as he saw Peter, who was looking squarely at him and standing straight, with his best menacing posture. Peter was pretty good in the menacing posture competition too, and Luther got the message fast.

He reached over, slammed the passenger door of the pickup and pulled into the traffic, which was obviously not moving away from the police station fast enough for him. Mary looked at the elaborate pickup, but what caught her eye was the vanity plate: S-69-X.

Laura followed Mary's gaze and smirked. "Yeah, that was what he wanted all last night: SEX and 69."

Luther had managed to get around the traffic now and screeched off, yelling something about a "fucking bitch," but the remaining words were lost to the listeners and to posterity. Mary suspected that they would not be much missed by either.

Laura turned away to smile at Jerry. "Did you miss me, lover?"

Mary expected Jerry to answer with some negatively framed phrase after what he had told her the night before, but he smiled at Laura and simply said, "Yeah. Know what I miss most?"

Laura smiled and became even more seductive, if that were possible. "I can guess," she said.

Jerry smiled too. "The cooking," he said. "You made the best pancakes I've ever tasted." Jerry remained silently smiling, as Laura's face registered first surprise, then disbelief, and finally bewilderment.

Jerry said nothing for a moment, but just as it appeared Laura was about to speak he said, "This is Mary, Mary Burke. She and I are running an ice cream shop here. And this is Captain Peter Morgan with the state police. This is Laura," he added, looking back at the astonished faces of Mary and Peter.

When the shock was just beginning to subside, Jerry spoke again. "You'll probably want to see Angie and talk to Peter." He motioned toward the captain, and then handed Laura the plastic bag he was holding. "These are the things I was telling you about. Angie's, I think. You may as well have them now. Too bad about Angie."

Jerry looked sincerely saddened, but Laura registered no emotion at all.

Mary recognized that plastic bag he had given Laura. It was from the pharmacy they had been in yesterday, the pharmacy that sold razors and shampoo and cheap jewelry, too. Laura had been promised jewelry, and she had received it. Mary considered this for a moment, and came to the conclusion that it was just what she deserved. Then she began to wonder how much of this had been anticipated, and how much was purposefully planned by Jerry.

"We'd better get started with this," said Peter.

# Chapter 31

Jerry and three other people in various stages of shock entered the police station. Inside Peter was met by a young female officer, trim and pretty, with naturally blond hair. The contrast was all the more obvious as Laura began to recover from the shock of being told her pancakes were her most memorable quality.

"This is Sargent Patti Larson, Miss Stewart, and she'll take a statement from you and have you identify your sister," said Peter.

"Yeah," said Laura, smirking first at Sergeant Larson, with a pitying look it seemed to Mary, and then she smiled at Peter.

"I got what I came for," she said, holding up the plastic bag of drug store jewelry, "so let's get it over with."

She cast a look at Jerry, who smiled and ignored the look and the woman, and Mary thought that Laura had not gotten what she had come here for. She had not even come close to getting it, and probably had never come close in all the time she had known Jerry.

"I'll need to talk to you when you're finished, Miss Stewart," said Peter.

Laura looked confused for a moment as she watched Jerry, as if she didn't realize that it was she to whom Peter was speaking. She cleared quickly though and replied, "What? Oh, yeah. Sure. Where do I have to go?"

"With me," said Sergeant Patti Larson. "Let me get a little information first." Patti didn't seem envious in the least, and Mary could see no reason she should have been as the two walked away. She did wonder why Peter wasn't conducting this part of the investigation, since she thought it would be at least a little important. The question was answered before she could ask it, however.

He turned to Jerry and said, "I have been asked to come with you, Jerry, to be interviewed by some other officers investigating this case. Officers from a different agency."

Mary winced. "What different agency, Peter? The government has so many agencies and they're all different or all the same, I can never remember which one it is."

"I have been asked not to tell either of you who it is you'll be speaking with, but I assure you, you'll remember this agency, Mary," said Peter, with the faintest of smiles. "I convinced them that you should accompany Jerry. They thought that you might need to be interviewed as well, and I thought...well, something about *lambs being led to the slaughter*, was what I was thinking about." Peter looked pointedly at Jerry.

Jerry wasn't at all nervous, which seemed to reinforce Peter's concern about those lambs and their slaughter in Mary's mind.

"Maybe we should do that now," Jerry said. "So you can be ready when Laura is done. I'd like to say goodbye to her, too." Mary realized this statement had a double meaning: that Jerry might want to say goodbye to an acquaintance, or that he might want the acquaintance to be gone. She wondered which one Jerry meant.

"Yes," said Peter. He led them to the same room they had been interviewed in before, in the back of the station. The same table was present, but additional seating had been brought in, along with additional people. Present now were the two "crime scene boys" that had been at the shop; was it really only yesterday morning? They had been dressed in civilian clothing then, but were in uniform now. The uniforms were not very flattering, and seemed to Mary to have been designed to conceal any femininity that might try to show itself. No wonder Peter had trouble keeping their gender straight.

There was another young man in uniform as well, trying to stand as far away as possible from the central figure in the room. This figure was seated behind the table. He was about thirty or thirty-five, Mary's age, dressed in a suit, and looking very severe. There were several chairs in the room, but this man was the only one seated. It was as if no one else wanted to be seated in his presence, and Mary wasn't at all interested in sitting or doing anything that would slow her exit from this room when the first opportunity presented itself. Even when the suit indicated they should sit, with the wave of his hand in the direction of the chairs in front of the table, everyone remained standing.

"I'm Donald Blanchard, with the Drug Enforcement Agency," he said as he motioned. "Please be seated, and make yourselves comfortable."

Mary declined the seat, and as for being comfortable, that was impossible right now.

"I can show you my identification if you wish," he added.

Jerry spoke first. "It's okay with me if it's okay with you, Mr. Blanchard."

"Why wouldn't it be okay with me?"

"I don't know what your required procedures are in Nebraska. It's probably different than it is in California. If this is just about talking, and you're not going to use any of the information gathered here, then identification won't matter." Jerry smiled at a slightly uncomfortable Mr. Blanchard.

He produced a badge immediately, and placed it on the table in front of him. "I think I should get an ID from you too; Mr. Wilson is it?"

Jerry looked quickly at the badge as Mary became nervous, remembering that Jerry had had no ID on him the morning of Angie's death. Jerry reached into his pocket and pulled out a wallet and then extracted his California driver's license, an ID from the West Side Rehabilitation Center, and a faculty card from the Berkeley School of Law. All bore his picture. Mr. Blanchard looked at them and began to speak when Jerry scooped them up again and handed them to the young officer in the corner.

"You'll want to make copies of these for your record," he said. The officer was both surprised and silent, but finally took the cards and looked around at his superiors. Mr. Blanchard was of no help, being as surprised as the young officer was, and only Peter was able to smile a slight but satisfied smile, and nod to the young man. The officer turned to leave the room and Jerry spoke again.

"Remember to copy both sides..." he looked at name badge now, "Mr. Larson?"

"What? Oh, yeah, okay. Thanks. I'll be right back."

Jerry wasn't finished. "We met a sergeant named Patti Larson just a few minutes ago. Is she your sister?"

"Oh, no, man. She's my cousin, Patti."

Donald Blanchard was recovering, "Copy the ID's and bring them back here—Larson."

"Yes, sir," said Officer Larson, and left quickly.

While Jerry was meeting Officer Larson, Mary was looking at the scene, and then at the badge, and then at the items on the table next to it. There were three small plastic baggies containing what looked like—well, bath salts. More significantly, there was a small gun next to these.

Donald Blanchard followed her gaze. "Mr. Wilson. We have been asked to investigate the death of a young lady who was killed here yesterday. An acquaintance of yours, one Angela Stewart."

Jerry frowned. "I've never heard her called Angela, only Angie, and I never did know her last name."

Donald looked at Peter. "You said, Captain Morgan..."

Peter cleared his throat. "Her sister is here at this moment. She will identify the victim. The fingerprints are all preliminary. It was Mr. Wilson who said she was Angie Stewart."

Donald shifted his gaze back to Jerry and looked as if he was about to speak when Jerry beat him to it. "It is Angie I saw, and as I said, I never heard her called anything except 'Angie.' She got mail addressed to 'Angie Stewart', not to Angela Stewart, just 'Angie'."

When no one spoke, Jerry added, "That will be in the transcript of my initial statement, Mr. Blanchard."

Donald looked at Peter, who turned crimson, clearly indicating that what Jerry asserted would be in his transcript, might not be there. "I will—" began Peter.

"Yes, you will," said Donald.

He looked back at Jerry as Officer Larson returned with copies and the originals of Jerry's identifications. He didn't seem to sense the tension, but merely smiled and handed the originals back to Jerry.

"Thanks, man," Jerry said.

"No problem, dude." The glare from Donald silenced further conversation.

Donald looked at Peter again and then spoke. "Perhaps we should have the local police handle the investigation of the death. They are capable of that, perhaps."

Peter was crimson again, but this time embarrassment was mixed with anger.

"That's a good idea," said Jerry. "Federal agencies aren't always able to get local people to co-operate in investigations like this. Captain Morgan will handle it much better." It was a statement, not a challenge, but Donald seemed to take it as the latter. He stared long and hard at Jerry.

While he was staring, Mary was looking again at the items on the table in front of him: the small gun, and three packets. They had obviously been left out in plain sight, perhaps because it was thought that their presence would unnerve Jerry? Thought by Donald Blanchard and by someone who knew Jerry already, and thought he was easily made nervous? Peter maybe? Mary thought maybe both of them had been wrong to think that. Jerry was the least nervous of all who were present in this room.

Donald began to speak. "Do you recognize these items, Mr. Wilson?" he asked, indicating the items on the table.

Jerry looked at the packets for only a second. "Bath salts," he said. "Probably from Carlos."

Donald cleared his throat. "Carlos?" he asked. "Is that a street name, Mr. Wilson?"

Jerry looked at him. "I've never heard it in the street language, but might be somewhere. A lot of the language is local. You can tell by paying attention to the context." Jerry was actually lecturing Donald Blanchard now. "This is probably merchandise sold by Carlos. Carlos Starr. He works the south side of Huntington Beach."

"You come from Huntington Beach, don't you, Mr. Wilson? So you would know about that, am I correct?"

"Of course," said Jerry.

"Did you buy these from Carlos?"

"No." Jerry said no more, and didn't appear to be in the least bit anxious.

"But you do recognize these?"

"I think so," said Jerry. "There's a 'C' written on them, and that's Carlos' trademark. He's good, and he likes to advertise. A real entrepreneur. If I can look at the back I can be sure."

Everyone looked at the packets now, and everyone saw a small "C" on each. Not very obvious until one looked for it, but definitely there when one did look for it.

Donald stared at Jerry, and then at a paper on the table in front of him, and then at the two embarrassed crime scene boys. "Will there be anything on the back of them?" he asked.

"There should be," said Jerry, "if they are Carlos' stuff. May I look at the back, sir?"

Donald smiled. "Of course," he said.

It wasn't clear what Donald expected Jerry to do, but he looked disappointed at what he did do. Jerry looked at the ID cards he still held in his hand, selected the California driver's license and using it, not his fingers, he turned it over with a quick flick. He never touched the packets with his fingers. On the back of the packet was an elaborate star

"Carlos," said Jerry. "Some of the other dealers can imitate the 'C', but the star is very fancy and hard to copy."

"Oh," said Donald. "Do you have an opinion as to what these packets contain, Mr. Wilson? We think they might be illegal drugs."

"No," said Jerry. It wasn't clear which question Jerry was answering until he looked up at Donald and spoke again. "There won't be anything illegal in these."

"Are you sure, Mr. Wilson?"

"Pretty sure," Jerry replied. "Carlos never has the illegal stuff in his trade. He's way too smooth for that. You can check with your regional office out in Southern Cal. They're familiar with Carlos. Carlos Starr. Ask to talk to a guy named Felix Poor or his partner, Nancy. They'll know what Carlos is up to."

Donald was getting a little flustered. DEA agents can get that way when the interview is not going according to their script, and this one definitely wasn't going according to his script.

"You better write that down, Mr. Blanchard," said Jerry. "Felix Poor or Nancy." He looked at the clock on the wall behind Donald's head and added, "Ask for Felix. Nancy will be surfing this time of morning. Today is Thursday, right?"

When no one answered, because the interview wasn't going according to anybody's script, Jerry shrugged and said, "Nancy surfs every Thursday morning. She's not too bad, either. She'd be better if she took care of her board."

Donald was desperately shuffling through his papers when one of the crime scene boys asked, "Were we going to get a sample? A drug screen, sir, and a DNA swab?"

"Yes, yes," said Donald. "Would you mind giving us a urine sample, Mr. Wilson?" he asked, producing a small plastic container with a screw-on lid from his briefcase.

Mary began to speak, but Jerry just took the container before she had a word out, unzipped his fly and pulled out what had been beneath it. He was in fact not wearing any underwear. He then filled the container with urine and screwed on the cap, placing the closed container on the table in front of an amazed Donald Blanchard before he put himself back in his shorts and zipped the fly.

The response was mixed. Mary was surprised, but perhaps not as much as she would have been had she not known Jerry already. She did look closely though. The crime scene women rendered a mixed opinion. One was clearly surprised, but was trying to peek around the obstacles to get a closer look while the other was frozen, eyes wide and mouth dropped open.

Her eyes and mouth were not nearly as wide as were those belonging to Donald Blanchard, however. "Yes…. Ah…"

Officer Larson looked at Jerry with a mixture of surprise and admiration. "Awesome," he whispered.

Peter was surprised as well, but he was also the first to recover. "My guess is that Mr. Wilson is willing to provide a specimen, and while the procedure is not what we're accustomed to here in Nebraska, I think we can say it was collected under the supervision of…well, let's just say it was supervised."

Chapter 32

There was a silence now as the astonishment had not yet faded. Peter finally cleared his throat and said, "Perhaps I can clarify a couple points regarding my investigation now, if that's all right with you, Mr. Blanchard?"

He didn't wait very long for a response, since none appeared to be forthcoming. "You recognize the packets, is that correct, Mr. Wilson?"

"Yes," said Jerry.

"And you do not know what is in them, but suspect it is not an illegal substance, am I correct again?"

"Yeah," said Jerry. "Felix will know though."

"Felix Poor? I'm not familiar with the DEA procedures," smiled Peter. "Some of them seem unusual to me, but will Felix have tested Carlos' merchandise? Is that done to all the dealers in Huntington?"

"Oh," said Jerry. "Not the dealer's stuff. Mostly that information comes from the overdoses that show up at the hospital, or the morgue too, of course. But Carlos is different. Everyone knows what he's selling."

"I'm sure the DEA understands." Peter cast a look at a still silent and bewildered Donald Blanchard. "But I'm not as familiar as they are. Why is Carlos Starr different?"

"He has cards printed up with the list of what's in his salts. Advertising. That's Carlos, a real businessman." Jerry shrugged.

"Really," said Peter. "I'm getting an education here today." The surprise was returning to the faces around him, and it was clear Peter wasn't the only one getting an education.

Jerry grinned a little. "There's a rumor that Carlos mails the cards to Felix and to the hospital ERs."

Peter just stared in disbelief. "Carlos sends his cards to the DEA?"

"Just a rumor," admitted Jerry. "They always have 'em though."

Peter whistled. "I'm really out of this loop. Why would a drug dealer send information about what he's selling to the DEA, and if they know he's selling, why don't they...well, stop him?"

Jerry shrugged. "Carlos does it as sort of a public service, so if someone comes in...well, they'll know what they took. The hospitals like that, and the clients like it too. If they get into trouble they can just tell the ER they took Carlos' stuff, and they know what was in it. Works all the way around."

"And the DEA knows and doesn't do anything?" Peter was incredulous, and looked first at Jerry and then at Donald, who was as incredulous as he was embarrassed.

Jerry shrugged again. "They really couldn't do much. You see, it's not illegal. Bath salts are changed so often, with herbals and stuff, that no one can keep up with it. Besides, people are going to use, and there isn't really any way to stop them from using. Making it illegal hasn't accomplished a thing. Right now prescription drugs, legal prescription narcotics, kill as many people as all the illegal drugs sold. At least with Carlos they're getting a clean product, not like the stuff coming up from San Diego or Mexico."

"I guess you might be right," said Peter, shaking his head. "So, would Angie have known this too? About Carlos, I mean? Could she have purchased these same or similar packets from him?"

"Yeah," said Jerry. "Angie got a lot of her salts from him." He shrugged and seemed to be considering adding something and Peter seemed to sense this, and waited.

Jerry looked up and said, "Ya see, Carlos deals salts, but he pimps on the side, too. Angie could sometimes trade for the salts that way." He shrugged.

"Her services for his services?" asked Peter.

"Yeah," said Jerry. "She would work the street for him, but not with Carlos, of course. Carlos never did it with Angie or with any of his other girls."

Peter frowned, as if he were considering something too. "You don't think Carlos had sex with Angie then."

Jerry shook his head. "Carlos is gay."

"Oh," said Peter. He looked around now, but most pointedly at Donald Blanchard. Donald offered no indication that he was ready to begin his investigation again, so Peter continued his.

"This is an important question, Jerry." He paused briefly. "The gun on the table. Do you recognize that?"

"No," said Jerry.

"Can you tell me anything at all about it?"

"Looks like a .22. Easy to carry, easy to hide. It's the kind street workers carry."

"People like Carlos or Angie, perhaps?"

"Carlos, yeah. I don't remember Angie ever packing."

"But if she did, for some reason, would this be what she would 'pack'?"

Jerry nodded. "Probably, but I don't think she would. I mean, she never did back in Huntington." For some reason it seemed to Mary that Jerry was suggesting that if Angie hadn't needed to 'pack' in Huntington, she wouldn't need to in Nebraska.

Donald was recovered now, recovered enough to interfere with Peter and what had been an interesting and informative discussion about the woman who had died a little over a day ago, and about her lifestyle and why she might have come to Nebraska to die. "If I may ask a question or two, Captain? Do you know where these things were found, Mr. Wilson?" he said, indicating the gun and packets on the table in front of him.

"No," said Jerry, turning his attention from Peter toward Donald.

"They were found in the top drawer of the dresser in your room, Mr. Wilson." Peter winced, and so did both of the crime scene boys. Mary looked around her and thought that Peter might have been a little upset that Jerry was being implicated, but the crime scene investigators had no reason to be upset except that divulging this bit of information was neither helpful nor "standard procedure."

If Jerry was upset, it didn't show. "Oh," he said.

"Does that surprise you, Mr. Wilson?"

Jerry thought for a moment. "Yes. I don't see why anyone would have put them there."

Donald drew himself up straight and asked, "Did you put them there, Mr. Wilson?"

Mary raised her hand, just like she did in grade school when she would ask permission to go the bathroom. She was smiling now though, something that never accompanied asking to go to the bathroom in grade school. "May I ask a question, Mr. Blanchard? Is Jerry being charged with anything? Or to put it another way, should there be an attorney here?"

"And who are you?" asked Donald.

"I asked first," said Mary.

Peter smiled. "This charming young lady would be Mary Burke. I think I mentioned her to you, Mr. Blanchard. It was she who received the call from Prentiss Forrest that prompted her to call us and led to the discovery of the body of the young lady."

"Not fair, Peter. He didn't answer my question," scowled Mary.

Donald was getting annoyed. "There are no charges...yet, Miss..."

"Burke," said Mary.

They were staring at each other now, and Donald wasn't winning. Jerry looked up at him and then quickly at the crime scene boys. "May I ask a question?"

"What?" said Donald.

"I would like to ask a question, sir," said Jerry patiently.

Donald's interview wasn't going by the script again, and he was clearly having trouble with Jerry's question.

Peter cleared his troublesome throat and said, "It would be fine with the state police, if it is okay with the DEA."

Jerry seemed to think this was an affirmative answer and asked, "Were there any fingerprints on the packets or the gun?"

Jerry looked quickly at Donald as he began to sputter, and then Jerry quickly shifted his gaze to the crime scene boys as their faces registered surprise and then embarrassment.

"I'm not going to answer that question, Mr. Wilson," stammered Donald.

Jerry shrugged and nodded. "No fingerprints. I didn't think there would be any." He looked up first at Donald again, and then the two ladies.

"I didn't say there were or were not any fingerprints, Mr. Wilson."

Jerry smiled slightly, and looked around him. "Do you ever play poker, Mr. Blanchard?"

"What?"

Jerry shrugged. "I played a little. With some guys I surf with, and a couple of them were kind of professionals. One of them was a dealer in Vegas, as a matter of fact." He chuckled a little. "A card dealer that is, and he always said: *your eyes are the mirror in which your cards are reflected.*"

There was silence now until Jerry said, "I wonder why anyone would wipe the fingerprints off the packets and then put them in my dresser drawer?"

Mary smiled. "I wonder about that too, but I think that this interview might be over, don't you, Mr. Blanchard?"

"What? I...yes, but I'll need to talk to you further, Mr. Wilson, and to you too, Miss..."

"Burke," said Mary.

Peter smiled. "I have one more question, if that's permitted." He was looking at Mary, not at Donald.

"Go for it, Peter," she said.

"Did you win, Jerry? At the poker, I mean."

"Usually." Jerry shrugged.

Peter smiled. "I thought so."

# Chapter 33

They were all still standing except for Donald Blanchard. He sat at the table with a gun, three packets of bath salts, and a plastic cup containing urine in front of him.

Jerry smiled and turned to Officer Larson. "You'll have to label that," he said, pointing to the urine container."

"Oh, yeah," said Larson.

Jerry must have appreciated the hesitancy, because he immediately began giving instructions. "You'll have to label it with my name: Jeremiah Peter Wilson." He then spelled Jeremiah.

"Now put my date of birth on it. September, thirty, nineteen seventy-eight. Check it against my driver's license. Then put today's date as the date collected, and the time it was collected."

Larson was concentrating, and Jerry waited until he had finished.

"Show it to me, but don't let me touch it, okay?" Jerry read it quickly and said, "That's great, man. Sign your initials on it. Then you'll need a plastic baggie to put it in. They usually have special bags for that, so no one can tamper with the spec. Do you have one, Mr. Blanchard?"

Donald began to fumble in his briefcase, and Jerry turned his attention to the crime scene boys. "Maybe you have one?"

One of them produced a baggie with a double seal and a large area on the front to write on. "Thanks, Tess," said Officer Larson.

Jerry smiled at Tess and then turned back to Officer Larson. "Now put the same information on the baggie, except that the time is the time you put the spec in the bag."

Again there was a delay while Larson laboriously wrote, and Mary wondered why someone besides Jerry wasn't doing this. Peter was just watching and smiling.

"Now," said Jerry, "you carry that with you until you give it to the next person to take responsibility for the spec. Watch them as they initial it with the date and time they got it. Always use the baggie, too. Some people get creeped out handling urine, even in a closed container." He shrugged as if to say he found this incomprehensible, and Mary thought he probably did.

Jerry turned to Donald again. "Will you be taking the specimen, Mr. Blanchard?"

Donald looked aghast, and then looked at his very expensive briefcase.

"We can process that, if you wish," said Peter.

"Yes, yes, please," said Donald, who was obviously someone who was "creeped out" by urine in a closed container, even when it was inside a double-sealed plastic bag.

"Maybe you can give that to Tess now," said Jerry, turning to Officer Larson. "Make sure she dates and times it," he added, winking at Tess, who winked back and then blushed ever so slightly as she took the baggie. Officer Larson watched her very closely as she dated and timed and signed.

"Oh, and Mr. Blanchard," said Jerry, and indicated the packets and gun on the table. "I didn't put these in that dresser drawer."

"What?" said Donald.

Jerry smiled. "You asked me if I had put them in the dresser drawer, and I never answered you. I didn't."

Jerry seemed to think this was all that was needed and turned to Mary. "I bet Laura is finished by now, so we better get going if we're going to catch her. She won't hang here long."

Peter smiled. "I'll be with you in two minutes if you can try to convince Laura to wait that long."

Mary nodded, and she and Jerry left the room, with Peter smiling, Donald fumbling, Larson looking after them with a mixture of gratitude and admiration, and Tess looking with a little admiration and a little lust as well, Mary thought.

"You were really good, Mary," said Jerry.

"What?" said Mary.

"All that stuff about getting a lawyer when you are a lawyer."

"I was talking about a real lawyer. One who passed the bar exam" Mary shrugged.

"Well, if I need a lawyer, I'm going to ask you."

"You may need better than me if Blanchard decides to go after you, Jerry."

"He seemed like a nice guy," Jerry replied.

"He didn't," said Mary. "He seemed like a flaming asshole."

"Well, yeah, but apart from that he was pretty nice."

When Mary stared at him in disbelief he continued. "You know, Mary, DEA agents have to act like that. It's not their fault, it's part of their job."

"You're so exasperating, Jerry. Is there anyone you don't think is nice?"

"Well, yes."

"Who? Laura?"

"It's the drugs with her. That's all."

"Okay. What about Rufus and Billy, who tried as hard as they could to kill you? Are they nice?"

"They just need to learn about violence and the damage it does to people who act violently, don't you think?"

"No, that's not what I think. Who do you think is not nice, Jerry?"

Jerry shrugged. "I'm not sure Aunty May is very nice."

"May? She's batty, for Christ's sake. When you're batty, you can't apply the niceness scale, Jerry."

"She had Dexter flatten all Rufus' truck tires."

"That's because she's batty. It's not because she's not nice."

"But Rufus really loves his truck. It's like the most important thing to him, and flattening his tires was just cruel."

"You're as batty as May is, Jerry."

Jerry's battiness might have received further examination, but they were joined now by the crime scene boys. "Excuse me, Mr. Wilson, but we forgot—"

"*You* forgot," corrected her partner. "

"Yeah, whatever, someone forgot to collect a DNA sample from you. Can I do that now?"

"Sure," said Jerry.

"It's just a swab," she added quickly. "Of the inside of your mouth, not your..." Embarrassment silenced her as her partner produced a swab.

When she reached for it, however, her partner pulled it away saying, "I'll collect it."

"I can do that, Tess," was her response.

Mary was amazed. Two police officers arguing about who would get to swab the inside of Jerry's mouth. Way too much drama, she decided.

"Even though I'm not an attorney, Jerry has asked me to provide legal advice, and therefore I'll decide," Mary said, looking at the two of them.

After only a couple of seconds, Mary reached over and took the swab and said, "I'll collect the specimen. Open wide, Jerry."

"But..." began Tess.

"You just swab the inside of my cheek, Mary," said Jerry.

"I know that." Mary glared at him. "I watch TV too, ya know." Before the officers could say another word, Jerry opened wide, and Mary swabbed, and then placed the swab in its container, handing it back to the disappointed crime scene boys.

"There you are," Mary said. "Now go play with your DNA."

"Wow," said Jerry. "That rhymes. I didn't know you were a poet too, Mary."

"What?" replied Mary.

Jerry looked admiringly at her. "Now go *play*, with your *DNA*. It's a poem, isn't it?"

Mary's look mixed surprise with disbelief, and she was about to speak, as soon as she could think of anything to say in response to this. The words that she was considering were not going to be poetic.

Tess beat her to it. "You're so cute, Mr. Wilson," she sighed. Her partner seemed to silently agree.

Mary's look shifted to Tess, with an increase in the disbelief, and possibly the surprise as well. She was still trying to think of something to say in response to this scene, which was rapidly become farcical if not criminal, when Peter arrived.

"Has Laura come out yet?" he asked.

Chapter 34

"No," said Mary. Neither poetic, not farcical, but she could not have competed in either league. The crime scene boys were hanging around still, for no apparent reason except to provide the farcical stuff if any more were necessary.

Patti Larson joined them a few moments later with Laura. "I have a statement," Patti said, "and Miss Stewart did identify the body as her sister, Angie Stewart."

"Miss Laura Stewart," Patti looked at Laura, "didn't wish to make any arrangements to claim the remains at this time. She also didn't want to have her fingerprints or a DNA sample taken at this time either." Patti looked as if she attached some significance to this, but left the audience to draw their own conclusion.

Laura didn't seem to feel there was any significance at all, or at least that any explanation was necessary.

"I've got a plane to catch. Are the police going to provide me with transportation to the friggin' airport?" Laura asked.

"I'm not sure we can do that, Miss Stewart," said Peter.

"Then how am I...Maybe you can give me a ride, Jerry honey? How about it, lover?"

Jerry smiled. There were several reasons why Jerry couldn't give her a ride, starting with the fact that he didn't have a car, and ending with the fact that not even Jerry was that stupid.

Jerry proved that he wasn't that stupid in the next second anyway. "I have to open the ice cream shop, but maybe Mary can give you a ride, Laura." He turned to face Mary now and added, "You said you had an errand to run in the city anyway, didn't you?"

Mary was surprised that Jerry made such an offer, and that she suddenly had an errand, which she didn't have a second ago. She almost said that she would love to ride in a car to the airport with Laura as soon as hell froze over, but was stopped by the look on Jerry's face. It wasn't the look of someone who was asking to be relieved of an onerous task, but that of someone who was asking if Mary, too, thought it was a good idea to ride to the airport with Laura, even if hell was still toasty warm.

It took only a few seconds for Mary to understand that Laura might well provide information to her that she would never provide to Jerry or any police officer, and that this could be the only opportunity that anyone would have to get that information from Laura. Once she left Nebraska she might disappear, and be beyond the reach of anyone.

"Sure," Mary said. "Going by there anyway. Can someone give Jerry a ride to the shop?"

Both crime scene boys volunteered at once, but Peter smiled. "I'll drop Jerry at the shop," he said. The disappointment of the crime scene boys was matched by the disappointment of Laura, but met with a little satisfaction on Mary's part. She wasn't quite sure why, but she was glad it was Peter who was driving Jerry around.

"If I can take a couple of minutes to go over your statement, Miss Stewart, you can get going," said Peter, indicating they should go toward the back of the station. He also indicated that Patti should accompany them.

As they disappeared into the back, the crime scene boys departed too, casting glances at Jerry as they did.

"So, are you setting me up? Or do you think Laura will talk to me about her sister more willingly than she will to you or the police?" asked Mary.

"It's just that—" began Jerry.

"She won't talk to the police and she won't want to talk to you. She has something else in mind for you, doesn't she?"

Jerry just nodded.

Mary looked to where Laura had just departed and said, "She doesn't seem too upset about her sister, does she?"

"I'm not sure," said Jerry.

"Not sure that she isn't really upset? You think that maybe she's devastated by it, but putting on a brave front for all the world to see? I think that's a pretty long reach, Jerry. There is no actor in all of California that good, and acting is not one of Laura's talents. She doesn't hide anything. Transparency seems to be her main talent, in fact." When Jerry remained silent, Mary said, "Okay. Am I missing something about Angie's sister?"

"It's just that—"

"Yes. It's just that...what?"

"Well, Laura has used two names to me, Smith and Jones, and she got mail to another name and...well, why does anyone think she's telling the truth about who she is now, or about whether she's Angie's sister? I just wonder who she really is. Maybe Angie was just a friend, or maybe she was an enemy even, and not a sister. Laura might be acting the way she is for a very logical reason. Maybe she's acting like she's not upset about Angie getting killed because she isn't upset. That's all I mean."

Mary was amazed, and impressed again with Jerry. This was getting monotonous. "But Stan said...she's on probation, they must have checked her identity...I mean, why...?" Mary was silent for a minute and then said, "There are ways to take care of all those things, aren't there Jerry?"

"I don't know." He shrugged. "But there are ways to do anything."

Peter was returning with Laura and Patti now, and Laura didn't look like she was intending to be here much longer. "Let's get the fuck out of here."

"Thank you for your assistance, Miss Stewart," said Peter. He turned to Mary and asked, "Are you sure you can drop Miss Stewart at the airport, Mary?"

"Yes," Mary replied.

"Then let's get going," Laura said. She looked at Jerry and added, "See you when you get back to civilized California, lover, if Hicksville, Nebraska hasn't rotted you to shit, that is." She moved to hug Jerry, but he beat the move by extending his hand to shake hers.

An awkward moment followed, and then Laura turned and left without a hug or a handshake. "Come on, for Christ's sakes," she said after her, and Mary smiled and walked away as well.

"I'll see you later, Jerry," she said, loud enough for Laura to hear.

"We better get going too, Jerry," said Peter.

"I can drop Mr. Wilson off, if you want me to, Peter," offered Patti with a smile.

Peter smiled too at the attractive young police officer in front of him. "I'm not that busy, Patti, and I wanted to talk to Jerry a little anyway." He paused and then asked, "You're transferring back to Kentucky I heard."

"Yeah," said Patti, and she was a little embarrassed. "Back home."

"I heard you were engaged, too," smiled Peter.

"Well, not yet, but soon...I hope. Joe is my high school sweetheart."

"Lucky guy. Say hello to my brother, Hank, will you? He's another Captain Morgan, but with Kentucky's staties."

"That's where I'll be working, Peter," she smiled. "Thanks for your recommendation."

"That's what I heard. Hank is lucky to be getting a good officer like you."

"Thanks, Peter."

Peter turned to talk to Jerry, and Patti walked away, and Peter didn't look after her to admire.

Chapter 35

Peter and Jerry went out the back of the station to Peter's car, not the police cruiser, but his own car. As they got in Peter said, "With all the rumors flying around about this case, I thought we should be less conspicuous."

They climbed in and Peter began to drive toward The Ice Cream Shop.

"I wanted to thank you, Jerry," Peter said.

"For what?"

"For making Donald Blanchard...well, for assisting him in realizing that the state police are not totally incompetent."

"Oh," smiled Jerry. "Mr. Blanchard did most of that himself."

Peter looked over at him and wondered if Jerry intended what he said to have the two meanings that it did. That Mr. Blanchard had realized that himself, but also that his own incompetence had made it clear that the state police were not the losers in the room.

"He messed up some stuff too," said Jerry.

"Yes. I wanted to talk to you, Jerry. Semiofficially, so if you don't want to answer, you don't have to." Peter paused, and then added, "And if you would rather have an attorney present we can arrange that, too."

Jerry smiled and said, "I think I'll ask Mary to be my attorney, but I don't think I need to have her here right now. Did you know she graduated from law school, Captain Morgan?"

Peter frowned. "Yes, I knew that, and apart from the fact that she can't really practice, not having passed her bar exam, I think you have made a good choice. You have made one mistake, though."

Jerry looked at him apprehensively, but Peter smiled back at him. "I hate being called Captain Morgan. I'm a good Baptist boy, and I don't drink, and being called—"

Jerry cut him off. "Yeah, alcohol is just another drug, really. I don't drink either. So should I call you just 'Captain' or something?"

"Just call me Peter, okay?"

"You sure? I mean, you don't mind?"

"I'm sure," smiled Peter. "I have a question for you…Jerry."

"Okay...Peter."

"Good," Peter replied. "This is serious now, Jerry. Did you know Angie was here in Nebraska before we found her dead?"

"No," said Jerry.

"You hadn't seen her here at all, is that right?"

"No," repeated Jerry.

"When was the last time you did see her?"

"It's been maybe six months ago. I heard she was trying to get in touch with me, back in Huntington, but...well, I tried a little, but we never connected. I didn't really want to connect with her."

Peter nodded, and considered the conversation and where it was headed. "I know I have sort of already asked this question, Jerry, but I have to be certain we're not misunderstanding each other. Did you have sex with Angie in the day or two before we found her dead?" Peter blushed a little, thinking how silly this last question was, but also how different Jerry was from the people he was used to talking to. He didn't know how the question could possibly be answered any way except the obvious way, obvious to him, but maybe Jerry could have had sex with Angie and not have "seen" her or "know" she was in Nebraska in some strange use of their shared but differently used language. In those novels and magazines he'd read in his youth, the men were always bedding some stranger only to discover she was someone they knew or some craziness like that, as if it were likely or even possible that someone could have sex with someone that they knew and not recognize her. He shook his head. The attitude and the language were so different in California.

"No," said Jerry. "I haven't had sex with anyone since I came to Nebraska," he added as if he were reading Peter's mind. "I haven't had sex with anyone in, well, three or four months."

Yes, thought Peter, *attitudes are different.* Peter would never have been so open about his sexual activity as Jerry was right now to a man he had just started calling by his first name a minute ago.

"Did someone have sex with Angie before she died?" Jerry asked.

Peter frowned and considered that he had only known Jerry since yesterday, and there was no reason to trust him.

"I'm not sure I should answer that question."

Jerry looked at him. "It's the only reason I can think of that would make you ask me if I had sex with Angie. The coroner would have found that by now, I think, but..."

"But?" asked Peter.

"There might be another reason you're asking me that question, and..."

"And?"

"Well, it's your eyes," smiled Jerry.

"My eyes?"

"Yeah," said Jerry. "You would be really good playing poker. Way better than Donald would be."

"Oh," smiled Peter. "Let me help then," he decided. "We'll shoot that scene again, from where you asked me if anyone had had sex with Angie, okay?"

Peter eyes widened and his face took on a look of shock. "What? How did you kn———...I can't answer that question, Jerry!"

Peter returned his appearance to its normal controlled self and said, "Was that any better?"

"Yes," smiled Jerry. "Except that..."

"Except that what?"

"Well, if you can act that well, how do I know you aren't still acting?"

"You don't, Jerry, you don't. But the coroner is not a very good actor, and he seems to think Angie had sex within a few hours of her death."

"Vaginal sex?" asked Jerry.

"Ah," said Peter, who was acting embarrassed now, or maybe he wasn't acting. "Why ...?"

"Oh, it's just that Angie really liked...well, kinky stuff, so you might want to make sure they check everywhere. That's all."

Peter frowned. "Would 'everywhere' mean the same thing in Nebraska as it does in California?"

"Well, yeah. I think, you know: anal, and oral and Angie liked to—"

"I'll have them make sure they check everywhere," Peter cut Jerry off, possibly because he was getting tired of "acting" embarrassed, or maybe he just didn't want to go for an Oscar today.

"There might be more than one, too," said Jerry.

"More than one...?"

"Person."

Peter thought a moment and added, "If she did, and if we can find out with whom, we might have come a lot closer to finding her killer."

"Maybe," said Jerry.

Peter looked quickly at him before returning his attention to the road ahead. "Why do you say 'maybe'?"

Jerry shrugged. "It's just that Angie had sex with...well, she sold it, and used it, and a lot of the guys she had sex with..."

"She gave 'casual sex' a much broader meaning? Is that what you're suggesting, Jerry?"

"Yeah," said Jerry. "She didn't even know half the guys, and I can't think of any of them who would have cared enough about her to have killed her. Not anyone in California. She just wasn't worth it." He shrugged in despair.

"The DNA sample you gave today will be used to verify that you didn't, Jerry. I'll be glad when it does."

"Oh," Jerry replied, without much interest. He perked up an instant later and looked at Peter. "Why is that?"

Peter shrugged. "I guess I don't want you to be the one who killed Angie."

"Oh," said Jerry again. "I thought maybe you were worried about Mary." He was smiling now.

"Mary?"

"Yeah, ya know. That she wasn't getting to like someone who had had sex with someone like Angie."

Peter considered this a moment. "Is Mary getting to like you, Jerry?"

"I hope so."

"Well, I'll be as mad as a...a drunken Baptist if anyone hurts Mary. She's definitely worth a murder, so be careful that you're not the one who gets murdered."

Peter was serious only a few seconds and then he smiled, and Jerry smiled too. "I'll be careful, Peter, and if someone hurts Mary, I'll help with the murder, okay?"

They arrived at The Ice Cream Shop and Jerry got out of the car. Peter was about to drive off, but Jerry just stood there, and finally Peter asked, "So, are you going in?"

"Oh, yeah. In a minute."

Peter waited, but Jerry made no move. "Do you need some help or something?" Peter asked.

"No," Jerry replied, but still made no move toward the shop.

Peter looked and then got out of the car and said, "Let's go in and make sure everything is all set, okay?"

"Well..."

"Let me have the key, okay? And I'll check it out. In case you're nervous."

"I'm not nervous, it's just that...well, Mary didn't give me a key."

Peter frowned now and Jerry added quickly, "But I can get in all right."

"How are you going to get in, Jerry, without a key?"

"Oh, I...well, ya see..." Peter was looking questioningly at Jerry. "You have to promise not to tell anyone," Jerry finally said.

Peter watched with growing concern as Jerry walked to the door, took out his multiple tool, selected a narrow blade and knelt by the lock. He inserted the blade, shut his eyes, and then began to hum a soft monotone. To Peter's surprise the door popped open only a few seconds later.

"Simple one," Jerry said. "That's why I didn't lock Aunty May's shop. Locks don't keep people out of anything. Don't tell anyone I can do that. People get nervous when they know you can jimmy open any of their locks." He smiled, and went into the shop.

***

Meanwhile, Mary wasn't having a simple one. She and Laura were driving toward the airport, and Mary couldn't decide whether she wanted Laura to talk or stay quiet. They were both silent for a while, but as they neared the airport, Laura decided the issue for her.

"So, have you done it with Jerry yet?"

160

Mary waited a moment and decided she wasn't going to let this woman shock her. "No," she said.

"Too bad, but you'll be very happy when you do." When Mary made no response, Laura continued, "Best I've ever had, and he can fuck for hours. God, it is great." Laura bent her head back and laughed as Mary mentally noted that her sex with Jerry was still in the present tense.

Laura looked at her quickly to make sure she was listening, Mary thought, and said, "We do it every night, sometimes every day, too."

Mary looked at her and smiled, but said nothing. *Over the top, Laura honey. Way more than anyone would believe.*

"Yeah, he's great." She tossed her head back again and then looked for a reaction from Mary. Mary just nodded.

"Hey, pull into this rest stop, will ya?"

Mary pulled into the rest stop. It was just outside the airport, with fast food, expensive gas, and dirty restrooms. Mary wondered which Laura wanted.

"Pull over there, away from the cars," she said. As Mary did, Laura pulled out a hundred-dollar bill from her purse.

"No, babe, I ain't offerin' to pay for the ride. This is what Luther paid me for last night. Want to hear what he had me do for him to earn this?"

"Not necessary," said Mary, as Laura rolled the bill into a straw.

"Didn't think so." She was pulling a mirror out of her purse now, and put a line of white powder on it and then using the hundred-dollar straw, sucked the line into her nostril, something that Mary had only seen in the movies.

"You want a line?" Laura asked.

"No," said Mary.

"Didn't think so," Laura smirked condescendingly. "One more for me and then I pay you, okay?"

Laura did her second line, then laid back in her seat. "Great," she smiled. "Only thing Angie and I fought over was who got the last line. That and who got Jerry, that is. We fought over him."

She lay there glassy-eyed for a minute or so, and then stirred to life. "Pull up to the gas pump, sweetie, and let me pay for the ride."

"Not necessary," said Mary.

"Ah, but sugar, I want to," Laura smiled.

"Let's just—"

Laura smiled. "Let's just call a cop and tell him I found this coke in your car, bitch. How's that for a plan? Now pull over to the fuckin' gas pump, will ya, sweetie?"

Mary hesitated for a minute, but decided there were more witnesses at the gas pumps. "Okay," she said.

She pulled to the pump and a middle-aged attendant came over to pump their gas. "What can I do for ya?" he asked Mary.

Laura leaned over and handed him a credit card. "Fill it up, sweetie."

The attendant smiled at her, took the card and began filling the car's half-full tank.

"Okay, Laura," said Mary. "We're driving to the airport from here; no stops, no coke and no friggin' games, got it?"

"You want ta have the cops—"

"That's just what I was going to ask you. I'll take a chance on walking away if you will. Shall we see who spends the rest of her life in jail, or shall we see if we can get you onto an airplane out of here? Your choice."

Laura scowled but said nothing, and the attendant returned with the card, a receipt and a smile. "Only took half a tank," he said. Mary handed the card and receipt to Laura and she signed, handing it directly to the attendant.

"Have a good trip, Mrs. Porter," he said, as he went to the next car.

Mary looked at Laura and then pulled back onto the highway.

Laura smiled at her. "Yeah," she said, holding up the card. "Luther has this wife, ya see. Visiting her sister he says, but I wondered. I wanted to leave her a present though, you know, a little lingerie I thought she might like. Luther liked it when I was wearin' it, so I put it in with her panties along with a little cocaine. Put one of my skirts in her laundry, too."

Laura lay back in the seat. "Luther's going to pay for that trick. Ya think he'll get to the laundry before his wife comes home from her sister?" She laughed out loud now. "And I found this card of his wife's in with her panties. Even swap; my thongs for her card. Luther is going to fly me home first class, and his wife might just believe he didn't give this to me, instead of believing that I stole this, which is what he'll try to tell her. Poor, stupid Luther. He deserves it."

Mary looked at her quizzically now. "How are you going to get on the plane without an ID to match the name on the ticket?"

"Oh, babe, you need an education. She left her friggin' passport there too, dumbass that she is, married to Luther." Laura pulled out the passport as they were pulling into the airport. "What do ya think?" she said, showing the passport to Mary. It wasn't that good a likeness, and Mary suggested that to Laura.

"Oh, shit, sweetie. I'll pull my hair back, chat with the hayseed on security about my terrible hairdresser and she'll buy it. Ya see, the government likes to be hiring the *persons of color*, and I'll get in line with one of them."

When Mary's face showed a lack of understanding, Laura shook her head. "Come on, babe. Ya know how they say the *persons of color* all look the same to us? Well, we all look the same to them. Those poor slobs are pulling down a stinking salary and they're supposed to catch me getting onto an airplane? Get real."

Mary shook her head and vowed to get even with Jerry for this trip. "Which airline?" she asked.

"Doesn't matter." Laura looked over at Mary. "You screwin' that Captain? He's kinda cute."

Mary wished she could think of something clever to say, but it was too disgusting to even bother. "No," she said.

"I got a present for him, too, but you first."

Mary began to feel a little apprehension, but they were stopped at the terminal with two state police officers within ten feet, so unless Laura had a small .22 on her, it was probably safe. She hadn't been here when Angie was killed, either, so that should be calming as well.

Laura reached over and shoved the plastic bag Jerry had given her at Mary. "You can have this. Angie had no taste in junk jewelry, and Jerry is dumb as dirt. This is stuff only a hayseed would wear." She pulled out a large and gaudy necklace to prove her point, and then shoved the bag at Mary. "Only thing Angie had that was worth anything was the locket she wore and they didn't give that to me, her only sister. Damned, fuckin' cops."

Laura scowled for a second before continuing. "Here is my return ticket to California," she said, and handed that to Mary as well. "Maybe you can get some money out of that, if you cash it before they find out it's stolen, too. I'm flyin' first class today."

As Mary looked at the ticket, Laura got out and walked toward the terminal. A few steps away she turned and said, "Almost forgot the cute captain. Tell him to ask Luther how his semen got inside Angie, if he wants to hear something interesting. Stupid bastard didn't even use a condom on a friggin' whore like her. Oh, and make sure you mention that there's cocaine in the top drawer of his wife's dresser, too. Fuckin' bastard."

By the time Mary looked up, Laura was inside the terminal. When she looked at the ticket Laura had given her, she read that it belonged to *Sally Smart,* and the arrival date had been three days ago.

"Laura was here when Angie was killed," she said almost aloud, but the only one there to hear her was a state police officer.

"Move it along," he said.

# Chapter 37

"But officer—" Mary began.

"Move it," he repeated.

"There's a woman who just went into the terminal that could have—"

"And you're stopped in a no stopping zone, so move it." The belligerence was becoming very apparent.

"You don't understand."

"It's you that doesn't understand, now move it or I'll—"

"Raise your blood pressure to the same extent that you're raising your voice and then you'll have a stroke, but no one will notice because you're not in a *no stroking zone* and furthermore, you have not been burdened with the cerebral tissue that's necessary to have a stroke in the first place. It's encouraging to me to be reassured that our airports are attended to by such as you." Mary smiled and added, "Especially since I don't fly very much."

There was silence on the part of the state police officer as Mary pulled away. She found parking in the short-term, read *very expensive* for short-term here, parking area and ran into the terminal. Once there, she tried to get the authorities to move quickly, but there were no state police and no *no stopping zones*, so things were moved along with excruciating slowness. That's actually not true; they moved not at all. Several low-level administration people listened and said she would have to take this to someone higher up, and those higher up said they were busy but would talk to her as soon as they could. When Mary tried to convince them it was important, they said they were sure it was, but.... No time frame was suggested, and Mary began to wonder if it would be in the current year or not. She then considered her parking fee, and decided that she might try to bypass the normal channels of non-communication.

She walked around the terminal, but saw no evidence of Laura. There was a VIP lounge, but of course she wasn't allowed in there, and after some consideration, she decided that Laura would not be allowed in the VIP area either. She finally walked up to one of the agents who wasn't busy at that moment, some accident of scheduling she was sure, and shoved Sally Smart's ticket at her.

"There's a woman who used this ticket to get here, but is buying or likely has bought a return ticket, and I need to—"

"Oh," interrupted the agent, "and you want a refund. Sure, this ticket has a cancellation option."

"No, that's not—"

"Let me run it through the computer to make sure, okay?"

Mary leaned slightly toward her in order to emphasize her words. "I need to find this woman. Can you please help me?"

"Oh, you don't need to find her, unless you want cash. I can have the refund mailed."

Mary was having one of those *out of conversation experiences* and looked around quickly to make sure the agent wasn't talking to someone else. "That's not what I want," she said. She then pulled out her own ID and handed it to the agent. "I'm Mary Burke, and this woman is implicated in a murder."

"Here?" asked the clerk.

"No, not here. Back in—"

"Oh, that's a relief." She looked only casually at the ID Mary had handed to her and said, "I can't really give you cash without Miss Smart signing the ticket. If you want cash you'll have to get her to sign."

"But that's the problem," said Mary. "I need to find her. She's—"

"Oh, I can have the refund mailed if you can't get her to sign."

"I have to find her."

The agent looked at Mary with condescension and patience. "You don't understand, do you? I can refund the ticket to the address given when the ticket was purchased if you can't find her to get her to sign the ticket. Do you understand?"

Mary understood a great deal more than the agent had told her, beginning with the fact that she was never going to get anyone to look for Laura until it was too late to find her because the planet would have spiraled into the sun by then, or whatever the final moments of life on this miserable orb were going to be. In a flash of insight that was light years ahead of anywhere that was even close to where this agent was, Mary asked, "What address would it be mailed to? So I can make sure that will be all right."

The agent looked at her computer screen and replied, "Thirty Six Janson Way, in Huntington Beach, Cal—"

"That will be fine," said Mary, taking the opportunity to finally interrupt someone else.

"Don't you want to verify the zip code too?"

"No," said Mary, "but I think I'll keep the ticket and—"

If there was an interruption competition, Mary was clearly outclassed. "Oh, I'm sorry. I didn't understand." Clearly a gross understatement. "If you're going to keep the ticket, I can probably cash refund it and just keep a copy of your ID."

Mary was a little bewildered, but a little curious too. "How much is the refund?"

"Oh, it's been used for one-way already, and there's a ten percent charge for refunding it, and we're not allowed to refund the prepaid bag charges so..." she looked at the computer screen, typed in a few entries and then looked up smiling at Mary. "Two hundred and ninety-five dollars. Do want that in cash now?"

Mary was flooded with a mixture of greed, ethics, and astonishment. Astonishment won quickly. "You can give me the money if I don't give you the ticket, but you can't give me the money if I do give you the ticket? Is that right?"

"Well, I would cancel the ticket, of course," replied the agent, as condescension returned to her attitude.

"Of course," said Mary. "But if Sally were to sign the ticket, you would still cancel it before I got any money, right?"

The agent concentrated for a moment and then said, "Yes, that's right."

Mary was getting far too mischievous now, and she smiled and said, "Can I borrow your pen?"

The agent looked at her pen as if it were the most valuable object in her possession, which it might be, Mary thought.

"Just for a second, and just here at the counter." She handed Mary the pen with some fear it seemed. Mary took it, and smiled as she moved down the counter a step, although she wasn't sure she really needed to. Her suspicion was verified when she returned a second later after scrawling on the ticket.

"I'm so sorry," said Mary, "but I didn't notice that Sally did sign the ticket." She showed the ticket to the agent, hoping the ink was dry enough that it wouldn't smear, having been on the ticket less than ten seconds.

"Oh, I didn't notice that either," said the agent. "I can give you cash."

"No, that's all right," said Mary, smiling. "Just checking is all."

"So, would you like the refund to be mailed?"

Mary could not understand why this wasn't confusing to this agent, since it was all so baffling to her. "I'm not sure Sally will get it if it's mailed," she replied.

"Of course not," said the agent.

When Mary looked at her she continued, "Mr. Forsyth would. He's the one who purchased the ticket."

"Forsyth? At Thirty Six Janson Way in Huntington Beach, with whatever the zip code is there?"

"I told you that you should verify the zip code, didn't I?" said the agent with a very scolding smile on her face.

"Yes you did, and you were correct," said Mary. "By the way, what is Mr. Forsyth's first name again?"

"I can't give out that information, Miss Burke!" replied the agent.

"No, of course not," said Mary. "I'll just hold onto the ticket until I can get his first name then."

As Mary turned to leave the agent said, "Okay, and thank you for flying with us today."

"I didn't fly with you today," Mary replied.

"Oh," said the agent, frowning. "Well then, thank you for flying with us, whenever that was."

"Have you worked here for very long?" Mary had to ask.

"Oh, no," said the agent. "I just transferred from the security department." She swelled with pride. "I used to work for the FAA checking people's IDs when they went through the security checkpoints, but they said I was better qualified for this position."

"Oh," said Mary, realizing that Laura had probably had no problem boarding her plane with whatever ID she had used.

As she walked away, she decided she had spent enough time here, and more than enough money on the short-term parking. Peter was the chief investigator anyway, and he was the one trying to move up to Major Morgan, so let him earn it. She probably should have called him right away, and now she had another call to make too.

Chapter 38

Mary retrieved her car and paid her parking fee, which didn't turn out to require mortgaging her house. This was fortunate, since she didn't own a house, but the parking fee made her wish she had taken the cash just offered, even though Mr. Forsyth might need it. Laura had given it to her, after all, and Mary wasn't sure why she had done that, but was sure she shouldn't trust Laura.

Once outside, she drove to the front of the terminal and stopped in the No Stopping Zone to write down the information she had acquired: Sally Smart, arrived three days ago, ticket purchased by someone named Forsyth, unknown first name, at Thirty Six Janson Way in Huntington Beach, with an unknown zip code. But she had to let Peter participate in the investigation too, for his self-esteem. Then there was Luther probably Porter, with a registration tag S-69-X. Vanity had a very high price. Everyone would remember that tag. When she called Peter she would mention the cocaine and the charge at the gas station outside the airport.

First, however, she had to wait for the state police to tell her to leave, and he did that almost as soon as she had finished writing.

"Move it," he said, as recognition began to spread across his face.

"I just wanted to make sure you had not had a stroke, officer. I'll be leaving," said Mary, and drove away.

She drove toward her shop now. At least she thought Jerry would not be destroying it this time, but she didn't think she would have a large enough profit to compensate for the parking. She would have to at least offer to pay Jerry something for his help, too.

She called Peter, gave the information she had, which when she gave it sounded like far less than she thought it had been. Laura was on a plane going somewhere, possibly California, using someone else's name, but she wasn't sure whose name, and she had probably been in Nebraska for three days, or at least someone using Sally Smart's ticket had. She was a little more positive when she came to Luther.

"Yes, then there's Luther," she said. "Who dropped Laura off this morning."

"What about Luther?"

"Well, Laura said she had sex with him, although I declined the offer to hear the detailed account. Hope you're not disappointed, Peter."

"No," he said. Mary had expected a little banter, but none was forthcoming. Most unlike Peter.

"Laura also said, and this was a gift especially for the cute captain she met today, that Angie might have some of Luther's semen within her vagina."

"Really," said Peter. "Perhaps not in her...well, Jerry had suggested it might be in other places too, based on Angie's interest in kinkiness."

"Oh," said Mary. "Laura has cocaine with her, if she hasn't used it all, and Luther's wife's credit card and passport. Her last name is Porter, at least that's what the gas station attendant called her when she charged half a tank of gas for me. I didn't get a look at the card or passport long enough to verify that. I think Laura might have been just checking to make sure the card would go through all right."

"Could be. I'll ask Luther about the card and the encounter with Angie. It might be possible to get him to give some information if I tell him his wife's card has been stolen, rather than that his latest sexual encounter is now dead."

"Angie is probably not his latest. Laura is surely that one. If he hasn't had another since he dropped her off. You remember his registration tag, don't you?"

"Hard one to forget," replied Peter.

"Yes," said Mary.

"One more question, Mary. Do you like Jerry?"

"Yes, I guess so," Mary said, a little surprised by the question.

"Well," said Peter. "I like him too, but I told him I would kill him if he did anything to hurt you, so let me know if I need to commit any felonies, okay?"

"What?" asked Mary.

"Gotta go now, and see if I can catch Laura" said Peter. "Too bad you couldn't have gotten them to hold her at the airport."

"There wasn't enough brains at that airport to fill a thimble, Peter. What was that you said about Jerry?"

"Don't be so old-fashioned, Mary. No one uses thimbles to measure brains anymore. Everyone is metric now." With this he hung up and left Mary to ponder, and to make her second call.

Mary did ponder briefly. Peter was acting strange, with no lewd remarks about the sexual comments, and then his questions about whether she "liked" Jerry. Maybe he had been hanging around Jerry too much.

Her next call took a little effort. She didn't have the number, and she was driving home at a speed that didn't exactly conform to the suggested speed for this highway, but she had been advised by the state police to "move it" so she was. When she finally got connected, Frank was glad to hear from her. He even remained glad when she told him what she wanted him to do.

"You're retired police and good at the computers, Frank, and I need to sort this out."

"Yes, okay. Just a little identity shifting is all it is."

"But it may go pretty deep, Frank. She's on parole in California. Can you get into the records you'll need to access?"

"I can try. I'm retired probation myself, so I'll recognize the subtleties in the record. The things said and not said. When do you want this?"

"Is tonight too soon?"

"Yes," chuckled Frank. "Way too soon, and I have a date tonight. Joan and I are going to a movie."

Mary scrunched her face. "How about after the movie? I'll buy you a late supper?"

"That important. Yeah, okay. We can meet at a restaurant named Maria's and I'll show you what I have, how's that?"

"Okay. Thanks, Frank. Is Joan coming too?"

"Yes, if that's all right with you."

"Yeah, sure. I just wanted to know if I should get a date for tonight."

"No need to do that, Mary."

"I think there's someone I can get."

"Oh, no, Mary, it's all right if you don't have anyone to ask. We can just do the three of us."

"No, Frank. I think I can get this guy I met...well, yesterday, really, but I've known him for...well, almost a year, and from high school too. Anyway, I think he'll come along."

"You don't have to get a date, Mary. I'd love to see you anyway, and I want you to meet Joan."

"Frank!"

"Yes?"

"I'll have a date tonight. End of discussion. See you at Maria's at a table for FOUR."

"Yeah, sure. Movie's out at ten or so, and if you can't—"

"Don't say it, Frank. I can get a date tonight."

"Yeah, sure. See you then."

Mary hung up and scowled. All right, she was thirty-five and had been a little slow in the personal relationship area, but she could get a date. Her sex life had been less in the past few years than Laura or Angie would have accomplished in a night's work, but she could still get a date. She wasn't over the hill, even if her father was trying to marry her off to the first guy who had shown any interest, even if he didn't know a thing about him. She could get a date. Even if that date would have to be Jerry, she could get a date. End of discussion.

Chapter 39

She was driving into her little town now, making the plans for the evening. She realized she was looking forward to it, and maybe even to having a date with Jerry. She also realized she was assuming he would go, but she figured she could convince him if he was reluctant. She stopped by her apartment on the way by to pick up some clothes for herself, and for Jerry. She decided just to bring his backpack rather than pick something out for him. He didn't have that much, and he probably couldn't get into Aunty May's house anyway.

When she arrived at The Ice Cream Shop, Jerry was serving a small group of teenage boys who were chatting about surfing, of course. They were laughing and asking questions and Jerry was telling them all how great it was. A few people were at the tables, too, but it was approaching the lunch hour, and things usually picked up a little then.

"Hi, Mary," said Jerry. "How'd it go?"

Mary smiled, but decided to play her trump card right off. "You owe me on that one, Jerry."

"Oh," he said. "I guess Laura can be pretty—"

"It wasn't at all pretty, Jerry." Mary smiled. "And you owe me, and this is what you owe me. I have to meet with a friend tonight and he's bringing his new girlfriend, and I'm bringing you."

"Oh, wow," said Jerry. "It's like a double date, isn't it?"

"Well sort of, but—"

The crowd around Jerry began congratulating him.

"Way to go, man!"

"Awesome, just awesome."

"And with Mary, She's really ho——" This last speaker stopped suddenly and looked at Mary with a slight blush. "She's a very nice lady, I mean."

"Yes," said Jerry, "She is." He smiled, and Mary blushed, and the crowd around Jerry slapped him on the back and high fived him and paid for ice cream and left the shop murmuring words to Mary on their way out.

Mary smiled now too, and handed Jerry his backpack. "I thought you might want to change before we go. Clean jeans and shirt...and...and underwear, for God's sake." She put on her best angry face and added, "And socks, too."

"Yeah, sure," said Jerry. "Special night. Where are we going to go?"

"This is just about Angie and Laura and whether...don't make more of this than it is, Jerry. We're probably going to a place called Maria's in the city. Just a little, casual Italian place, but you have to dress nice."

"Nicely," corrected Jerry.

"What?"

"I have to dress *nicely*," said Jerry. "It's an adverb if it's modifying the verb: to dress. I think I might have a friend that works at Maria's."

"A friend *who* works there, you mean? People are *who*, not *that*. You have a friend working in a restaurant in Nebraska? Do you have a friend everywhere, Jerry?" smiled Mary, "Friend or none, you do need to dress nicely for my friend, and this is just about investigating, so please don't get all excited about it."

"Of course not," said Jerry. "It's just a date. A double date, really. Our second date though. After last night."

"Last night wasn't a date, Jerry," said Mary.

At that point another customer walked in. "Hi, Jerry," he said.

"Oh, hi, John," Jerry replied. "How are ya?"

"Doing okay, an' you?"

"Hi, Dad," said Mary.

"Oh, hi, Mary. Didn't see you there."

"Probably because you weren't looking for me, your own daughter in her own ice cream shop. Why would you?"

"Now, don't get all bunched up, Mary. I came by to talk to you and Jerry too, of course, about you, of course."

"Why are you talking to Jerry about me, Dad?"

"Just trying to make sure his intentions are honorable. Looking after my daughter."

"What about *my* intentions? Aren't you worried about Jerry?"

"Oh, Mary," said her father. "Word has it that you have been asking him out every night since you met him. Don't you think you might do better playing a little hard to get? Mature men like that sometimes, ya know."

"It's only been two nights, Dad."

"An' you only met him yesterday, Mary."

"Last night doesn't count."

"It counted for me," said Jerry.

"You don't count, Jerry," said Mary. "Weren't you here to make sure Jerry's intentions were honorable or something, Dad?"

"Well, yeah, that's right. Thanks for reminding me. Are your intentions honorable, Jerry?"

"Yes, I think so," said Jerry.

"Good," said John. "Not too honorable I hope."

"Dad!"

"What?"

"I'm thirty-five and I can take care of myself."

"You're thirty-five and you haven't done all that well so far. I thought maybe you needed some help. I was just thinking you might be happier married, that's all."

"Married to whom?"

"Oh, I'm not sure you need to be picky."

Mary shrugged. "Maybe you're right. Mom certainly wasn't very picky."

"Now don't be criticizing your dear departed mother, Mary. She was married at your age."

"But she was married to you, Dad. I thought you told me not to point out her failures, the principle one being you."

"And she was so proud of you, too. Wounds my heart to hear you say all those nasty things about her."

"Dad!"

"Look, Mary, can Jerry and I talk a little? The whole world does not revolve around you."

"No, you may not talk to Jerry!"

John shrugged. "Be careful of her, Jerry. She can be kind of moody sometimes, and for no reason at all."

Jerry just nodded and smiled.

"But now that we're talking about her mother, I have something I wanted to show you." John looked at his daughter, who was quietly contemplating patricide, when another customer came in to delay the murder. Only for a few minutes, she hoped. Mable Snyder was closer to her father's age than to Mary's, and might not understand the acute necessity for this particular murder. That was the trouble with today's society: they took homicide so seriously, when it was often just the most merciful solution to parent-child disputes.

"What can I get for you, Mrs. Snyder?" Mary asked.

"Oh, hi, Mary. I was hoping to talk to Jerry."

"Of course, if my father is done talking to him. Jerry has a pretty busy schedule, but I think he can squeeze you in. Maybe I can get you some ice cream while you wait?"

"Well, I guess that would be all right," said Mrs. Snyder. "Just a small—"

"Maple walnut?" offered Jerry.

"Why yes, that's right," said Mrs. Snyder, smiling.

"I knew that too," said Mary.

John smiled. "Of course you did, Mary. She's a good catch, Jerry." Jerry nodded and Mary scowled.

"Now Jerry," John continued, "I have something to show you. It's Mary's mother's engagement ring."

He opened a small box, and Mary turned with a half-filled small cup of maple walnut. "Mom's engagement ring?!"

"Just showin' Jerry," said John. "I'm not suggesting anything."

"Dad!" said Mary, waving the half-full dish at him.

"Maybe you ought to let Jerry finish scooping the ice cream, Mary?" said Mrs. Snyder.

"It's a real nice ring," said Jerry, looking at the ring and then at John, and finally at Mary. "I can finish with the ice cream if you want, just let me put my clothes in the back." Jerry picked up the backpack and started toward the back of the shop.

John looked at the backpack and asked, "You're not makin' Jerry move are you, Mary?"

"What?"

"Maybe he can stay with me?" offered her father. "Ya know, I've got some pictures of Mary when she was a cute little kid. I can show them to ya, if ya want."

"No you can not!" said Mary

"You and Jerry are living together?" said Mrs. Snyder. "That's a good idea, Mary. I wish I'd done that with Phil. I would have gotten divorced a lot sooner if I had."

"I'm not living with Jerry, Mrs. Snyder. He's just staying at my apartment."

"Oh," frowned Mrs. Snyder. "I thought maybe you were staying at his place. Do you really think you should be moving him into your place so quickly? Maybe slow down a little so you don't look too desperate."

"I'm *not* desperate!" said Mary.

"Of course not, dearie," consoled Mrs. Snyder.

"Ya see, Mary," said John. "Mature people think a woman should play a little hard to get."

"Mature people!?" said Mary. "We're talking about Jerry and you, Dad, not about mature people."

"There are no mature men," said Mrs. Snyder. "They are all just big children."

Mary waved the half-full dish again and turned to Mrs. Snyder. "Never were truer words spoken."

"Yes," Mrs. Snyder replied, "but maybe half a dish is what I should eat today. Before it's an empty dish, I mean." She snatched the ice cream from Mary's hand before anyone could move to interfere.

Jerry emerged from the back in time to see it happen though. "I can give you the rest if you want it later," he said, "and I don't think Mary is ready for an engagement ring yet, John."

"Soon, though, and I'll have it when she's ready."

"A friendship ring first," said Jerry, pulling out a dollar bill.

"Now that's a nice idea, Jerry," said Mrs. Snyder.

Jerry folded the bill quickly and when he was done there was a ring, which he put on Mary's finger before she could pull it away. "Ya see? The eye above the pyramid is right there on top," he said, swelling with pride.

"That's nice," said Mrs. Snyder. "Childish too of course, but nice," she added, looking not at Jerry but at John before taking a taste of the maple walnut.

"Thank you," said Jerry, as a new group of customers entered the shop. Among them was a six-year-old girl.

"Oh, Mama, look at Mrs. Burke's ring!" she cried.

"Show it to her, Mary," said John.

"It's a friendship ring," said Jerry.

"It's so pretty," said the six-year-old. "And it looks like a dollar bill!"

"It is a dollar bill. Jerry made it," said Mary. "I can give it to you if you like it."

Everyone was appalled at the offer except Mary, who hadn't realized giving her friendship ring away was any problem, and Jerry, who seemed to think that the young girl deserved a ring of her own.

"I couldn't take Jerry's ring from you, Mrs. Burke!" the young girl cried.

Jerry smiled. "Of course not," he said. Everyone looked at him, but he didn't seem to notice. "Mary's fingers are bigger than yours are."

Jerry then took out another dollar bill and folded it in front of her to her amazement, and only a little less amazement in the rest, fashioning a ring like Mary's. He tried it on her finger, but removed it and refashioned it. When he was finished, he placed it back on her finger. "Perfect," Jerry said. "Now we're friends too."

There were screams of delight and hugs and then her mother offered to pay for it or at least give Jerry a dollar to replace the one that he had used. "Oh, that's okay," he said. "You can't buy friendship, you know...or a friendship ring. You can buy some ice cream, though."

She did, and the tip she left more than matched the dollar ring her daughter took, but by then there were others coming for ice cream and leaving with rings too, and soon they were coming for rings and leaving with ice cream. Jerry helped serve the ice cream, in between making the rings, and steadfastly refused to be paid anything, always providing his own dollar bills.

The age gradually crept up, and soon teenagers and young or even middle-aged adults were asking for and getting rings. Mrs. Snyder had left with one. Business began to match yesterday's tallies as the draw on the rings replaced the draw of the "grass," and Mary had to admit there was the draw of Jerry. People were leaving large tips, too.

Jerry was a friend to the children, charming to the ladies, and one of the boys to the men. To the men he talked about surfing of course, but also about fishing, although he admitted to all that he had never so much as put a line into the water. No one seemed to mind.

Near suppertime it began to slow, and Bill and his brother Louis came in. They looked nervous for some reason, and when Mary asked what she could get them, neither answered. Finally Louis looked at his brother with disgust and approached Jerry.

"Bill here was wondering if he could get a ring." The fifty-or-so-year-old Bill blushed deeply. Louis cast another look at him and added, "Not fur himself, but he's got himself a girlfriend."

Jerry smiled. "I know what that's like," he said, and winked at Mary. "Too soon for an engagement ring, but the perfect time for a friendship ring, right?"

"Yeah," said Bill.

"Well, what size is the finger it'll be going on? Mary's size, or maybe a bit bigger?" Jerry reached over, taking Mary's ring-clad finger and showing it to Bill.

"Yeah," he said. "A bit bigger."

Jerry fashioned the ring, tried it on first Bill's and then Louis' finger, and they were impressed.

"Now," said Jerry, "ya want ta see a really neat trick?"

"Sure," said Louis.

"Do you have a twenty?" asked Jerry, and Louis looked in his wallet and produced a twenty-dollar bill. Jerry folded it in half and then in quarters, smoothed it, and then put it in the pocket of his shirt. He then looked behind Louis and said, "Thanks. Can I help the next person in line, please?"

Louis and Bill first stared and then stammered. Bill looked behind him, but there was no one else in line of course, and by this time Mary was looking at Jerry too. He smiled and pulled the twenty-dollar bill out of his pocket, handing it back to Louis. "I can't believe that one works every time."

Everyone laughed, but mostly Louis and Bill. They offered to pay for the ring, which Jerry refused. "Buy some ice cream for the lady," he said, pointing to the ring. "That'll impress her."

"Good idea. We should have some here before we go, though," said Bill, looking at his brother.

Chapter 40

John had hung around for an hour, chatting and gossiping, but finally left, saying he had to go to the office. This left Bill and Louis eating ice cream, the only customers in the shop. Mary and Jerry were behind the counter, with Mary relating the high points of the trip to the airport to Jerry. "So she pulls me into a rest stop, does a couple lines of coke...is that the right way to say it?"

"Yeah," said Jerry, "snorting is used, too."

"Yeah, so then she insisted we pull over to get gas and pays using Luther's wife's credit card. She had stolen it when she was planting her clothing for the wife to find. Setting Luther up royally, I'm not sure why, but she was, and she had the wife's passport, too."

Jerry just nodded.

"So anyway, then we are at the terminal, and she gives me her ticket into Nebraska, saying I might be able to cash in the return flight. She gave me back the jewelry you bought her, suggesting that I might wear it, but no one with any taste would be caught dead...well, I have it in the car if you want it back."

"Did you touch it?" asked Jerry.

"No," said Mary. "Laura showed it to me and I'm sorry, Jerry, but that's the one thing we agreed on. It is not something I would ever wear. Maybe Angie?"

"No," said Jerry. "But you didn't actually touch it yourself?"

"No. Touching it wouldn't have made it look any better. So finally, as she's walking into the terminal, she says that Luther had sex with Angie the night she was killed!"

Jerry just nodded, and Mary wondered if he understood what she was saying, or believed it, or was just so used to this kind of thing that it didn't affect him. "She said that?" Jerry finally asked.

"Yeah. That Luther's semen was in Angie."

"I wonder how she knew, unless she talked to Angie, or..."

"Or?"

"She was there."

Mary was puzzled. She had been so overwhelmed by the revelation that she had never thought about how Laura knew, or even if she really did know. "Maybe she didn't know. Maybe she was just trying to get Luther into the really deep weeds, ya think?"

Jerry frowned. "Too easy to check that out, so it probably is true, but how did she know? And to be so sure of it that she would get you to tell..."

Peter came in at that point.

Mary looked up and asked, "Any luck getting Laura's flight?"

"No," sighed Peter. "None of the names we know she was using are on any flights out of that airport. Mrs. Porter did get a big cash advance at the airport, but didn't fly out of it. You sure she took a flight out?"

"She said she was going to," Mary answered. "Maybe she bought the ticket with cash."

"She probably flew out," said Jerry. When Peter and Mary looked at him he added, "She won't want to be around here. This is not her turf. She won't feel comfortable here. Might have hitched a ride or something, but she was at the airport already, so that makes the most sense. She's not that clever, either, to make up an elaborate subterfuge."

Mary at least was impressed that Jerry was clever enough to use the words *elaborate subterfuge* correctly in a complete sentence. "So, where is she?"

"On her way to big L.A.," said Peter. "Ya think, Jerry?"

"Yeah," he smiled. "That's where she'll feel comfortable. You're a poet too, Peter. Is everyone in Nebraska a poet?"

When Peter looked at him, Jerry added, "On her *way* to big *L.A.* It's a poem, right?"

"Jerry has this thing about poets, Peter," said Mary.

"Okay," smiled Peter. "But we can't catch her without knowing what name she's using, or at least what flight she's on. And we don't even have her fingerprints yet, to see if she has any matches from the shop where we found Angie, or in May's house. We don't have enough to get a warrant. She could have been the one who killed Angie and planted the gun and packets of bath salts in Jerry's dresser."

"You think they were planted then?" asked Mary. "Blanchard seemed to think they were left there by Jerry. Was that gun the murder weapon? Blanchard never did say."

"Ballistics says it was, and I know they were planted," said Peter. "I went to the room with Jerry to pack his clothes and I saw him empty *all* his underwear and clothes out of the top dresser drawer.

"When we left, it was empty for sure. Blanchard doesn't believe me, but I know nothing was there. Of course Carl was running errands with May, so anyone could have gone in and planted them."

Jerry just shrugged. "I have Laura's fingerprints if you want them."

"You have what?" asked Peter.

"They'll be on the jewelry I gave her," suggested Jerry.

"And a hundred other people that looked at it in the store before you bought it," said Mary.

"I washed it at your apartment this morning to make sure there were no other prints on it," said Jerry. "Only Laura touched it, since you didn't. Can I borrow your phone, Mary? Maybe I can get Tess to rush the prints for you, Peter. You can verify them later when you get the official ones from Washington, but you know these are really hers."

Mary handed Jerry her phone, although she wondered why Jerry was calling Tess and not having Peter call her, but then she realized that Tess might rush something more quickly for Jerry than for Peter anyway. She also noted that Jerry dialed the number directly, no directory assistance, and Tess apparently answered herself, since he didn't ask to speak to her.

"Hi, Tess. This is Jerry."

"I'm good. You?"

"That's good."

"Yeah, I'll be at The Ice Cream Shop this afternoon."

"Oh, yeah. If you want a ring I can make it for you."

Mary and Peter were beginning to look annoyed.

"Look, Tess. Wondering if you can do me a favor. Peter has some cheap jewelry that has got Laura's fingerprints on it, and I thought you could lift 'em today, and maybe compare 'em to the specs you picked up at the shop where you found Angie."

"No," said Jerry. "Not plastic, just really big gaudy pieces of glass. Easy to pick off the prints, that's why I choose it, so it would be easy and it's...well, really ugly, so I figured Laura wouldn't keep it."

"No, I didn't know that part for sure, but I took a chance she wouldn't keep it, just throw it away. Lucky Mary was smart enough to get her to give it to her."

"It's over here at the shop, if you want to come by now."

"Okay," said Jerry, and hung up.

"Tess'll be by in a couple of minutes to pick up the jewelry, Peter."

"And we'll have some prints to work with. If we can find Laura, we'll be all set."

"What about the Luther connection?" asked Mary.

"I got his address from his registration tag and went out there. I told him about his wife's missing credit card and asked him politely to check to see if anything else was missing. He went straight to his wife's top dresser drawer, and when he opened it there was a packet of cocaine on the top of a couple pair of red thongs. The panties under them were much more conservative in their nature. The store his wife bought them in didn't have the word *Secret* in its name."

"So you nabbed him?" asked Mary.

"Yes, and printed and DNA'd him," smiled Peter. "We'll know for sure about him and Angie in a day or two."

Mary smiled and Jerry nodded, but he was on the phone again.

"Hey, Stan," he said.

"Oh, I'm having a good time out here, except for poor Angie."

"No, not my own shop. One with this really nice lady, Mary."

"Well maybe. Her dad likes me."

"I'd love to have you meet her!"

Mary frowned. "Stan will have to come to Nebraska if he wants to meet me."

Jerry smiled. "She said she would love to have you come out to Nebraska for a visit and meet her, Stan."

"He can stay with me, Jerry," said Peter. "It would be too crowded over with you and Mary."

"Unless he comes tonight it won't be 'Jerry and Mary'," said Mary.

"Peter said you can stay with him, Stan," Jerry said.

Jerry looked at Peter and said, "He wants to know if you surf any, Peter."

"In Nebraska? Fishing is the closest water sport we have. I can show him how that's done."

"No surf here, man, but Peter will show you how to fish, okay?" Jerry said.

Mary and Peter were beginning to look at Jerry with annoyance on their faces again when Jerry said, "Look, Stan. It's about Laura. She said she came out here to ID Angie, but it looks like she may have already been out here when Angie was killed."

"Yeah, I thought that was strange, and anyway Peter couldn't hold her, no warrant and no jurisdiction." Jerry smiled and nodded at Mary as he said this.

"Well, she's likely headed back to Huntington I'm guessing, but we can't figure what name she's using, so we can't tell what flight she's on."

"Yeah, I thought since you would recognize her and can get some sort of a warrant real quick, you might be able..."

"That's it. Look, she told Mary she was flying first class and probably paid cash, so maybe a flight out of here that's large enough to have a first-class section, and she would pick a direct flight if there is one. No other airports in this area she could fly out of either."

He looked at Peter and Mary, who shook their heads.

"Great, Stan, and I'm looking forward to seeing you."

"Oh, yeah, he's right here. He wants to talk to you, Peter," said Jerry, handing him the phone.

Peter took the phone and spoke, "Captain Bradshaw? This is Peter Morgan."

"Oh, sure, Stan. This is Peter."

"No, no luck getting a trace on her here. We have a ticket for a Sally Smart that she gave to us and that has an arrival date three days ago. Purchased by a Mr. Forsyth at..."

"Yes, that's the one. You know him? James is his first name?"

"Really. VIP buying tickets for..."

"Yes, very interesting."

Peter cast a quick look at Jerry and said, "I have the preliminary phone report for the number Laura has been using, and that shows several calls from this area over the last three days, so she probably was here."

"No, Jerry seems to think that it is her number."

"Yes, I think he would know too."

"Well, yes, as soon as it looked like it wasn't going to all fall into place easily, I started gathering all the information I thought we might need, including her cell phone records. Still may be one of our locals who killed Angie, but there are a lot of possibilities and I'd rather have ..."

"No. Angie had a phone on her, and we used that to contact Laura, but that number hadn't been used at all for maybe a week."

"Exactly. Sorry I can't give you more to go on, but..."

"No, we couldn't hold her and she knew it. She didn't want to wait around until we could, so my guess is that she's out of Nebraska by now."

"She wouldn't give us any fingerprints, but we have some jewelry that only she handled and we're lifting her prints off that to compare, but it would be helpful if you could..."

"Yeah, I've requested them from Washington, but they think the Nebraska State Police couldn't possibly have anything important going on."

"Of course."

"I'm looking forward to meeting you too, Stan."

Peter smiled and handed Mary her phone. "Stan thinks I'm doing a great job with this case."

"Stan thinks *we're* doing a great job, but you made one mistake, Peter," said Mary.

"What?"

"Inviting Stan to stay with you and teach him about fishing. Stan is gay."

Peter frowned. "You mean gay men don't fish, Mary?"

Louis and Bill had been listening to this conversation quietly, but now Bill spoke, "Gay men fish, Mary. You fish, don't you, Lou?"

"'Course I do. Who said I don't?"

"Mary did, just now."

Louis shook his head. "Ah, she's from Nebraska an' don't know no better. If she was from California like Jerry is, she'd know, wouldn't she, Jerry? Gay men fish same as everyone does."

Jerry just nodded.

Chapter 41

Tess was there a few minutes later. "Where's that jewelry?" she asked Jerry, although Peter was still sitting there. Mary produced the plastic bag and Tess put on her gloves and looked inside.

"Perfect," she said, holding up the necklace with its gaudy glass pendant. "If she touched this we'll get her prints."

She finally turned to Peter and Mary. "Great you got it from her, Mary, but you didn't touch any of these yourself, did you?"

"No," said Mary, as she was still trying to figure out how Jerry had figured out that this was what Laura would do with the jewelry.

"I'll have this for you in a couple hours, Peter, and a match on some of the prints from the shop if I can. All unofficial, since I don't really know these are that bitch Laura's prints, but maybe I can tell you if these match any that we picked up at the crime scene. Patti was tellin' me about Laura, and I'd really like to nail her."

"Yeah, thanks, Tess. We'll have official prints pretty soon."

Jerry frowned a little. "You shouldn't be so angry, Tess. It isn't good for you. Laura is just using too many drugs, that's all."

"And you shouldn't be so naive, Jerry. She's a bitch, and a little *tough* is what will help her see that she doesn't want to be a bitch any longer." Tess seemed sure of herself on this point.

"Well, maybe," Jerry conceded

Tess smiled and added, "And like, this is so great. Real crime scene stuff, just like on TV. Gotta go now, but I'll be in touch, Peter" she said, as she went out the door. "I'll come back for the ice cream later and the ring, Jerry."

"Maybe I better look like I'm busy too, before Tess steals all the credit," said Peter.

"You want your ice cream, Peter?" asked Mary.

"I'll be back for it," said Peter.

As he turned to leave he nearly ran over Mary's father, returning to the shop. "Sorry, John."

"Hey, Peter, I'll take his ice cream, Mary," said John.

"Okay, Dad. Shall I get Peter to pay for it?"

"Just put it on my tab, Mary."

Jerry looked at John and then at Louis and Bill, the only others in the shop right now. "You sure you want to do that, John?"

"What?" asked John.

"Well, ya see, it's just that..." said Jerry, speaking a little more softly and leaning slightly toward John while he glanced again at Louis and Bill. They had been ignoring the conversation until now, but were suddenly listening very closely. Jerry wasn't speaking so softly that they couldn't hear, but softly enough to make them want to hear.

"What?" said John again.

"Well, it's just that...well, you know. A lawyer who can't afford to pay for an ice cream? People might think...well, that if he has to beg for ice cream from his daughter, maybe he shouldn't be trusted with...well, you see what I mean," said Jerry, glancing again at Louis and Bill.

Louis was looking at his brother, and his brother leaned in to speak, "Ya know, Louis, I was going ta talk to John about drawin' up that will ya been tellin' me I need, but maybe..."

John spoke immediately and loudly. "Oh, I think I can pay for this one, Jerry."

"And your tab, too?" asked Mary.

John looked quickly at Louis and Bill. "Oh, sure. Forgot I had that. Will twenty cover it?"

"I think so," said Mary.

"Aw, here," said John. "Take forty, and keep the change on that too." He turned and smiled at Louis and Bill, who went back to their ice cream.

"So, did you come by just to pay your tab, Dad?"

"No, Mary. Things were kind of sl-- I mean, they're kind of busy at the office. That's what I mean," John said, and glanced quickly at Louis and Bill. "So I decided to take a break from the hectic pace I've been having lately."

"Yes, of course," smiled Mary. "It has been pretty hectic."

Louis and Bill rose to leave now. "Thanks for the ring, Jerry," said Bill.

"You want to take that ice cream for her too?" Jerry said.

"Oh, yeah," smiled Bill.

"You want just a dish, or maybe a sundae, or maybe.... Yeah, maybe a pint, so you can share it. That's real romantic."

"I don't know," said Bill. "Pretty full right now."

"You don't have to eat very much, just a few bites, but you'll be sharing it with her and she'll like that," smiled Jerry.

"Well...yeah, that's a good idea. Thanks, Jerry. I won't eat much."

Louis smiled and tapped Bill's stomach; not large, but not small, either. "He'll eat his share," he said, laughing as his brother frowned.

Jerry filled a pint and they left, leaving John as the only customer.

"Thanks, Jerry. That coulda ruined my business if it got around," said John.

"How is business, Dad?" asked Mary.

"Oh, you know. Not much for a small-town lawyer."

"So what did you come by for, Dad?"

"Oh, just checkin' to see how things are going with you and Jerry, that's all." He winked at her.

"Well, we haven't consummated the relationship in the two hours since you left. As a matter of fact, I took your advice, Dad," said Mary, "and I'm playing hard to get."

"Well, if that's all right with Jerry," offered John.

"Why wouldn't it be all right with me?" asked Jerry. When no one offered him any reason, he put a serious expression on his face and said, "You know, John. It's not about sex."

John blushed and Mary had to chuckle at him. "Yes, dear father of mine. Some mature men prefer a meaningful relationship to casual sex."

John was only slowly recovering, and Mary finally took pity on him. "You were partners with May's husband, George, weren't you, Dad?"

"Well, yeah. Shared the same office and all, but not the same clients."

"Or the same secretary?"

"Oh, you mean Jessica?" asked John. "We shared her secretarial skills, meager as those were, but George was the only client on her social calendar."

"That's good," said Mary, "because I would have to cut your balls off otherwise."

Her father smiled. "Jessica wasn't at all interested in me or my balls, and not much interested in George, either. It was the money for her, always and only the money."

Mary frowned now. "This whole thing seems to have started with the money George took with him when he left with Jessica. That's what got Prentiss into the shop. Maybe George didn't take it with him."

"Well, I don't know," said John, "but I'd be surprised if Jessica would have left without the money in her hand, and I don't see how she would have left any behind."

"But Prentiss said she did. That's what he was looking for when he went to the shop," said Mary.

"Don't know about Prentiss," said John. "That boy is capable of getting anything confused."

"But Dexter got five hundred from May. Where did she get that kind of money from?"

"To flatten Rufus' tires," added Jerry.

"How did you know that?" asked Mary.

"Oh, Jasmine told me about it. She was talking about Francis and how she liked him, but didn't like Dexter and I asked her why. She said he was bragging about flattening Rufus' tires, and she didn't think that was very nice."

"Shit," said Mary. "Prentiss knew about it, and now Jasmine knows about it and tells you about it, Jerry. Why hasn't Rufus heard about who flattened his tires?"

"Maybe he has heard about it?" offered Jerry.

John shook his head. "If Rufus had heard who flattened his tires, Dexter would be dead."

"Got to agree, Dad," said Mary. "But what I want to know is where May got the money to pay Dexter."

"Not from the trusts, that's for sure," said John.

"You're sure, Dad?"

"Yup. You see, I'm not dumb. I could see that there was something going on with George and Jessica, and George was pullin' together all the money for Jessica, so I...well..."

"You what, Dad?"

"Well, I called May and talked to her. Ya see, she never liked George. Never really trusted him, either. That's why she never changed her name when she got married. Stayed a Wilson. So when I suggested she tie the money up in trusts and things like that, she agreed right away. Seems George didn't have much himself, it was all either in May's name or in real estate, but he'd been trying to get as much as he could. May and I tied it up pretty tight.

"'Course George could have gotten it if he had the time to challenge the trusts, some of it bein' community property, but Jessica wasn't going to wait. I kinda thought that would discourage her altogether, but it didn't. I think she thought there was more money left than there was."

"So all their community property is still in the trusts?" asked Mary.

"Yeah. Her brothers are trying to get at it, and of course making sure she doesn't spend any, but I still keep a close eye on it. They won't get it while I'm watching it, even if May can't get it until George is legally dead."

"That'll be next year, right?" asked Mary.

"Maybe a little longer, depending on how the court decides to determine George's last verified sighting. Five years if they use section 25-205, but of course you know that, Mary. Says ya only got five years to bring an action, and George ain't done that yet."

"Five years," said Mary.

"No one's even heard from George in five years, if ya discount the postcards." John shrugged.

"The postcards," said Mary. "Prentiss said he got one from Florida somewhere. Are there others?"

"I got one. Just something about 'Having a great time' and signed by George. No mention of where he was or anything. Strange," said John.

When Mary looked at him he added, "Usually when someone disappears there are rumors or sightings. Bank accounts get requests for verification and stuff like that. After four years they have to be running out of money, but none of that's happened. I keep a close eye on it. Not much else to do when I'm not worrying about my daughter."

"And there's no need to spend any of your precious time doing that," said Mary. "You think George is still alive?"

"Might not be," said John. "Jessica might have buried him and taken all the money. 'Course she hasn't shown up anywhere either, but I haven't been watching for her as closely as I have for George."

"But she would have no reason to hide," said Jerry.

"Unless she buried George in sunny Florida after he sent his postcards," suggested Mary. "How many postcards were there?"

"I got one and May got one. She was yelling about how he was worse than the devil himself for sending it to her. Waving it around and showing it to everyone who would look at it. That was when she really went over the edge."

"And it was from George?" asked Jerry.

"His handwriting and signature. I'd recognize it after sharing a practice with him all those years."

"Could Jessica have forged the postcards?" asked Jerry.

"Jessica?" said John. "She couldn't write like George. No way. She even tried to forge his signature one time, on one of his checks it was, and the bank wouldn't even look at it. That should have got her fired, but ended up with her getting promoted to George's bed."

Mary shook her head. "So it looks like George and Jessica took what money they could and ended up in Florida, and then disappeared."

"Yup," John shrugged. "Ya see, May was really suspicious, and so she kept all her own money, from the store I mean, in cash, and locked up somewhere."

"In the store I heard," said Mary.

"That's what I heard too, but May never said anything to me. Maybe 'cause I was George's partner, she didn't really trust me either, or maybe she didn't trust anyone."

Mary looked at Jerry. "But there's no money in the store now, is there Jerry?"

"I didn't find any. One locked fridge, but I looked in there 'cause there was this musty smell in the shop. The fridge was empty."

"May let you look inside it?" asked John.

"I didn't ask Aunty May," admitted Jerry.

"You said it was locked, though," said John.

"Jerry is not inconvenienced by locks, Dad," said Mary. "But more to the point: Where did May get the money to give to Dexter?"

"Not from the trusts," said John. "Jerry may not be inconvenienced by locks, but the bank has those trusts locked up with a lock even Jerry couldn't get into. I would have seen it anyway."

"She must have gotten it somewhere," said Mary.

"Must have," said John. "Maybe Jessica left a little behind. Maybe May had a stash hid that George didn't find?"

"But where is she stashing it?" asked Mary.

"I don't think it's in the shop," said Jerry.

"And I don't think she could hide it from Rufus and Billy in the house. They're in there snoopin' around all the time," said John. "May doesn't get around too well now, so...well, I don't know where else there is."

"Snooping around for what, I wonder?" said Jerry.

"Anything they can sell, I suspect," John answered.

"I wonder if they think May hid some money from George and Jessica too," Jerry frowned.

They had little time to think as a batch of teenagers came in looking for the rings they'd heard about.

Chapter 42

The crowds started coming in and the rings were made and given and the ice cream sold, and Mary began to wonder what Jerry would do for an encore tomorrow. Business was almost up to the speed it had been yesterday, and the tips were enormous. By closing time at nine, they were ready to close. Jerry had taken over serving and let Mary count as he had last night, and while it was still busy he kept up with ice cream and rings and cheery comments. When the sign on the door was turned to say "CLOSED" it had been the best day she had ever had.

"Time to get dressed for the date, Jerry," Mary said.

"I'll clean up while you change. Won't take me a second," he replied.

"Underwear and socks, Jerry. Remember that. I don't want to have to check, either." Mary smiled and took her clothes into the back to change.

She emerged a few minutes later wearing a dress. The shop was clean, and Jerry was smiling. "You look great, Mary," he said.

Mary blushed slightly. "What, this old thing?" she said, swishing the dress she was wearing.

"Looks like...like 'California Girls'."

"What?"

"You know, *I wish they all could be California girls*, The Beach Boys. It was written by Brian Wilson in '65 during his first LSD trip. Still a nice song, but I never knew how nice it was until I saw you tonight." Jerry smiled and Mary blushed again, and didn't have any idea what to say.

Jerry shrugged and said, "I'll get changed now too. Brian isn't any relation to me, by the way."

As Jerry went into the back, Mary recovered enough to realize that Jerry and Brian shared the same last name.

Jerry emerged a few minutes later as Mary was putting the cash from the day into the bank sack to deposit, "Over two thousand tonight..." she started to say. Jerry was dressed in tan slacks, a colorful button-down shirt over a dark-red tee, but tucked in and buttoned. He had on shoes and socks as well. It looked like he had shaved again, and his hair was clean and pulled back into a miniature ponytail.

"You look great, Jerry," Mary said.

"Not really, but if I'm going to be with you tonight I have to dress up, you know."

Mary smiled. "Did the Beach Boys ever record a song about California Boys?"

"No," smiled Jerry. "They didn't surf very much, either."

They dropped off the deposit at the bank and began the drive to the city, not much of a city, but the closest thing to a city in this part of Nebraska.

"So let me tell you what we're doing here, Jerry," said Mary, "besides going on a double date."

Jerry smiled as if to say that was the only important thing they were doing.

"Frank Gregorio is a friend of mine, and he's also a retired police officer; probation officer the last few years he worked on the force. He's good with the computers, too, so I asked him to find out who Laura and Angie really are."

"He might," said Jerry.

"Or at least he can tell us who they are not," said Mary, a little disappointed that Jerry wasn't more enthusiastic about the prospect of sorting out who the players were in this murder. "Laura was probably here when Angie was murdered so she's a suspect, right?"

"I think so," said Jerry. "But I don't know why she would kill Angie."

"I'm not sure why anyone would want to kill Angie." Mary realized that Jerry was still the principle suspect in most peoples' mind, and she wasn't sure why he wasn't in her mind, but she was sure that Jerry had not killed anyone.

"Stan may have picked up Laura by now," Jerry suggested. "I wonder why either of them was out here."

"Good question."

"I mean, I come out here, and then they come out here, and..."

"You think they were following you, Jerry?"

He just shrugged.

"Laura said you were the only thing besides the last line of coke that they ever fought over."

Jerry remained silent.

"So, why did you come out here, Jerry?"

"Oh. Aunty May asked me to."

"Asked you to?"

"Yeah." Jerry shrugged. "Last year she called me up and said she wanted me to come for a visit. I said yeah, and then she started saying it had to be right away. She even offered to pay my way out here, but of course I couldn't let her do that."

"But you did come, and you opened her shop to give away ice cream, right?"

"Well, yeah," said Jerry. "It was kind of strange the way that happened. When Aunty May started really pushing to have me come, I thought it might be that she was sick or something, so I came right out for a visit like she said. And then she started talking about how she really wanted to open the shop again. Like it was before her husband left."

"So you did?" asked Mary.

"Well, I couldn't sell groceries the way Aunty May had done. The inventory was too expensive. But ice cream isn't that bad. And it's seasonal, so I could come out here for a little while and help Aunty May run the shop, but be back in California for the landscaping, too."

"So you decided to put me out of business and spend all Aunty May's money doing it?"

"Well, I didn't understand about running an ice cream business, Mary. I didn't know it would hurt you when I did it. I just thought it was a nice thing to do for Aunty May. I spent my own money on the ice cream, of course."

"So May didn't pay to open the shop?" said Mary. "Maybe she doesn't have a stash of cash somewhere."

Jerry smiled. *"A stash of cash…"*

"Don't say it, Jerry," Mary said. "I didn't really mean to get all bent about the *ice cream war*. It all worked out and I've made *mucho dinero* having your help at the shop."

"Yeah," said Jerry. "I'm going to miss working there."

"Well, maybe you can keep working there if you want. Until you go back to California, I mean. I would have to pay you, though."

Jerry smiled. "That'd be great. And you don't have to pay me. I'll save money not buying ice cream for Aunty May's shop, and you can take me out on dates every night to pay me."

"I'll pay you a salary, Jerry…and maybe take you out on dates every so often."

"That's a deal."

# Chapter 43

They arrived at the restaurant named Maria's, and Frank and Joan were waiting. The maître d' knew Frank, and escorted them directly to a table near the back.

"Hey, Mary," said Frank, standing to seat her. "You look stunning tonight. This is Joan," he said, indicating the lady seated at the table. "She's a literary agent, helping me with my book."

"What book?" asked Mary.

"He hasn't decided yet," said Joan, extending her hand in greeting.

Mary took it and turned to Jerry. "And this is Jerry, my date," she said pointedly to Frank.

"Glad to meet you," said first Frank and then Joan.

"Frank has already ordered for us," Joan said. "He knows the chef tonight."

There was a server at the table now. "What may I get you to drink?"

"Just some wine," said Joan. "To go with whatever it is we're going to eat."

"Could I have some tonic water too?" asked Jerry.

"No mango?" said Mary.

"Not in a fancy place like this, Mary," said Jerry. Mary frowned at this. Only fancy places would serve mango juice in Nebraska. It must be different in California.

The server left, and Frank looked at Jerry. "So, how do you know Mary?" he asked. "Or should I ask how Mary knows you?"

"I work in her shop," said Jerry, before Mary could speak.

Mary experienced slight embarrassment at this revelation. "He was running a rival shop, so I put an end to that by recruiting him to work for me. It was pretty easy after there was a murder in his shop."

"That would be the murder of Angie, perhaps, with some last name that's still in dispute?" offered Frank. "Interesting. Shall we eat first and talk after the meal?"

"You tantalize me, Frank," said Mary.

"He's good at that," smiled Joan. "Maybe light banter before the meal is served, and that will enhance both the meal and the interesting information. How is it that you know Mary, Jerry? Just rivals turned partners in the ice cream war?"

"We knew each other in high school," said Jerry. "And then...well, my parents died, and I ended up moving out to California. Then my Aunt May asked me to visit, so I came back, and Mary and I decided we liked each other, or at least I decided I like her.

"That was on my first trip a year ago. Aunty May asked me to come back to run the shop again this year, but I wasn't going to come until I remembered Mary. I really came back to see her again. All my friends back in California thought I should."

"All your friends told you to come back to see Mary again?" asked Joan.

"Well, yeah." Jerry shrugged. "I talked a lot about her after my first trip."

"You didn't even recognize me, Jerry," said Mary without thinking.

"No, but I remembered you, and I remembered that I liked you."

"Oh, I like Jerry, too," said Mary, as she began to feel a little defensive. "He's the best surfer I know."

"Really?" said Joan.

Jerry smiled. "I might be the only surfer she knows."

"So, do you run an ice cream shop back in California?" asked Frank, smiling.

"I surf and landscape, but no ice cream in Huntington Beach."

"He works at a drug rehab center, too," said Mary, and immediately realized this sounded like Jerry was in rehab as well.

The conversation lapsed for a moment, and Joan looked around to rescue it. "That's an interesting ring you have, Mary."

"Oh," said Mary, looking at the friendship ring. "Jerry gave that to me. He made it himself," she added, before she realized how foolish that sounded when referring to a folded dollar bill.

"Surfing and landscaping and ice cream shop and makes jewelry," chuckled Frank.

"He teaches at Berkeley, too," Mary said.

"Well, not much teaching, really. Two classes a semester on street drugs and trash talk is all. I landscape and surf during the day." Mary was feeling as if she had to make Jerry admit that he was really successful or something to impress her friends, but Jerry didn't seem to mind that he was just a surfer, and wasn't cooperating with her at all.

Jerry smiled at Frank. "You were a police officer, is that right, Frank? Mary said you were a probation officer too. That's cool. Is that what your book is about?"

"His book is about whatever he's thinking of at the moment," smiled Joan. "Might be about surfing right now."

"Where'd you two meet?" Jerry asked.

"Well," said Joan, "I guess it's like you and Mary. We're both from this little city here in Nebraska, but hadn't ever met. I went to Las Vegas to teach a course on how to get a literary agent interested in you, and Frank came all the way out there just to meet me. He already knew how to get a literary agent interested, or at least how to get *me* interested. Then there was this murder, and he helped solve it and save me, and then I saved him, and then...well...just like you and Mary."

"Yeah," said Jerry. "Mary is the intelligent one though. Did you know she graduated from law school?" Jerry smiled with pride. "Taking a little breather before she takes the bar exam."

"I didn't know that," said Joan.

"She was pretty near the top of her class, if I recall," said Frank, looking at Jerry with skepticism, the way an uncle would look at his favorite niece's new boyfriend.

Mary was becoming a little more embarrassed, for herself and for Jerry, low man at this table it seemed.

"Vegas is nice," said Joan, sensing the tension. "Have you ever been there, Mary?"

"I have once," said Mary. "I lost too much money to go back again."

"Maybe you can take her, Jerry?" said Joan.

"Yes, that would be fun," smiled Jerry.

"Have you ever been?" asked Joan.

"Oh, yeah," Jerry said. "I play out there every couple of months or so."

"Do you win?" asked Joan.

"Oh," said Jerry looking a little embarrassed himself now. "I play poker sometimes, but well...it's not fair to take advantage of people, so I don't play very often."

"Take advantage of people?" asked Frank.

"Well, yeah," said Jerry. "If you learn to read their eyes, you can tell what they're holding. I learned to do that when I was playing with some friends and...well, one of them was a dealer in Las Vegas.

"When I got so I could beat him, I decided it was time to stop. You don't have to get every hand, you know, just often enough to win more than you lose. But that's not fair to the other people, so I don't usually gamble when I'm out there."

Frank was staring in disbelief, while Mary was trying desperately to think of some way to explain Jerry to these people, so it was only Joan who was left with words to speak. "So what do you do in Las Vegas, Jerry, if you don't play, gamble, I mean? If it's not too embarrassing to say here." Joan didn't look like it would be embarrassing for her.

"Oh," said Jerry, blushing a little now too. "I play. Jazz mostly, but I can back up the rock groups too, and even some pop if they don't have anyone else."

"You play jazz?" It was Mary who was asking, and she was immediately embarrassed that she didn't know this already.

"Yeah," said Jerry with a shrug. "Guitar is my favorite. I can do sax, too, but everyone can play a sax. I can do banjo and mandolin if they need that, but no one usually does. Not in Vegas."

"Really?" asked Frank. "You have to be pretty good to play Vegas, don't you?"

"Good, but not real good," said Jerry. "Vegas is where everyone retires to. Performers, I mean. They call it becoming a 'resident'. When they get tired of touring, but can still draw a crowd, Vegas is their home." He shrugged again. "Huntington is different."

"How so?" asked Frank, sounding genuinely interested.

"Well, you see, the clubs there cater to the people from L.A. and down toward the south, and they're pretty knowledgeable about the music. You have to play well or they'll know it, and you won't get to play for them."

"So you're pretty good?" asked Frank.

"I guess," admitted Jerry. "Some of my friends and I have a pretty regular gig up in L.A. and Huntington too, of course. We recorded a few songs. That sort of thing."

"So are you famous, or are you going to be famous?" asked Joan.

"Jazz players don't get famous," smiled Jerry. "They get cool, and that's all. If you want fame, don't play jazz. If you want to play the best music this country ever produced, that's jazz."

He smiled now, and looked as if he were playing some of the best music the country had ever produced in his mind.

That music was interrupted by the wine steward, a lady about Mary's age, with red hair and a pleasant smile that seemed to linger longer on Jerry than on the others. "Can I pour for your approval, sir?" she asked.

Frank smiled and nodded, but the wine steward looked at Jerry again before removing the cork and handing it to Frank. She then poured a small amount into Frank's glass for him to "approve", which he did. She then poured for the others, but when it was Jerry's glass she was about to pour, he turned it upside down. She smiled at him, a puzzled smile, and then retreated to the bar.

"You must be driving, Jerry," offered Joan.

"No," said Jerry absently, and looked at the bar. He turned back to smile at Joan and said, "Excuse me. I'm going to the chamber where even the king goes alone." He rose, nodded slightly to them, and then placed his napkin on his seat, indicating that he would be returning.

"*Where even the king goes alone* where?" asked Frank.

"The little boy's room, Frank. To pay the water bill, to powder his nose, or whatever men do in there. Where did you find him, Mary?" said Joan.

"Oh, it's like I said.... He—"

"He's adorable. So nice and interesting, and interested in us, too. And handsome!" said Joan.

"I don't know," said Frank.

They all looked over to see Jerry chatting with the wine steward, or maybe she was the bar maid now. She was smiling, and then making gestures of surprise, and then she leaned over to hug him. Finally she pointed down the nearby hall and Jerry proceeded, and she followed.

"Yes, I'm sure there's a reason for that," said Mary, with visions of Sandy and Jasmine in her head.

"Oh, the two of you," said Joan. "Jerry is cute, but you can beat her off, Mary. Offer to arm-wrestle her."

They watched as Jerry emerged, followed by the wine steward. They both returned to the table, but the wine steward stopped to speak to the maître d', who looked at their table and nodded. As she approached the table, the background music changed from the Italian folk to a jazzy piece.

"Oh, Jerry," she said. "I didn't recognize you all dressed up and everything, and here in Nebraska. I thought you might like some California wine. Wanta try this?" she said, holding up a bottle that said something about Napa Valley on the label.

"I brought extra glasses," she added, holding up three wine glasses.

"Sure, Kathy," said Jerry, turning his wine glass right side up.

"Okay then," said Kathy, as she pulled the cork out, discarding it this time. She looked at Mary as she began to pour, not a small taste but full glasses. "How are you doin', Mary? It's been ages, hasn't it?"

Jerry looked at Mary's bewildered face. "You remember Kathy. She went to high school with us."

"Kathy?!" said Mary. "You had—"

"Yeah. Black hair, and way too much makeup. But I was young then. You haven't changed a bit, Mary. Still gorgeous without even trying. Color me totally jealous."

Kathy finished the pouring of the wine. "Try it," she said.

"I didn't recognize her at first either," said Jerry, as he picked up his glass and let the wine touch his lips as the others tasted theirs. None of Jerry's was swallowed.

"Good wine," said Joan. "So, Kathy, you didn't recognized Jerry?"

"No," shrugged Kathy. "He looked familiar in that way that people look when you know them from somewhere else."

"It's been years," said Mary. "I still don't believe it's you. You look so different."

"Yeah, well, that's Jerry's fault." She struck a casual pose as she looked around the near-empty restaurant, deciding that it could do without a wine steward or a bar maid for a few minutes. "When I turned thirty, my creep of a boyfriend decided to go out to California. It was back a couple years ago, and like a ninny, I decided to go with him. I don't think he wanted that, but anyway, one day he went to work and never came back."

She shrugged. "So I'm like, destitute in Huntington Beach, California, and who do I run into, but Jerry. What was the name of that rehab again?"

"West End," said Jerry.

"Yeah, well, Jerry told me to clean up and he'd see if he could get me a job and, well...I did, and he did. First serving tables and then bartending at this club he plays at. A couple years he starts playin' in Vegas every so often, and I tried to talk him into getting me a job there, but instead he finds me this job back home."

"You like it back home, Kathy?" asked Joan.

"I do now. Didn't then. I thought Jerry was rad." She smiled, and Jerry blushed. "Playin' jazz at night, and surfin' the day. Counselin' at the rehab and even teaching at the Berkeley School of Law. And he's the grass specialist for...what was the name of that company you worked for, Jerry?"

"Zen Landscaping," said Jerry. "We own it, really."

"Yeah," said Kathy. "Ya know people would call askin' for him special. 'Course that's California." She shrugged. "They are crazy about their grass in Southern Cal."

"The grass specialist?" asked Frank.

"Lawn grass, Frank. Seed and sod, you know. Not marijuana. No one calls that *grass* anymore," said Mary.

"Well, I knew that too," said Frank.

"They still call it grass here in Nebraska sometimes," said Kathy. "Only thing wrong with Jerry was Laura."

"Laura?" asked Mary.

"Yeah," said Kathy. "She was loony tunes all right. And Jerry was living with her."

"Living with her?" asked Frank.

"Yeah, well in his apartment. Nothing sexual between them, except in Laura's mind. Poor Jerry was just too softhearted to throw her out. And then to top it off, Angie shows up and she makes Laura look like the most normal person on earth."

"Angie? Laura's sister you mean?" said Mary.

"I don't think so," Kathy said.

"That's what—" began Mary.

"Why don't you think they were sisters, Kathy?" asked Frank.

"Just didn't act like it. Laura was like looking after Angie sometimes. Keeping her from screwin' up too bad, but...well, one time Laura says it's her birthday an' she goin' to celebrate, and Angie asks her when it is."

Joan smiled. "Lots of sisters don't remember when their sister's birthday is."

"Yeah, I guess," said Kathy, "but Laura didn't seem to think Angie should remember it. Like she just said, oh it's two days from now, like there was no reason Angie should know when it was. Strange a sister wouldn't know, and strange a sister wouldn't expect her sister to know. You could ask 'em."

Mary looked down at the table as Jerry said, "Angie is dead, Kathy."

"Oh, wow," said Kathy. "An OD?"

"No," said Mary. "She was shot to death a couple days ago."

"Oh, wow!" said Kathy. "Was that Angie that was on the news? They didn't give her name, but...well, she was always living way too close to the edge."

# Chapter 44

The meal arrived and Kathy was about to leave when the owner, Louis, came over. "Hey, Frank. How come ya didn't say you were friends with the celebrities?"

Frank looked at Louis, but recovered quickly. "Friend of a friend, really. Jerry, do you know Louis? He's the owner." Jerry rose to extend a hand.

"Jerry Wilson from big old California and Las Vegas, too," Kathy said, and smiled at Louis.

"Yeah, I play a little," said Jerry.

"You sound pretty good," said Louis.

"You've heard him play?" asked Joan.

"Sure," smiled Louis. "You have too." He pointed to the music somewhere above him. "What's this one called?"

"*Surf's down,*" said Jerry. "I'm doing the guitar on this one and Stan's on keyboard."

"Stan from the Huntington Beach Police?" asked Mary.

"Yeah," said Jerry. "He's okay on keyboard." Jerry shrugged, making it clear that okay meant not that good.

"So, I wanted to talk to you, Jerry. You interested?"

Jerry seemed to know what the talk would be about, although Mary was having trouble, and Frank and Joan seemed totally puzzled too. "Later, maybe, after we eat. That be okay?"

"Sure," said Louis. "See if you guys can talk him into it and I'll buy you dinner. We close at one tonight." Louis and Kathy walked away smiling. It looked as if Louis might be one of the reasons Kathy didn't mind being back home.

"I had them bring a vegetarian marinara, too," said Jerry, blushing a little. "I don't usually eat meat." He then began to pass the pasta and sauces around the table, along with the chicken and meatballs, and people began to serve themselves and eat.

"No meat in ice cream," said Joan.

Jerry smiled and nodded. "If we have to leave by one, maybe we had better hear what you think about all this, Frank."

Frank sampled the meal he had before him. "It is interesting. What do you really know about these two ladies who may be sisters, Jerry?"

"I like ice cream, but this is really good too," said Jerry, looking at Joan.

He took another bite and turned to face Frank. "I was moving into a new apartment in Huntington, closer to the landscaping garage we use, and Laura was getting evicted. She asked if she could stay a few days 'til she got her act together, and...well, that turned into three months. She never paid much rent, but she cooked a little. She was using a lot, and I tried to get her into treatment, but that went nowhere."

"Using drugs, you mean?" asked Joan.

"Yeah," said Jerry. "She worked the streets and dealt the drugs sometimes I think, but none of the reputable dealers wanted to have anything to do with her."

"Like Carlos?" asked Mary. She turned toward Frank and Joan to add, "Carlos is a reputable dealer."

"Yeah," said Jerry, as if he were talking about a restaurant or laundry service. "Carlos would pimp for her, but he never let her deal his drugs. He couldn't trust her. Anyway, she was gradually sliding down, and even the dealers weren't willing to sell to her because she didn't pay.

"Then Angie showed up. Actually, Laura brought her around, and she must have had some money, because Laura had some money, and I don't think she could have gotten it anywhere else except from Angie."

"When was this?" asked Frank.

"Six or seven months ago, maybe. Laura still stayed at the apartment for another month or so, and Angie was there a couple of times, but I...well, I wasn't comfortable there, and I was going up to Berkeley and that's six hours driving, and then out to play in Vegas too, so I wasn't really there too much. I'd stay with Stan, too."

"Your apartment, and you left it for them?" asked Joan and Jerry nodded, without any hint that there was anything unusual about this.

"They needed a place to stay, and I wasn't there that much." He shrugged.

"So maybe seven months ago, Angie shows up, and Laura suddenly has some money, not for rent, I'm guessing," Frank asked.

"No," agreed Jerry.

"And then they what? Just split? Free apartment and they left?"

"Yeah, well, I'm not sure it's important, but I may as well tell you the story." Jerry looked embarrassed as he glanced at Joan. "Sorry to be talking like this in front of you, Joan," he said.

Joan was surprised. "Oh...I mean, I've heard...well...well, I'm not going to leave. If Frank and Mary can...Well, just say it, and I'm sure I'll...Just say it, Jerry."

"It's just that Frank is a police officer and Mary already knows most of it, but I don't want you to think less of me for what happened."

Joan was still surprised, but managed to speak a little more coherently this time. "I'll not think any less of you, Jerry, although if it is really good, I'll suggest that you write a book about it."

Jerry shrugged. "You're a literary agent, aren't you? This isn't what a good book should be about. You see, Laura earned her money working the street."

"That would be prostitution, right, Jerry?" said Joan.

"Well, yeah, and she really liked to brag about how good she was, too. Most of the working girls couldn't care less. It's just another job for them. But Laura was always bragging, and she would...well, brag about me."

Whatever anyone had expected Joan to say wasn't what she said. "Well, I can understand that. You're a really attractive man, Jerry, and I can understand that a woman would want to brag about having sex with you." Jerry blushed and Mary giggled, but Frank nearly fell off his seat.

"I'm not propositioning him, Frank, but women can be the same as men are about their conquests."

"I guess so," said Frank.

"I'll not brag about you, Frank, and I'm sure you will be worthy of bragging about too. But I can see how Laura would brag about Jerry."

"But ya see, we never really had sex. A couple times when Laura practically—"

"Raped you?" offered Joan. Frank was crimson red now in his embarrassment, and Mary was giggling uncontrollably. Fortunately the restaurant was nearly empty now.

Jerry nodded. "Yeah, sort of."

Mary gained enough composure to say, "Jerry says he only wants to have sex with someone he loves."

"And that would be you, I hope."

Mary was now blushing a little. "Not me, yet."

"And Frank is waiting patiently too," said Joan. "We've only known each other a month now."

"That's the way it should be," said Jerry.

"Yes," said Joan. "Is the rest of this story interesting too?"

Jerry smiled. "Not really. Laura was always bragging, and we were at my club one night and she was doing her usual, and I just said that we hadn't had sex in like a month. When she said I was lying, I told her she was so wasted she wouldn't have known, and...well, she was wasted that night, and everyone pretty much knew it."

"And," said Joan. "You did use condoms when you were raped, right, Jerry?"

"Of course."

"Good," said Joan in her best stern motherly tone.

Frank cleared his throat. "Not to interrupt, but was Angie there when you...what would you call it, confronted, Laura?"

"Yeah," said Jerry. "They were hanging out together pretty much all the time by then. Anyway, next day she was gone, and so was Angie. They left some clothes behind, and I still have those, but I never heard from them again. I think Angie was trying to get to me a couple times, but we never connected. I never really tried."

"Hm," said Joan. "Kathy didn't think Laura and you were having sex either." She looked at Mary, not at Jerry. "So, what do you have to tell us, Frank?"

"I can add a few wrinkles to the drama," he smiled. "Laura has a hard time in the computer."

"Oh," said Mary and Joan simultaneously.

"I can't get into the police or government files, but what I do get suggests that there used to be a minor felon working L.A., who seems to match Laura's profile until about six months ago. She was named Laura Smith, by the way."

"That was what she told me her name was," said Jerry.

"Okay," said Frank, "but that might be the only thing she told the truth about. She had a few arrests for drug stuff and prostitution, which is illegal in California, but not in Vegas."

"Outside the city," Joan corrected.

"Yes, thank you," smiled Frank. "Trouble is, Laura Smith disappears, and not to Las Vegas, or at least there are no arrests, credit cards, drivers...well, I can find none of the usual traces present for anyone that's not a hermit. Laura Smith wasn't a hermit when she disappeared from the computer. She didn't die or anything, she just isn't there."

"She didn't die, so she got herself a new identity, that's all," said Mary.

"Only if she got herself new fingerprints, too. Laura is on the various watch lists, and she's in and out of the records that I can access. She had a couple court appearances even, but than seven months ago...well, her court appearances disappear. She isn't picked up for any felonies or misdemeanors or anything, but all of a sudden there's Laura Steward, who bears a striking resemblance to the Smith with the same first name."

"I'm not following this, Frank," said Mary.

"Neither am I," said Frank. "Whatever happened seven months ago is something I have no explanation for. Laura Smith disappears. And no one seems to notice it."

"How can that be?" asked Mary.

"It can't, not without some major work from the inside, anyway." Frank shrugged now. "The security on the computers is tight, so I couldn't get into it enough to know how or even what was done. Laura Smith is in the Los Angeles police records, and disappears, and Laura Steward shows up in Huntington Beach, but what is curious is that all of the Smith records seem to have stayed in L.A., and Laura Steward starts a fresh file in her new home. To do that, someone had to really do some major purging in the L.A. computers."

"Wouldn't they check her fingerprints?" asked Mary.

"They certainly would, but there don't appear to be any for Laura Smith. I can't get into her records, but apparently the *'no such person'* e-mails are not considered that big a deal. Huntington requested records, including fingerprints, from L.A. and got a *'no such'* back from them."

"Did Washington send the prints?" asked Mary.

"It doesn't look as if they were ever requested from Washington," said Frank. "That's interesting. It used to be standard procedure, and probably still is."

"What about Angie?" asked Mary.

Frank smiled. "You didn't ask me to look into Angie, but fortunately I took some initiative. Angie existed right along. Right along as of two or three years ago. I couldn't get any birth certificates or school records or anything like that, but she may have changed her name or something simple, and I didn't really have time to look into it. I will." He winked.

"She has no background, though. No family or that sort of thing right now, and her name seems to have been Steward in all the records I did find. She's had a couple problems with the police, but nothing major. She does seem to have a source of income as you suggested, Jerry. When she gets into trouble she gets a lawyer; her own lawyer, not a public defender. Laura is the puzzle, and I don't think Laura and Angie were sisters."

"Wouldn't someone, I mean some person, have noticed that Laura wasn't there? That she wasn't in the computer?" asked Joan.

"The L.A. police are not going to be too concerned if she isn't on the street anymore. They might not even notice. She wasn't on probation in L.A.; that happened in Huntington. But the requests for records? Someone from Huntington asked for them and didn't get them, and someone looked for them in L.A. and didn't find them. I don't see how they couldn't realize that the records had been erased, unless they were told not to notice."

"Told not to?" asked Joan.

"Whoever did this was a very ingenious and probably a very powerful individual."

"Who?" asked Mary.

Frank shrugged. "The guys who hack into computers can get past any security if they really want to, but it has to be worth the effort. Then there are the people involved. Someone is making sure no one asks why Laura Smith is suddenly no longer in the system. Even her fingerprints are no longer in the system. This could be done, but only with a great deal of effort, and Laura doesn't seem like the kind of person someone would go to this much effort for. Someone got her out of L.A. and down to Huntington Beach, but, and this is important, without giving her any money. Then Angie comes along with the money."

They were quiet for a moment. "Any ideas, Jerry?" asked Frank.

"I didn't know Angie that well, but Laura...well, I don't think anyone would have gone to any effort at all for her."

"But it was Laura they made the effort for," said Mary. "Could she have been blackmailing one of her clients?"

"Maybe," said Frank, "but it's still a lot of trouble. She would have had to have the client first, too. She wasn't very discreet either, which means if she had a client who cared whether he was named by Laura, she would probably have already told everyone about him."

Jerry shrugged. "I don't think Laura had any clients that were like that."

"What about Angie?" asked Joan.

"I don't know about Angie," said Jerry. "I didn't know her very well. She was wild and seemed to think it was all just fun or something. I don't know, but I don't think she would have gone to any trouble for Laura, either."

"But someone killed Angie," said Mary. "Could it have been Laura? And why would she have killed her?"

"Maybe Stan picked up Laura and she can tell us what's going on," said Jerry.

"Tell him to find out why Laura has two names and isn't in the LAPD computer anymore and that may give him a lead," said Frank.

Mary thought a moment. "There was that guy who bought her ticket for her, or at least for Sally Smart. James Forsyth. Could she have been blackmailing him?"

"Or could he be her sugar daddy?" asked Joan.

"Ask Stan," suggested Frank. "He's local. He'll know. He's a local cop who is doing the job he's paid to do. He probably doesn't even know the records are missing, because he doesn't need them. Laura Steward gets in trouble and he knows who she is, so the records don't matter."

"So it's not Stan who's hiding Laura's records," said Mary.

"Stan couldn't have done this," smiled Frank.

Louis was at the table now. "Time to close, paisanos. What do you think, Mr. Wilson?"

Jerry smiled. "The food was excellent. What would you like me to do?"

"Well," smiled Louis. "I've been thinking of a Sunday brunch kind of thing."

Jerry just nodded.

"Maybe a few hours, late morning to early afternoon. I could maybe pay a couple hundred."

Jerry looked pensive a moment. "I'm union so it would have to be union pay. I don't want to get in trouble with them."

"Yeah, well, okay," said Louis.

"And the minimum time is four hours, with two half-hour breaks. I sometimes play through the breaks if I'm into the music, but the breaks are in the agreement, okay? That's standard and I don't—"

"You don't want to get in trouble with the musician's union," smiled Louis. "Neither do I. I don't know as much as you, though. This is my first real, what do you guys call it: a gig?"

"It's a 'gig' for me," smiled Jerry. "It's a job or a booking for you. I'll get my own guitar and amps. Just music, no vocal, and just me to start. You'll have to have room for me, and if you want a platform you'll have to provide it. I provide the instruments and me, that's all. If you want more players, I get to pick them, not you. You'll have to decide about things like requests and tips, but whatever you want is good with me. I don't usually drink alcohol so it would be helpful if you let the bar staff know that so they don't let people buy me drinks. Oh, and I'll have to make sure it's okay with Mary for me to take the time off from the ice cream shop."

"Okay," said Louis, with just a hint of bewilderment. "Should you start this Sunday?"

"I don't know," said Jerry, and looked at Mary. "Can I start this Sunday, Mary?"

"I don't know, can you start this Sunday, Louis?"

There was silence for a minute until Louis said, "I can start this Sunday."

"Can you get the word out that quickly?" asked Joan.

"Well..." began Louis.

"I can help spread it around the computer if you want, Louis," said Frank.

"Yeah, sure. That'd be great, but can he do it this Sunday?" Everyone first looked at Jerry, who looked at Mary, and everyone turned to look at her.

"Well, I can manage the shop for a few hours, for God's sake. Jerry can play here and then come to the shop, and play there, maybe."

"Your shop ain't in the city, is it? I don't want any competition with my gig here."

"It's not a 'gig' for you, Louis, just for me," corrected Jerry.

"My ice cream shop is outside the city, Louis," said Mary.

"Good. Ten to two, and thanks for spreadin' it on the computer, Frankie. Come by on Sunday, okay? And don't worry about tonight's meal."

With this Louis turned to leave and Joan said, "I'll put a sign up in my office window, Louis."

"And I'll put up a sign in my window, too," added Mary.

"Oh, yeah, thanks," said Louis, waving.

Chapter 45

"You know, this meal tastes even better now that it's free," said Joan as they walked toward their respective cars.

"So we'll make up a couple of posters," she continued. "I have a friend at a print shop who can have them by tomorrow afternoon, and I'll drop one or two out at your place, okay, Mary?"

"Sure. Only two days, but Jerry has already got a bunch of groupies out our way," said Mary, with more enthusiasm than she thought she would have. This meeting was supposed to have been about a murder, not a "Jazz Gig."

"What shall we put on the poster, Jerry? *From Huntington Beach and Las Vegas*, and...well, do you play in L.A. or San Francisco?" asked Joan.

"In L.A. sometimes," said Jerry.

"What's your group called?" asked Joan.

"Jazz Surfers," said Jerry.

"Everything is about surfing for Jerry," said Mary.

"Not everything," objected Jerry.

"Okay. What isn't about surfing?"

Jerry looked puzzled for a minute and Mary finally said, "This could take a while, Joan. Can he get back to you on that?"

"Sure," Joan nodded. "And you're the lead artist in Jazz Surfers, right?"

"Well, not—"

"Of course," said Mary.

"I don't want to hurt the other guys' feelings, ya know," Jerry replied.

"Who is better than you?"

"Well..."

"Truth is truth, Jerry. Stan isn't that good on the keyboard, is he?"

"Well..."

"Are any of the others as good as you are? All I heard on that piece in the restaurant was an awesome guitar and some other guys backing it up," said Mary.

"But the other guys—" began Jerry.

"So it's Jerry Wilson, star performer with Jazz Surfers, from Huntington Beach, L.A. and Las Vegas," said Mary. "No relation to Brian Wilson."

"Who is Brian Wilson?" asked Joan.

"The Beach Boys, Joan," said Frank. "Ya want some help setting up on Sunday, Jerry?"

"Yeah, sure," said Jerry. "About nine maybe."

"The Beach Boys?" said Joan as they walked away. "They were a rock group, right?"

"Let me write up the stuff for the poster, okay?" replied Frank.

"Why?" was the last thing Mary heard Joan say, and she didn't hear Frank's answer.

"At least we don't have to get up early tomorrow morning, but we'd better get this murder solved before Sunday." She slipped her hand through Jerry's arm without thinking as they walked to her car and Jerry smiled, but did nothing to remove it.

"Ya know, Mary," he said.

"What, Jerry?" Mary replied.

"You should take the bar exam."

Mary stopped for a second to look at him. "Maybe," she finally said, and they walked to the car and drove to her apartment.

They settled in once they arrived, and Mary thought ever so briefly about a different sleeping arrangement, but dismissed it at once. Jerry was a nice guy, and he had moved from the *never in this lifetime* list to the *maybe sometime* list partly because Joan had thought he was so "adorable", but he would be gone soon, back to California and the California girls, and Mary would miss him a little, and...well, it was better not to get involved. Jerry settled on the couch without any attempt at anything else anyway, and Mary wondered if he would have been interested if she had been interested.

"I'll sleep in my underwear tonight," he said, pulling the covers he had neatly folded that morning over him. "Good thing you thought to have me wear them."

"Yes," said Mary, thinking that she had made the right decision on underwear and sleeping arrangements.

Jerry removed the last fragment of doubt when he said, "You can have the shower in the morning since I showered yesterday and won't need to shower again. I'll wear the same clothes tomorrow since all my stuff is at the shop anyway."

"Yes," said Mary again, and headed for her room. She turned as she entered and smiled. "Good night, Jerry." Her smile expanded and she added, *"Sleep tight, and don't let the bed bugs bite."*

Jerry smiled as if this were the most natural thing to say. "Good night, Mary."

Mary settled into her bed and decided not to think of anything tonight. She was tired and she could sleep in a little in the morning, and Jerry would be there in the morning too. It turned out that Mary was wrong. At four in the morning, after only two hours of sleep, her phone rang.

At first she thought it was a dream, and then she thought that someone should answer that annoying phone, and finally she woke enough to realize that she was *the someone* who should answer it. "Hello," she said.

"What?"

"You want Jerry? Who the hell is this?"

"Oh, hi, Stan. Captain Bradshaw, I mean. That was my TV you just heard. I wish they wouldn't use that horrible language on all the shows now. What, oh Jerry, yeah. You already asked for him once, didn't you? He's sleeping in the next room. *Alone* in the next room, the same as I'm sleeping *alone* in this room. Let me get him for you."

Mary stood and faced the dilemma. She was in her nightgown, which was less than she would ever have let Jerry see her in, but her robe was somewhere in the back of her closet, and to put on anything else would take a lot longer.

She quickly decided that making Stan wait *a lot* longer would probably encourage him to think there was *a lot* more going on in her bedroom, and she didn't want that thought to get any more traction than it already had. Maybe Stan would be calling her father next? Maybe Jerry wouldn't notice her nightgown? Maybe she should just give Jerry the phone?

So a few seconds later she was standing over a sleeping Jerry, nudging him and saying, "Jerry. Jerry! Wake up! It's Stan, and it's..."

She put the phone to her ear and said, "What time is it in Huntington, Stan?"

"Oh, only 2:00 a.m. there. A much more reasonable hour. Take the phone, Jerry."

She handed it to Jerry, who was looking at her, half-asleep, but looking as if he was noticing what she was wearing.

"The phone," Mary said again.

"Oh, yeah," said Jerry. "That's a nice color for you, Mary. The blue matches your eyes."

Jerry put the phone to his ear. "Hi, Stan. Whazzup?"

Mary thought of looking for her robe, but the damage had already been done to her modest image, and she wanted to know what crisis in the California surf could be this important. She did sit in the chair, not on the couch next to Jerry at least.

"Oh, you did get her," Jerry said, waking completely now.

"First class? What name?'

Jerry looked again at Mary and she began to feel just a little uncomfortable at his wide-eyed stare. "Mary Burke?!" asked Jerry.

"What about me?" asked Mary.

Jerry held the phone away slightly. "Laura was flying using your name, Mary. That's all."

"Did she charge it on my credit card?!"

"Did she charge it on Mary's card?"

Jerry listened and then shook his head. "Not on your card, but she did have your driver's license."

Mary was already going through her purse and produced her license. "I have it right here," she said.

Jerry looked up and said, "Wow. Not that one, Mary. It was a California license."

"But I don't have a California license."

"She doesn't have a…. Oh. Stan thinks it's fake," he said, holding the phone slightly away again.

He put it back to his ear and frowned. "Who did you say?"

"Wow," said Jerry. "I've heard of him, but why..."

"Well, you're going to hold her anyway, right?"

"What do you mean?"

Jerry sat listening for a long time now, and Mary thought he might have been disconnected or something, but finally Jerry just said, "Wow."

"Oh, yeah? Really? Okay. Yeah, we got to go back to bed, but call back, okay?"

"What? Sure she can, but tell her she has to wax, okay? Make sure you tell her to do that, Stan."

"Yeah, later, man."

"Back to separate beds, in separate rooms, Stan!" yelled Mary. "Oh, hell, what's the use? Jerry, you're going to have to get a cell phone, so people can call you without calling me first."

Chapter 46

They sat for a few seconds, with Jerry frowning and looking at the floor, not at Mary in her nightgown at least, while Mary wondered first if he was thinking about her, and then what he was thinking about if not about her, and finally why he wasn't saying what he was thinking about.

"What are you thinking about, Jerry?" she asked.

"What?" replied Jerry, looking up.

"The call? You remember, it was just now? From Stan? At four in the morning, Nebraska time that is. What was it about?"

Jerry looked at her and she added, "Not my nightgown I hope."

"No," said Jerry. "It is pretty, but..."

"I'll make it simple then. Not the nightgown. Hide your disappointment, Mary," she said. "Who has to wax, and is waxing really popular among the women in California? It's losing popularity here in Nebraska I think."

"Oh," said Jerry. "It's Nancy. I don't think she waxes, but I can ask. Anyway, she asked if she could borrow my board and I said sure, but she never waxes hers. Her board I mean. That's why she wants to borrow mine, so I asked Stan to—"

"I just knew it would be about surfing," said Mary. "So now on to the unimportant part. Laura (I'm guessing), flew first class (probably not that important, but typical of Laura), to California using my name and my California license, (which I'll have to remember to cancel as soon as I get one), and was picked up by Stan? Is that pretty close?"

"Yeah," said Jerry.

"And how did she get a driver's license in my name? And before she came out here, which was probably before Angie was murdered, and before you had even met me again?"

"Well," said Jerry. "I told everybody I was coming out here to see you again."

"You told Laura that?"

"Not Laura. I hadn't even seen her in months, but she probably heard from someone. Ya see, all my friends think I should have a girlfriend."

"Even Laura and Angie?"

"Well, no. I think they think I *shouldn't* have a girlfriend, or that the girlfriends should be one of them. I kept telling them how great Mary Burke was."

"But you didn't even recognize me when we met, Jerry. You didn't even remember my name."

"But I remembered you. It's not just about physical stuff or names, Mary. It's about your karma."

"So it was my karma that you came back here for and the rest of me is just...we can straighten that out later, okay? So anyway, Laura somehow got a driver's license in my name, which she remembered even if you didn't, and flew out here for some reason I can't figure out yet, but I hope it wasn't my karma, and now Stan has her in custody, and he'll find out all about it, right?"

"Well, yeah, except that…"

"Except that what?"

"Well, Stan traced the ticket to this guy, James Forsyth, and he's a big real estate mover in Huntington Beach, *J. F. Realty*. Stan thinks he may be trafficking, too."

"Trafficking?"

"Yeah," shrugged Jerry. "Some of the construction stuff comes up from Mexico, and they think he has drugs in the shipments. Cocaine probably, but—"

"So Laura's got herself a sugar daddy?" interrupted Mary. "What little I know about Laura, and I don't really want to know any more, would be consistent with her choosing a rich drug dealer as her daddy."

"Stan didn't think that was it. Laura's not that good. He'd already been out to talk to this guy Forsyth about the ticket and said he wasn't too concerned about Laura, or his lawyer wasn't, until Stan mentioned that this all related to Angie's murder. I guess Mr. Forsyth lost it completely then, crying and then screaming and...well, his lawyer told Stan to leave and he did; to pick up Laura. Stan didn't know about the second ticket, the one with your name on it, until he picked Laura up."

"Okay, but Stan has Laura and will keep her until he can talk to Mr. Forsyth again, right?"

"Well, that's just it. Laura has a real expensive lawyer, and Stan thinks he'll push hard to get bail set and that Laura will—"

"Skip bail. Is that what they say?"

"Yeah, sometimes," said Jerry.

"So pretty soon Laura will be out again, and...can she get another one of my driver's licenses? Do they have a limit to the number of driver's licenses you can get in California? Nebraska does, I think."

"I don't think she can," said Jerry.

"Too much to think about on too little sleep. Good night for the second time this morning, Jerry," said Mary, and headed for her bedroom.

Jerry lay down on the couch and Mary on her bed, and both tried to sleep, but neither managed to even doze. It was Mary who found herself standing next to Jerry two hours later.

"Jerry," she said.

"Yeah."

"I've been thinking about this, and I think we have to do something about it."

"Well..." said Jerry, "I was thinking we should wait."

"Wait for what?"

"Well, it's just a little fast, that's all."

"What's a little fast? What are we talking about?"

"You know, about..." Jerry frowned, and his embarrassment made it clear what he was talking about.

"Sex?" said Mary.

"Well...yeah, I think we should wait."

Mary glared at him. "Yeah, I think we should wait, but that's not what I was talking about."

"Oh," said Jerry. "Sorry, but—"

"Oh, never mind," said Mary. "I'm not sure whether I should be flattered that you think about that with me, or annoyed that that's all you think about. I'm worried about Laura."

"Laura didn't mean anything to me, Mary. I told you that."

"Jerry! This is not about sex! This is about murder, for God's sake."

"Oh, Angie? She didn't mean—"

"Jerry! Stop it right now. Sex is not the only thing in life." Mary paused to look at Jerry, sitting bare-chested in his underwear, and she added, "It might be the most important thing in life, but it is not the only thing. Put your tee shirt on for God's sake. I don't sit around baring my chest, do I?"

"It's different for a woman," said Jerry, "and you're only wearing a nightgown."

"I couldn't find my robe," said Mary, as she looked at his tanned and muscular chest again and said, "It is not different for a woman, now put your tee shirt on and I'll get something to put over my nightgown too, if that will help."

Mary went back into her bedroom as Jerry reached for his tee shirt.

When Mary returned she had a flannel shirt over her nightgown, and Jerry was in his tee shirt.

"I'm afraid Laura is going be murdered if we don't do something," said Mary.

"Laura?"

"Yes, so get Stan on the phone and put the phone on speaker, so I can explain it to both of you."

Jerry took the phone she handed him. "You really think we should call him at this time in the morning?'

"Yes. He called me at four in the morning and it's four in the morning in California now, so call him. That's probably the time he likes to talk on the phone, don't you think?"

Jerry dialed and put the phone on speaker before a sleepy voice answered. "Hello?"

"Hello, Stan. This is Mary, and I'm sorry to wake you, even though you woke me two hours ago."

"Oh, that's okay. I've only been asleep about half an hour."

Mary shook her head, trying to get the logic in that, but finally just asked, "You're a good friend of Jerry's, aren't you, Stan? That would explain it."

"Well, yeah. Is that what you called about? I mean, are you serious about Jerry? I think he's a real nice guy and he needs a nice girl, too."

"He's also listening to all this since we're on speaker here, and that's not what I called about. I think Laura is in danger, and I want to tell you why I think that, so you can do something about it if you agree with me. Do you really think I should get serious about Jerry?"

"About Jerry? Yeah, I think so. What do you think?"

"Maybe, I'll call you later," said Mary. "Right now it's Laura I want to talk about. Is she still in custody?"

"She was when I went to sleep."

"That would be half an hour ago, right?"

"Thirty-five minutes now," said Stan.

"Yeah," said Mary, shaking her stubbornly logical head again. "Look, Stan. Laura is the mystery woman here. Why was she here in Nebraska? Why was she friends with Angie? Why does she have a high-priced lawyer in her corner now, and...Why?"

"Well—"said Stan.

"You're still asleep, Stan, so let me do some of the thinking for you, okay?"

Mary interpreted the pause that followed to indicate agreement and continued. "This guy James Forsyth is buying tickets for Laura, right? Could he also be the source of the money Laura started showing up with back a few months ago? Someone messed with the computer records, someone rich and powerful. Could that have been Forsyth too?

"Maybe," continued Mary, "but he's not upset when she's about to be jailed. Why? Then there's Angie. She has her own lawyer when she gets in trouble, just like Laura has now. Could that be the same lawyer, by the way? I hadn't thought of that."

"I can check," said Stan, who sounded fully awake now.

"Anyway, everybody says Laura was looking after Angie, and that Angie was one wild child. Do you think that was exactly what Laura was doing? And do you think Laura would do that out of concern for a fellow human being, or... Well, Laura has money, and Laura has first-class plane tickets, and Laura is looking after Angie, and...am I the only one who thinks this is not a coincidence?

"And so the next piece of this early morning puzzle is why was James Forsyth supporting Laura? Was she his mistress and still working the streets? I'm no expert, but that isn't the way I pictured the mistress role among the wealthy, so Laura must be providing some other service, right? And the only other service we know she's providing is watching Angie, right? If she's watching after Angie, that would explain why she was here in Nebraska, wouldn't it? Was she following Angie here? Was that what James Forsyth was paying her to do?

"Okay, so next question: If James Forsyth is paying Laura, and what he's paying her to do is to watch after Angie, why is he doing that? You said he was really upset when he heard Angie was dead, right? So maybe she was something special to him. Not a mistress, but maybe a daughter or something?

"Does, or did, James Forsyth have a family member or something like that who could have been Angie? I have trouble seeing the wealthy getting upset about a prostitute, even in California. My friend out here, Frank Gregorio, can't find any record of Angie back beyond about two or three years."

"It does make sense of what didn't make sense," said Stan. "I couldn't figure this guy Forsyth getting so upset about...unless Angie was—"

Mary interrupted, "But why is he trying to get Laura out of jail? Is he still supporting her after she let Angie get herself killed? Or is he planning to pay her for screwing up? Is he the kind of guy who would feel an obligation to his employees even if they failed to perform their assigned task, or is he the kind that would kill them for their failure?"

Jerry spoke for the first time. "Stan. I was wondering why Laura came to ID Angie at all. I thought it might be the jewelry, but maybe it was to ID her as someone she wasn't, so she could have a little time before Forsyth found out she screwed up, ya think?"

"That makes sense," said Mary. "And Angie had a locket on, didn't she? We still have that. I wonder whose picture might be in it?"

"I wonder," said Stan. "Look, can you...?"

"Probably not, whatever you were going to suggest," said Mary. "But you can get Peter a picture of James Forsyth easy enough, and he can see if it looks like the picture in the locket, if there is one. Laura was annoyed that we hadn't given her that locket. Something is in it."

"Yeah," said Stan. "The picture will be on its way as soon as I can get to it."

"Does Forsyth know where Angie died?" asked Mary.

"Not from me," replied Stan. "He'll suspect it was in Nebraska since that's where he's been buying tickets to, but it will take a little time to track it down closer than that, especially since Angie is ID'd as Stewart. Her name isn't even mentioned in the news coverage yet."

"Maybe we had better get this murder solved before James Forsyth does track it down and starts to randomly dispose of suspects in a fit of vengeance."

"Yes," said Stan, neither confirming Mary's fears nor denying them.

"Laura had my driver's license and a ticket in my name, right?" asked Mary. "So am I in California now? Was Laura planning to set me up somehow? Was Angie in on it? Were they planning to get rid of their competition?" Mary looked quickly at Jerry.

Stan was quiet for a few seconds as Mary's anxiety notched itself up. "Forsyth is probably no longer fooled by Laura's game," he said. "He knows Laura used a fake name and that the ticket bought for 'Mary Burke' was used by Laura. He's probably the only one who knows exactly what's going on. Take care of yourself though."

"Stan," said Jerry. "Take care of Laura too, will you?"

"I'll try, Jerry. And Mary. Call me later, okay? About Jerry, I mean. Got to go now."

"Goodnight, Stan," said Mary, "and don't let the bad guys bite."

Stan hung up and Mary frowned for a moment. "Laura gave me her return ticket and told me to cash it in. I wonder if she wanted my name to be on the...?"

"But you didn't cash it in, did you?" asked Jerry.

"No," said Mary.

"Honesty is its own reward," replied Jerry.

"It might be today," said Mary.

# Chapter 47

They looked at each other until Mary said, "That was a good meal last night, and I enjoyed Frank and Joan, so why am I hungry?"

"Not enough sleep," offered Jerry.

"So should I get more sleep or eat something? And will I have to get dressed and go out to get something to eat?"

"Maybe get something to eat," said Jerry.

Mary looked at him and thought that maybe staying here might not lead to more sleep, even if they did use the bed. "Yes, food. We'll come back to shower, so I'm just going to get dressed in my bedroom, and you'll do the same out here. Knock on the bedroom door when you're finished, and don't knock on it for any other reason, okay?"

"What other reason would I knock on it for?"

"Exactly," replied Mary, and went into her bedroom before any other reason came up.

They were dressed and heading to Roses for breakfast a few minutes later. "Shall we call Peter and fill him in on what's happened in California?" asked Mary.

"It's early in the morning," said Jerry.

"You're right. We should make sure Peter is awake now, even if he doesn't want to be. Why should we be the only ones to be going without sleep this morning?"

Mary called but was disappointed. Peter was already awake. He did say he would meet them for breakfast.

When Sandy seated them, she offered Mary coffee and Jerry juice. "Coffee," he said.

"But isn't that caffeine stuff bad for you, Jerry?" smirked Sandy.

"I'm trying to learn to drink it a little," smiled Jerry.

"You're weird," replied Sandy, and left to get three coffees, one for Peter too, who arrived before she got back with the coffee.

"So, who gets to go first?" asked Peter, sitting and looking incredibly well-rested.

"That depends on whether you want me to fall asleep while I'm talking or while I'm listening," said Mary. "Maybe if you talk while I suck down coffee I can stay awake long enough to listen."

"I'll go first," interrupted Jerry. "Do you know if the locket Angie was wearing had a picture in it?"

"Yeah, I think so," replied Peter. "We were thinking we might be able to trace something that way, but now with Laura's ID, we won't..." He looked at Mary's face and her smug expression and said, "Or maybe we will?"

"Stan will be sending you a picture of James Forsyth so you can compare it to the picture in Angie's locket," said Mary.

"And James Forsyth would be the person who is buying Laura's airplane tickets and would be what to Angie?" asked Peter.

"Maybe her father," said Mary.

"Oh," said Peter. "I thought I was going to go first. If this is what you two are like without coffee, I may as well just surrender now."

"We're the meteorites in this game," smiled Mary. "One flash of brilliance and we're ready to drink coffee and listen to you, Peter."

"Okay," Peter smiled. "First of all, Donald Blanchard is a flaming asshole."

"I told you, Jerry, didn't I?" said Mary. "But that's not news, Peter. You're going to have to be more stimulating if I'm going to stay awake."

"The news part of it is that I'm expecting a call any minute from him telling me to pick up Jerry, so that will color the rest of the stimulating information and I hope keep you awake."

"You got me, Peter."

"Good. Next part is a little enticing too. The prints on that jewelry, only one set of prints, match some of the prints in the shop where Angie was found dead."

"Laura was there?" asked Jerry.

"It looks like. We don't have definite proof, since we don't have Laura's official prints yet and we can't be really sure there's only one set on the jewelry, but it sure looks that way according to Tess."

"That's interesting," said Mary, as Sandy came over with the coffee.

"You're saving my life, Sandy," said Mary.

"Any time," Sandy replied. "You know what you want?"

"Cheese omelets all around, Sandy," said Mary.

"I was going to—" began Peter.

"Have a cheese omelet," said Mary. "Make it easy for Sandy and safer for you. Now what else do you have, Peter? Wait until Sandy leaves to answer, okay?"

"I'm leaving already, Mary," said Sandy. "Boy, are you grouchy this morning or what? I just saved your life, remember?"

"But I'm still grouchy, so watch it. All of you."

With this Sandy left to contemplate the fickle nature of saving lives.

"Okay," said Peter. "I shouldn't be telling you any of this, so fewer is better. The next interesting part is that one of the places Laura put her fingerprints was on a packet of bath salts Angie had on her. A lot of prints on that, but definitely Angie's and the ones we think are Laura's."

"Carlos' salts?" asked Jerry.

"They had his 'C' and his *star* on them. Looked exactly like the ones they found in your dresser drawer, Jerry. That's another problem. Donald Blanchard has this theory that you're the dealer, Jerry."

"But Jerry's prints aren't on any of them, are they?" asked Mary.

"Donald is not dissuaded by logic," replied Peter. "He's advancing the theory that Jerry wipes off his prints so they can't be traced to him, and never leaves his prints on his packets of salts. That's why there are none on the ones in his dresser, and why his are not on the one found on Angie."

"Angie had only one on her?" asked Jerry.

"Just one, why?" said Peter.

"Not much for Angie to have on her. I wonder if the ones in the dresser were taken off Angie," Jerry replied, and frowned a little.

"You're right, Peter," said Mary. "This is not logical. If there were a lot of prints on the packet Angie had, but not any on the ones in Jerry's dresser, then a lot of people handled the one Angie had on her and probably the ones in Jerry's dresser until whoever put them there wiped off the prints. Was that person trying to make sure Angie's prints weren't on them so that no one would suspect she had handled them? If Donald thinks Jerry wiped off his prints before he sold it, it should be only Angie's prints on the one she had, and why would Laura's be on it at all? Did she handle it and then put it back on Angie?"

"Laura didn't kill Angie for the salts," said Jerry.

Mary frowned. "Look, Peter, this isn't making any sense. It could have been Laura except that...well, the way I have it figured, Laura was supposed to be protecting Angie."

"I don't know," said Peter. "What were those two doing here in the first place?"

Jerry shook his head. "Angie'd been trying to get in touch with me. When I came out here maybe—"

"She followed you?" asked Mary. "And Laura followed her?"

Jerry shrugged.

"That would explain why she was in the shop I guess, but who killed her? I don't see Laura killing her."

"No," said Jerry shaking his head. "I don't see Laura shooting anyone. She never packed in Huntington."

"She would have had to get a weapon here, and that would have been difficult for someone who was from outside. It wasn't licensed, but even so," said Peter.

Mary shrugged. "She didn't bring a gun with her from California, not on the airplane, and she would have had trouble getting one here and even more trouble putting it and the packets in Jerry's dresser. I don't think it was Laura, do you?"

Both men shook their heads. "Whoever put the packets and the gun in Jerry's dresser had to know where Jerry's room and his dresser were in the first place," Peter said. "Laura didn't know that, did she?"

"No. She couldn't have known," said Jerry.

Sandy brought the omelets and looked around the table. "Now let me see if I can remember who ordered which one. Oh, wait a minute; they're all the same, aren't they, Mary? Thank you for making it soooo simple for me. You know, Mary, you've been hanging around Jerry too much." She deposited three omelets in the middle of the table and departed.

"Or not hanging around him enough," said Peter.

"What about Luther, the friend of Laura and probably Angie?" asked Mary.

"Friend of Angie, definitely," said Peter.

"DNA is back this quick?" Mary said.

"Luther decided he was better off confessing. He and Angie and Laura, it seems."

"Oh," said Mary.

"That was like Angie and Laura," said Jerry.

"I can't figure this out," added Mary.

As Mary spoke, two other men came in and she looked up. "Rufus and Billy. Just what we need."

"Maybe you're right," said Jerry and got up, walking over to the table they were seating themselves at.

Rufus put on a display of antagonism, while Billy looked as if he were ready to leave.

"Sorry about that thing the other day," said Billy.

"What thing?" asked Jerry.

"You know that...well, that thing," said Billy again.

Jerry looked puzzled, and finally shook his head. By now everyone was looking at them, and Peter and Mary were standing to come over, as Jerry said, "I'm not...Anyway, maybe you two could join us?" He motioned toward the table where Peter and Mary were standing. "If you care to. I wanted to talk to you about the shop and Aunt May."

Billy looked hesitant, and Rufus looked defiant. "You buyin'?" he challenged.

"Sure," said Jerry, and turned to walk back over to the table.

Rufus and then Billy looked around, and somehow concluded that they had to follow Jerry if he was buying, and so they did. They pulled up two more chairs and sat.

"Mornin' Rufus, Billy," said Peter. Mary just nodded. Rufus and Billy made no effort to acknowledge the greeting.

Jerry smiled. "Prentiss Forrest found Angie dead in Aunt May's shop a couple days ago. He said he thought Aunt May had some money stashed in there. Do you know anything about that?"

The directness of the question seemed to take them off guard.

"She ain't got no money," said Rufus.

"We been lookin' all over for her money," said Billy.

"So you think she has some money stashed?" asked Mary.

"Well, yeah," said Billy. "'Specially after Dexter."

"You knew about Dexter?" asked Mary.

"Oh, shit," said Rufus, glaring at his brother.

"What?" said Billy.

"I don't want that to get around," hissed Rufus. "What'll people think?"

"But you did know about Dexter?" asked Mary again.

"That he flatted the tires on my truck? Yeah, sure. I ain't deaf, ya know. Everyone knew 'bout that."

"So why isn't Dexter dead?" asked Mary.

Rufus looked at Peter, not Mary, and shrugged. "I wouldn'a kilt him. It was that damned May anyway. She's such a bitch. She even made Jerry come all the way out here to open her shop up again, just so's we couldn't sell it. Weren't Dexter's fault. He was just doin' what May told 'im to."

"So you knew Dexter flattened your tires and you knew May paid him to do it. Is that right?" asked Mary. "And you what? Took pity on poor Dexter?"

"Yeah, but...well, I don't want people ta know that I'm a...well, that I'm some kinda wussy." Rufus looked really distressed.

"I don't think anyone will ever think that, Rufus," said Mary. "I know I'll never think that."

"Really?" said Rufus. "Thanks, Mary."

Jerry looked at them and added, "It is a truly wise man who chooses his battleground and does not let his opponent choose it for him." When everyone stared at him he added, *The Art of War*, by Sun Tzu." He nodded as if this explained it all, ignoring the blank faces that clearly contradicted him.

"You said May got Jerry to come out here so you couldn't sell the shop, Rufus, is that right?" asked Mary.

"Well, yeah. Shop's useless an' Prentiss wanted ta buy it, but May kept talkin' about openin' it up again. Me an' Billy finally said we wouldn't pay the taxes on it and she got really pissed. That was why she paid Dexter to flat my tires. Then she calls poor Jerry here to come out an' makes him open the shop ta sell ice cream, but a course Jerry don't know nothin' about ice cream." Mary nodded, and Jerry just blushed

Sandy arrived now, with coffee for Rufus and Billy and refills for the others. She looked nervously at them all and asked, "Do you want something to eat?"

"Sure they do," smiled Jerry, "since I'm paying." Jerry chuckled at this in spite of the fact that no one else saw any humor.

"They'll have what Jerry is having, won't you boys?" said Mary.

"Are you sure they will?" said Sandy.

Billy raised his hand, much like the little school boy who wished to ask a question.

"You don't want to eat what Jerry is eating, Billy?" asked Mary.

"Oh no, not that. It's just that I'm kinda hungry an'...Can I have two? Of whatever they are, I mean."

"Yes," said Sandy. "Is that okay...of course it is, isn't it Jerry?" She left immediately; proof that she, at least, had not mistaken Rufus for a wussy.

"Thanks, Jerry," said Rufus.

Mary shook her head. All the best of friends now. "So you knew about Dexter and you also think May has a stash of money, is that right?" asked Mary.

"Yeah," said Rufus.

"An' we can't find it," said Billy, with obvious despair.

"And I'll bet you've looked," said Mary.

"Sure have," said Rufus. "In the shop an' in the house, too."

"There's that fridge what's locked, Rufus," said Billy. "A big walk-in fridge, but we couldn't get the key from May."

"I opened that," said Jerry.

"How'd ya get into it?" asked Rufus, as if Jerry was his best friend.

"Jerry can do that," said both Mary and Peter simultaneously. They looked at each other, and finally looked at Jerry.

"Wow!" said Billy. "That's cool."

Peter cleared his throat. "Billy, Rufus. Does your Aunt May have a gun?"

"Sure," said Billy.

"She's...whaddya call it? Paradnoids?" offered Billy.

"Paranoid," said Mary.

"So she has a gun?" persisted Peter. "One that someone could find and use to shoot someone with?"

"Yeah," said Rufus. "Some sort of assault rifle, I think it is."

"An assault weapon?" asked Mary.

"Yeah," said Billy. "Big sucker, too. Every so often she'd get pissed and start taking out her gun and showing it around tellin' everyone she was goin' ta' shoot 'em."

He turned to face his brother now. " 'Member last winter she got all fired up? Dressed up in her winter coat with those crazy mittens a her's with the snowmen on 'em, waving that gun around. She couldn't a pulled the trigger on it with those mittens on."

"Yeah," said Rufus. "She finally settled down, and then she insisted everybody hold that damned gun so she could take pictures of us with it. Said she was going to send it on her Christmas cards next year." He shook his head in disbelief.

"She's gettin' worse," added Billy. "Caught her wanderin' around down the road from her house just a few weeks ago. Musta been half a mile away. Didn't seem ta know where she was, either."

"She's addled," said Mary.

"Yeah," said Rufus. "Billy and me have been trying to get her declared so, so's we can keep her in tow."

"Oh," said Peter. "You don't know anyone with a small handgun then? Brushed nickel and fake ivory handle? Neither of you have one like that, do you?"

Mary thought this was possibly the stupidest thing to ask someone who might have killed someone with a gun like that, but then again Rufus and Billy were among the stupidest people she knew. They might just answer the question.

"Sounds like George's gun," said Billy.

"George's gun?" asked Mary.

"Yeah," said Rufus. "George had one a' them .22's. Used it for when he had ta take a deposit ta the bank."

"But," said Mary. "Could he have taken it with him? On a plane?"

"Said he was going to take it with him," said Rufus. "Couldn't take it in his carry-on, but he had it packed into his checked-in bags somehow."

"So he took it, or he and Jessica took it," said Peter.

"Guess so," said Rufus. "Ta Florida, I guess."

"He got to Florida," mused Mary.

"Guess he did. Sent me a postcard," shrugged Billy.

"Me too," said Rufus. "His writin' it looked like ta me, an' one of those sticky labels with the address printed on it."

"Printed address?" asked Mary.

"Yeah," said Billy. "George always liked to send postcards to everyone so they knew he was a big spender on his vacation. Didn't like to write out the addresses though, so he printed 'em all up on the computer at his office before he went, and then just put 'em on the cards."

"Yeah," chuckled Rufus. "Heard tell he forgot his address book one time and couldn't send any postcards an' it really pissed him off, so that's when he started printing 'em out in advance on the computer. Thought it made him look really important, he said."

"He printed out labels to mail postcards when he was running away with his secretary?" Mary was astounded.

"Naw," said Rufus. "He'd have Jessica print 'em out. He was real proud a foolin' everybody, 'specially ol' May."

Mary shook her head. "So do you think the murder weapon went to Florida with George and Jessica, Peter?" she asked.

"There are a lot of brushed nickel faux ivory handled twenty-two caliber handguns out there."

"If George didn't take it, that bitch Jessica woulda," said Rufus. "She knew what she wanted, and knew how ta get it."

Billy nodded his agreement as three more omelets arrived.

Chapter 48

They ate with little conversation. Jerry paid, and Rufus and Billy left, thanking him again.

"Soooo," said Mary. "You're friends with Rufus and Billy now, Jerry. Wouldn't 'a believed that could happen."

"They're all right," said Jerry with a shrug. "Didn't hurt Dexter anyway."

"True," observed Peter.

"But did they help us get any closer to the murderer?" asked Mary.

"If you consider that we were not anywhere close to figuring it out before, they haven't really moved us any further away," smiled Peter.

"Okay, so what do we know?" asked Mary, and began at once to state what they, or at least she knew. "Angie and Laura come out to Nebraska, maybe together or maybe with Laura following, planning to slander me somehow and get Jerry. They screw around with Luther, probably just practicing group performances for when they could get at Jerry, and then what? Angie and Laura go to the shop, maybe looking for Jerry? Maybe together or maybe separately? Maybe Angie went and Laura followed? Does that make sense?"

"I don't think they went together, or they both would be dead. There was no car there either, so someone must have dropped Angie off. Laura must have had a ride to leave in though, so maybe she came after Angie was dead, ya think? I can't see Laura shooting Angie, but I can see her following her there and finding her already dead," said Peter.

"I don't think Laura would kill Angie either," said Jerry.

"I don't see Laura killing the golden egg-laying goose. I think Laura knew she was supposed to keep Angie safe, and she wouldn't have done anything so stupid."

"No," said Jerry.

"So she must have followed Angie, and she must have found her dead," said Mary.

"Makes the most sense," said Peter.

"And then she either handles the packet of salts or has already handled it, but decides to make an escape plan," said Mary. "She spends another night with Luther, plants some incriminating evidence for his wife to find, or maybe to tell the cops about to get them onto Luther, I don't know, and what next?"

"Well," said Peter. "She identifies Angie as her sister, and if we didn't...well, if you didn't track down the guy who bought her a ticket out here, we might never have figured out who she really was. Laura said she was Angie Steward and that's her ID back in Huntington Beach."

Jerry sighed. "She probably never thought anyone would figure out who Angie really was. That happens a lot, and if Mary Burke had cashed in the ticket and Laura used the fake driver's license to fly home—"

"*Mary Burke* would have been in the deep weeds," answered Mary. "But what were they doing there in the middle of the night? Prentiss was after the money, but Angie shouldn't have needed any money and Laura...well, neither of them would have known about May's money anyway."

"I think they might have been looking for me," said Jerry.

"Maybe," said Peter. "But so far there's no reason for Angie to end up dead."

Mary shook her head again. "So Angie is there, and Laura is there, and Prentiss is there and someone else who kills people is there and...and what is in that shop that's drawing people like a magnet? Even crazy May is dragging Jerry out here because her brothers are trying to sell it. What is it with that shop?"

"Maybe we should take a look at it," said Jerry. "Is it still a crime scene, Peter?"

"No," said Peter. "Neither is the house, so you can move back there, Jerry, if you don't get arrested."

"No, he can't, Peter," said Mary. "He's staying with me."

"Okay," said Peter. "Let's go."

They took Mary's car at Peter's suggestion, to draw less attention, leaving his cruiser out in front of the restaurant. As they drove, Peter got a call. He looked at it and said, "Donald. I think I'm out of cell range, aren't I?"

"Could be," said Mary.

When they arrived, there was no one in sight. "Should we tell May we're going to look around?" asked Mary.

"Just upset her unnecessarily," advised Peter.

They went inside with the dim light from the outside to guide them. They left the lights off. On the floor were the crime scene markers, still outlining the place where Angie's body had lain.

"Tess should have removed that," said Peter.

"She was busy," said Jerry.

"Is that the locked fridge?" asked Mary, pointing to a walk-in refrigerator with a chain looped around it and two padlocks on it.

"Yeah," said Jerry. "They were pretty easy."

"Can you open it now?" asked Peter.

"Yeah, but I already had it open. There was this musty smell you see, and...well, I can open it if you want."

"Yes," said Peter. "I'm sure the crime scene boys opened it too."

Jerry looked at it. "I don't think so. I put tape over the locks to keep them clean and the tape is still there. They might have put it back on, but they...I'll open it."

Jerry took out his multi-tool and knelt, and then began to hum his soft monotone. It was almost hypnotizing to watch as first one and then the other lock dropped into his hand, as if they had never been locked at all. He opened the door, and Peter shone his flashlight in to reveal—nothing. It was completely empty, as Jerry had said it was. What wasn't empty were the hands of the person standing behind them. They held an assault weapon.

"What the hell are you doin' in here?" said May Wilson, as she pointed her gun at them. If she were a good shot she could take them all out before any of them could get to her.

"You been messin' around here too much," she said. She smiled now, and raised her weapon slightly, firing off a dozen shots above their heads.

"So you'll know I can use this," she said, and smiled more broadly.

"You can't get away with killing us and expect no one to find you, May," said Peter.

"Wanta bet? Bet your life on it, maybe? Prentiss ordered this gun on the Internet and had it delivered here. He don't know that, but that's what the order will say. His fingerprints are on it, and so are Rufus' and Billy's; and mine are not." She looked quickly at her hands, and they all looked with her. She had gloves on her hands. None of her fingerprints would be on this murder weapon.

"May," said Mary. "You don't have to—"

"But I want to," said May, her weapon pointed at them again.

"Jerry is your nephew, May."

"Yeah, an' he was supposed ta keep that fool Prentiss from gettin' this shop an' findin' what's in it, but what does he do? Brings that hussy out here from California."

They could see the sneer on her face as she mockingly mimicked what Angie must have sounded like. *"All I want to do is leave that gorgeous Jerry a note.* Stupid whore! Pussy full of semen an' a pocket full a drugs. She was real disappointed when she found me here instead of you. The bitch saw what I had hid here.

"You want ta see the note she was goin' ta leave ya, Jerry?" May threw a piece of paper on the floor in front of him, but Jerry made no move.

"Not that interested in her, is that it, Jerry? Got yourself another whore, just like my husband did, is that it? You don't look a bit like Jessica, Mary."

"May," said Mary.

"Shut up, all of you. Get into that fridge, now!"

"Aunty May," said Jerry, looking at her and then beyond her. Looking for his karma in darkness, it seemed. "You're sick, and you're doing something that will hurt you." He began to sway back and forth on the old floor and it began to creak with each movement; the rhythmic creaking of the old boards beneath his feet and the slow, soft words Jerry spoke would have been soothing if they were not facing an assault weapon held by crazy May Wilson.

"Shut up, you fool," said May. "That don't work on me."

"You're only going to cause yourself more pain, Aunty May," said Jerry, as if he didn't understand that she was about to kill him.

"I'm going to cause *you* pain," said May, moving her gun just a bit to point it at Jerry. The gun was pointed at Jerry, with Mary and Peter on either side of him. Maybe if they moved at once, May wouldn't be able to kill them all before one of them reached her. Jerry would surely be one of the dead. May was pointing her gun directly at him, and likely Mary and Peter would be dead too. Not much chance, but it seemed like it was the only one they had.

The wind blew through the open door of the shop, rustling the papers on the counter and the misspelled sign on the door as Jerry kept up the slow rhythm of his sway with the boards creaking beneath him and his voice coming softly. Coming softly, but not reaching the woman with the gun. There she stood, with only darkness behind her, like the devil herself; but still Jerry calmly swayed and spoke. Peter and Mary couldn't look at anything except the sneering face of the woman who was going to kill them.

"You don't have to do this, Aunty May. You killed Angie, but that was because you were frightened, wasn't it?'

May sneered out of the darkness, "It's you who should be frightened, Jerry. But you're not smart enough to be frightened. Maybe I should kill your friend first, to show you how frightened you should be." She didn't move her gun from Jerry or look at Mary, but somehow Mary knew the friend was she and not Peter. Peter seemed to know too, and began shifting away a little to give himself a little advantage when he rushed her.

"Stay where you are!" yelled May, without moving her gaze from Jerry.

Jerry smiled and swayed and the boards creaked louder, and Jerry's soft voice said, "It's over, Aunty May. It's all over, now." Then he yelled it: "Right Now!"

As May raised her gun to shoot, even before Jerry had finished speaking, he began to lean toward Mary at his right. May shifted her aim to follow, but when she did her gun slid into the hand coming from behind her. That hand pulled the weapon rapidly upward, and the shots that May fired all splintered into the timbers in the old ceiling.

In another second, Donald Blanchard held May with one hand and held the weapon that had almost killed them in his other hand.

# Chapter 49

"A couple things," said Donald. "First, I think you should place this woman in custody, Captain Morgan. I think this weapon may be illegal under the federal ban on assault weapons. Second: will someone tell me what the hell is going on here? And third: why doesn't anyone show me the least bit of respect?"

"That's three things, Donald," said Mary, "which is one more than a couple."

May Wilson was struggling now, yelling at her loudest. "They are all out to get me! Wait until George gets home! He'll straighten you all out! Trespassers in here trying to steal my money!"

"Now, now, May," said Peter. He spoke into his cell phone, "Hello, Carl. An ambulance out to May Wilson's place, and get Tess out of bed, too, for a crime scene. And we'll need a couple of officers to go with May at least as far as the hospital."

"You're not taking me to any hospital!" yelled May. "You all workin' for that hussy Jessica. It's her that's behind this. Wait until my husband gets home! He'll have you all in jail, especially you!" she spat at Peter.

Mary placed her hand on May's arm and she finally collapsed into a sobbing, quivering relic of the woman who had almost killed them all a few minutes ago and who **had** killed Angie a few days ago. That's how she remained until the ambulance arrived to take her to the hospital. She went with them quietly, almost as if the fury of four years had finally been spent.

"Make sure she gets to the hospital, Carl," said Peter, "and don't let her go shopping this time."

Peter chuckled and Mary did as well, partly to release the tension. May would be placed in a hospital, and maybe get some help or maybe not, but she was no longer a threat to anyone.

They were still waiting for the crime scene boys when May left. "That was pretty impressive, Mr. Wilson," said a relaxed Donald. "I thought you saw me in back of her, but I had no idea how I could get close to her without her noticing me. Pretty sure she would shoot me if she noticed me, or shoot you."

Jerry shrugged. "I knew these old floors were creaky and that you couldn't walk on them without making noise, so I figured I should make enough noise to keep May occupied." He shrugged again as if keeping a crazy woman with an assault weapon "occupied" was nothing special.

Peter was amazed, however. "How did you even know we were here?" he asked Donald.

"Oh," smiled Donald. "Astute detection is all that was. You see, when I called you about...well, when I called you, never mind about what, and you didn't answer, I was driving by that pub downtown and I saw your cruiser parked in front. I was a little pissed...well, my motive was…well, never mind. I thought you were in there, but when I went inside a server, Sandy I think her name was, told me she thought she heard you say you were going out here. I came out here to see...to see if I could help you fix your cell phone. That's it," he smiled. "Those cell phones are always failing when you need them most."

"And Jerry noticed you and you saved our lives," said Mary. "You could have waited a couple nanoseconds longer to save us, but..."

"Pretty cool," said Donald. "Did I hear her say she killed Angie?"

"Yes," said Peter. "Paranoid, I guess. She had some money hidden somewhere and probably thought Angie was trying to get it. Angie was just caught in the wrong place."

Peter bent now and picked up the paper May had thrown at Jerry with his handkerchief and looked at it. *"I will love you forever,"* he said. "It's evidence in this crime now, but I'll see that you get it back," said Peter, looking at Jerry.

Jerry wasn't paying attention. He was walking around, looking at the floor. "I wonder where the money is?" he asked, but didn't look up.

"Maybe there was no money," suggested Peter.

"There was enough to pay Dexter," said Mary.

"Maybe in the house?" Peter shrugged.

"No," said Jerry. "Aunty May said I was supposed to keep Prentiss from finding what was in this shop. That's what she said, so it must be in here."

Mary frowned.

"I guess it doesn't matter now," said Peter. "I'll tell Tess she'll have to look at this place a little closer than she did the first time. May will be hospitalized, I'm sure, and for quite a while, so there's no rush on this."

"They won't let her out, will they?" asked Mary.

"She won't run for it, she can barely walk," Peter said.

"She can handle an assault weapon," said Donald.

Mary frowned again. "It just isn't adding up right, Peter. What do you think, Jerry?"

Jerry looked up from the floor and asked, "Do you think Aunty May is really crazy?"

"She acted crazy," said Peter.

"Acted," repeated Mary.

When no one said anything she continued. "Look, Peter. Someone killed Angie, right?"

"May said she did, or practically said she did."

"But not with that assault weapon. With the gun someone put in the top drawer of the dresser in Jerry's room."

"Yes," said Peter. It looked as if he were starting to speak again, but stopped as if he realized that what he was about to say made no sense.

Mary continued. "Someone put that gun there, and someone took the packets of bath salts, but only three of them, leaving one on Angie, to make sure she was tied to Jerry; took them and cleaned off the fingerprints and put it all in Jerry's room. Someone did that, and then someone got Carl to leave this place unguarded so that everyone would believe that anyone could have put them there.

"The person who did that wasn't crazy; cunning, yes, but not crazy. And she figured a way to get Rufus and Billy, and Prentiss, to put their fingerprints on her assault weapon, too."

Peter and Donald began to stare at Mary as Jerry began to shift his weight on the floorboards again. He finally looked up and said, "There seems to be something under here. It sounds empty under here. Can we lift up these boards please?"

"This is a crime scene," said Peter.

"I don't see any crime scene tape yet," said Donald. "Let's take a look, shall we?"

They were all pulling at the boards now, each trying to outdo the other, but the boards were not held very firmly. It was apparent that nails had been removed, and it took only a minute to uncover a ditch beneath them

Peter pointed his light into the darkness to reveal two bodies, now four years old, with a sack lying on top of them and their luggage beside them.

"George and Jessica?" asked Peter softly.

"That would be my guess," said Mary.

"That was the musty smell all along," said Jerry.

"Well I'll be damned," whispered Donald.

"That's likely true, Mr. Blanchard," said Mary. "All the good people are; but it won't be for anything you have done here today."

Donald looked first at Mary and then at Peter. "Perhaps you had better notify the hospital that May Wilson is not as crazy as she would like us to believe she is, and that she may be planning her escape at this very moment, don't you think, Captain Morgan?"

"Yes," said Peter, and he looked back at the bodies of a husband and his girlfriend, who had been killed four years ago.

"But the postcards?" said Peter.

"Are just postcards," said Mary. "May is pretty clever, Peter, so make that call to the hospital now."

# Chapter 50

It had been early in the morning when May had tried to kill them. It would have brought her score up to six if she had succeeded. She almost succeeded in escaping the hospital when everyone assumed, the police included, that she was just crazy old May Wilson. She had cultivated her image very well. She was dressed and walking briskly toward the exit when Peter's call came in, and she had to be run down in the parking lot before she was subdued and handcuffed.

"If he had called a minute later she would have been gone," was a frequently heard sentence that afternoon. Somehow the accolades went to Peter, and Donald didn't seem to mind. Neither did Mary or Jerry, in spite of their somewhat crucial role in it all. They found themselves in The Ice Cream Shop a little after noontime.

They were not alone, of course. News had spread fast in this little town, and today everyone was coming in for ice cream and the details of the amazing story of May Wilson. Mary's father was one of the first to show up.

"Brought that postcard you asked for," he said, handing it to Mary. "That's George's writing on it, I'm sure, and it's postmarked three weeks after he...well, after he was dead."

Mary turned the card over, looking at the pasted label with the address printed on it. She began to slowly lift the edge, and when about a half-inch was off she showed it to her father. "This was addressed before," she said, pointing to the writing beneath the label. "Looks like it might have been sent to May by George, ya think? There are a lot of stamps on it too. Enough to cover an old postmark."

"Well I'll be damned," said her father.

"Lot of that going around today," smiled Mary. She shrugged and said, "May probably got some of her old postcards that George had sent her from Florida, and put on new labels and new stamps and...I don't know, maybe she had a friend in Florida who mailed them for her."

Her father just shook his head.

Peter came by too, to tell them that Tess was *all kinds of embarrassed* missing two bodies in the crime scene she had investigated. Peter thought it was funny, but Mary realized that if Tess had found the bodies of George and Jessica, May would have never had a chance to try to kill her and Jerry. They hadn't died anyway, so maybe it didn't matter.

Peter said that Tess had determined that George and Jessica, yet to be officially identified, but everyone knew it was them, had been shot with a .22 at close range, and the bullets were still in them. Peter thought it would be the same gun that had killed Angie.

Mary and Jerry were having trouble keeping up with the business until Francis and Jasmine came by with an electric guitar and amplifier to loan Jerry. Jerry had called on Mary's phone as soon as they reached the shop. Mary was going to suggest again that he get his own phone, but decided that she could share hers for a little while longer. She still had his friendship ring on.

"Where ya want this, dude?" asked Francis, dressed now in untorn jeans and a short-sleeved shirt. His hair wasn't any shorter but it was clean, and he had shaved. Jasmine was dressed in jeans and a loose top, that didn't hide, but also didn't display too much of her. The top was covered by the windbreaker Francis had given her, in spite of the hot weather.

"It's busy today," she said to Mary. "Can we help?"

Mary decided they could, and it was soon crowded behind the counter and in front too, as people lingered to discuss the event. Jasmine and Francis scooped ice cream and asked questions about the sizes and how to wash the scoops, and all that stuff that Mary took for granted. She had to look at Jerry, who had much less trouble with these routine practices, even if he had no more experience.

Jerry was doing his share, but kept watching the guitar that sat in the corner. Finally Mary suggested that he set it up and try it out. He waited not another minute to take her up on the offer. Soon he was playing soft jazz outside in the sunshine, while people stood and ate, and soon were bringing their lawn chairs to sit and listen, and eat ice cream. People did that here, and many people carried chairs and such in the back of their cars, just in case they were needed.

Frank and Joan came by with the posters and stayed to listen too. Joan scrawled across the top of the poster: "Appearing On An Unannounced Schedule At The Ice Cream Shop."

Frank said that something must be happening in California because when he went online to try to find out something more about Angie, all the sites he had been able to access yesterday were now locked. "Someone is making sure there's no one getting to them," he said. "Someone in a very high, very powerful, and very official position."

Jasmine was chatty while Francis was intense about the task.

"So, like, my mother is so crazy," Jasmine said. "She keeps telling me I need to dress in like tight clothes and...well, you know. She says I'll never get the men to notice me if I don't like advertise. I mean, she's crazier than crazy old May Wilson by a mile. I don't want any men to notice me. I want Francis to notice me."

She cast an adoring gaze at Francis, who frowned and said, "Serving ice cream is serious business, Jasmine."

"Oh, yeah, of course, Francis," said Jasmine, as she turned to help the next person in line.

Mary had to marvel at this. The logic was totally turned upside down for Jasmine. May wasn't now, nor had she ever been "crazy." She had killed her husband and his girlfriend, and concealed the bodies in her shop. She kept the shop closed so no one would find the bodies, refusing to sell it. She had acted crazy to avoid any suspicion, and had somehow arranged that postcards be sent from Florida to convince everyone that George was still alive, and had gotten out of Nebraska. Then she just settled down to wait for the five years to pass so she could get the money.

When Rufus and Billy threatened to sell the shop, May realized that if someone else got that shop that sooner or later they would find George and Jessica, so she got Jerry to come open it up. That way they couldn't sell it to Prentiss or anyone else. Angie must have interrupted May as she was getting her money, or looking at her dead husband or some such thing. Maybe Angie went into the shop because she saw May in there and thought it was Jerry, or...well, they might never know for sure.

Whatever it was, after she had killed Angie, May set about pointing all the evidence to Jerry, her own nephew. Had she decided to get rid of Jerry by having him convicted of Angie's murder?

So Mary shouldn't have been surprised that she planned to kill Mary and Jerry and Peter too, with an assault weapon that had Prentiss' and Rufus' and Billy's fingerprints on it, but had none of her own. Three people who were suspiciously nosing around would be dead, and the three people who were likely to find what was hidden in the shop if it was sold, would be the obvious murderers. It was perfect. Had she planned this whole thing, or just taken cunning advantage of the events as they unfolded? She clearly didn't care how many dead there were when it was finished.

Mary was sure that Aunty May would have escaped when her plot was uncovered, if she had been given half a chance. She had probably hidden the money she did have somewhere distant enough from the house and shop so that she could get to it easily, without risking detection, once she walked away from the hospital or a psychiatric hospital, or wherever she was destined to go. Everyone knew she was "crazy" after all, and "didn't get around too well" so she wouldn't be locked up too tightly. Not really guarded.

Mary looked at Francis and Jasmine and thought that the final failure of Jasmine's logic was that Francis didn't mind her saying that he wasn't a "man". She didn't want to be noticed by any men, just by Francis who was what; not a man? Mary thought that Francis was a man and surely Jasmine thought he was a man, too.

"Do you have to charge extra if people want a scoop in a dish and a cone on top?" asked Jasmine.

"Yes," said Mary, and looked at the five-year-old waiting for the ice cream in a dish with a cone on top. "Except today. I'm alive, and I can give everyone a dish and a cone today."

"Just like Jerry," said Francis and Mary winced, but had to agree.

"Maybe we should start selling some food, too, Miss Burke," said Francis.

"Yeah," said Jasmine, handing the dish with a cone in it to the little girl reaching for it. Her mother paid and put more than enough in the tip jar to compensate for the free cone.

"Thanks," said the mother. "A little food would be nice. How late are you going to stay open this year, Mary?"

"I don't know. I'll have to consult my partner." She nodded toward Jerry, playing outside.

As she walked out, Donald walked up. "I heard there was good ice cream to be had here," he said.

"The best in town," smiled Mary. She pointed toward the shop, but Donald stayed beside her.

"That was pretty scary this morning," he said.

"Yes." Mary shivered in spite of the afternoon heat.

"That guy, Jerry Wilson, was pretty cool through it all, though." He nodded toward Jerry, quietly playing his jazz. Jerry had said that Donald was a nice person, and he had been right, as he had been right when he said that Aunty May wasn't nice.

"I got shot in the leg once. It was a case over in Kentucky. A friend of mine, Carla is her name, saved my butt that day."

Frank looked up from his ice cream and asked, "Carla Smith, maybe?"

"Yeah," said Donald. "Retired now. You know her?"

"Friend a mine," said Frank. "Small world," he added, and went back to his ice cream.

Donald shrugged and said, "I'll not be disappointed if I never get shot at again."

"Neither will I," smiled Mary.

"I just got off the phone with the people out in California. Seems this Angie was the daughter of some very wealthy real estate shaker. I was also told he was involved with some drug trafficking and prostitution, too, and that he had hired some hooker to watch his daughter. I guess when his daughter got killed, he decided that the hooker should be dead too, but the police slipped a ringer with a wire on her into the mix and...well, Angie's father may be seeing some real estate run by the State of California prison system. He really wanted to kill that hooker, and to do the killing himself."

Donald shrugged again and said, "I shouldn't be telling you this, but I wanted you to know that the risk you took today paid off. You should be proud."

Mary looked over at Jerry and said, "I am proud, thank you, Mr. Blanchard."

"Donald," he said. "Police captain I talked to in California said he had to convince the officer who slipped in on this guy, Forsyth, into taking a really big chance. This is the best part," smiled Donald. "Want to guess what he bribed her with?"

"No idea," smiled Mary. Donald was enjoying this too much for her to try to guess. "I don't know much about California and its cops."

"He promised her a surf board! Can you believe that? Not even a new one, he said, just one that belonged to a friend of his, but she wanted it bad enough to take the risk."

Mary stared at him. "Nancy?" she whispered incredulously.

"Yeah, I think that's what he said her name was. You must have heard already I guess. I'm going to buy a dish of ice cream now and listen to a little jazz. Strawberry is my favorite."

"I just knew it would be strawberry," replied Mary. "I'm afraid you can't buy any ice cream today. We have this special for DEA agents. If you save the lives of more than two people, you get a free ice cream. Only for that day though, but you can get any size, and in a dish with a cone too, all for free."

Donald smiled, and then said he was going to get that ice cream and then listen to that jazz.

As he went inside, Mary went over to where Jerry was sitting. She decided she would let Stan tell him about his surf board. She didn't think she could deal with a suicide today.

Jerry finished the piece he was playing and said to the crowd that he would be taking a little break. Several people asked if they could leave a tip for him, along with saying he was really good. Jerry told them the tip wasn't necessary, but that tips for the ice cream could be left inside in the tip jar in the shop. He also mentioned he would be playing at Maria's in the city, motioning toward the poster.

When the crowd had dissipated he said, "I've been thinking, Mary. Maybe I won't go back to Huntington right away."

"What?" said Mary.

"Well, yeah. I can work here in the shop and pick up a little money playing in the city and...well, there must be something I can do during the winter, don't you think?"

"And you're going to what? Give up surfing?"

"Well, I thought..."

"In a pig's ass, you will! You would be miserable. You would lose your karma, for God's sake, if you didn't surf. And besides, I would miss you."

"But that's..."

"You think I'm going to fly all the way back here from California just to visit you? Don't be so egotistical."

"But..."

"Look, Jerry. It was you who told me I should take the bar exam, and that means I'll have to brush up a little, since it's been six years, and what better place than Berkeley?"

Jerry frowned and then said, "UCLA?"

"What?'

"UCLA might be better than Berkeley. They have a campus not too far from Huntington," said Jerry. "But who'll run the ice cream shop?"

"We will, every summer. And train Francis and Jasmine to run it while we're away. You can play jazz while you're here, and teach at Berkeley, sell grass, counsel some people at the rehab, and teach me to surf when we're in Huntington. Simple enough, right?"

"Well..."

"Right. So that's settled. Now play something soft and sweet, and then kiss me, and then get Frank and Joan to buy you some decent clothes for Sunday. I'm not going to wear a friendship ring from someone who can't dress properly."

Jerry didn't play anything at all, but just reached over and kissed her.

The crowd smiled and sighed, and then applauded.

"What took them so long, John?" asked Mildred Snyder. "They've known each other for almost three days."

"Kids these days," replied Mary's father. "They're always movin' so slow. They think they're going to live forever."

Paul is an emergency medicine physician practicing at Lawrence General Hospital in Lawrence, Massachusetts. He lives in Georgetown, MA with his wife, Mary, of 40 years and two daughters. As he approaches retirement from medical practice he has become engaged in other pursuits, writing being among them. He has written a children's picture book about the adoption of his daughters titled: The Child In Our Hearts and his first novel: Mal Practice, a mystery of medicine and murder, has been given a Finalist Award by the IPNE (Independent Publishers of New England) in the 2014 Book Contest, Genre Fiction category. He is now opening a family business, an ice cream shop. This novel is not based on his experience in the ice cream business. He continues to write so watch for another novel soon.

www.ingramcontent.com/pod-product-compliance
Lightning Source LLC
Chambersburg PA
CBHW022123050726

47590CB00002B/374

9780990742401